Circle

Shadows of
the Night

WORDSWORTH ROMANCE

Circle of Fire

AND

Shadows of the Night

REBECCA BENNETT

WORDSWORTH EDITIONS

The paper in this book is produced from pure wood
pulp, without the use of chlorine or any other substance
harmful to the environment. The energy used in its
production consists almost entirely of hydroelectricity
and heat generated from waste materials, thereby
conserving fossil fuels and contributing little to the
greenhouse effect.

First published by Robert Hale Limited

This edition published 1994 by
Wordsworth Editions Limited
Cumberland House, Crib Street, Ware,
Hertfordshire SG12 9ET

ISBN 1 85326 500 4

Printed and bound in Denmark by Nørhaven

Circle of Fire

ONE

The house came unexpectedly at the end of the lane. Squarely built of grey granite slabs, it rose, huge and impressive, three-storeys high, from wide shrub-dotted lawns that sloped to the cliff-edge. Twin towers dominated either side. Below, the cliff dropped steeply away to reveal a curve of sand bordered by dark rocks, beyond which the sea stretched endlessly into the distance; while to the west the silhouette of the Lizard lighthouse was etched plainly against a cloudless blue September sky.

Bryony could only stare in amazement. So this was Penreath.

Picking up her handbag from the back seat of the car, she walked across the gravelled drive and climbed the steps to the front door, stepping inside on to soft deep-cream carpet. The walls were a perfect match, the faint pattern of the paper soothing and restful, emphasizing the atmosphere of quiet peace. A sparkling crystal chandelier hung over the well of a wide staircase that curved upwards in a smooth sweep to the landing above.

'Good afternoon. May I help you?'

Bryony was so intent on her surroundings that she hadn't noticed the reception desk to the right of her, or the pretty girl sitting behind it. No, she thought, pretty isn't the right word, but for the moment she couldn't think of one that would aptly describe the perfectly groomed candy-floss blonde hair and porcelain, almost doll-like, features. Had the receptionist, too, been chosen to blend with the decor?

'I'm Bryony Scott, the new osteopath.'

The girl's face smiled and Bryony wondered how she managed to do so without causing even the slightest crinkling of her skin.

'Ah, yes. Gavin told me you would be arriving. He said for me to apologize that he is not here to welcome you. Unfortunately, a meeting in Falmouth was most urgent.'

'Gavin?' Bryony enquired. Her interview had been in London and she had yet to meet the staff at Penreath.

'Dr Carthew. He will return in time for dinner tonight. Now, I show you your room.' The receptionist held out a slender white hand, its nails long, glowing softly pink. 'I am Astrid.'

So that explains the Nordic beauty and unusual way of speaking, Bryony thought, watching the girl climb the stairs. Wafer-thin too, but then, working for a health farm I suppose she has to be.

'Here you sleep.' Astrid opened a door at the end of a long corridor and to Bryony's delight she realized she was in one of the towers, overlooking the bay. Eagerly she crossed to the window, staring down to where white-crested waves rolled lazily towards the shore with a soft surge of sound.

'You like?'

She turned to meet Astrid's questioning eyes. 'I like very much,' she laughed.

The girl gave a slight shudder. 'For me, no. Too high. Too....' Her voice quivered. 'Too dangerous. I will arrange for someone to bring up your luggage.'

'Oh, don't bother, Astrid. I'll come down. There's not a

lot.'

One suitcase and a roll-bag to be precise, Bryony reflected. All my possessions. Not a great deal to show for twenty-four years of life. The fire had destroyed everything else.

And Tom.

A wave of grief swept through her, rapidly followed by a frighteningly familiar feeling of suffocation, making her lean her head against the cool glass of the window, breathing deeply, forcing the sharp salt air into her lungs, trying to quell her rising panic.

'You are ill?' Astrid's face was concerned.

Quickly Bryony shook her head. 'No … it's been a long journey and in this heat, even with the windows open, the car was airless.'

'I organize tea for you. You come down in one quarter of an hour. It will be ready then.'

When the door closed, Bryony sank on to the bed, exhaustion draining all the strength from her limbs. And her tears wouldn't hold back any longer.

Bryony bent her face over the washbasin, splashing it with cold water, staring up at her reflection in the mirror, hoping the redness of her eyes wasn't too apparent. I have to go downstairs. Face all those people. This is a new life. A new beginning. The past is over now.

But how can it be, she asked herself desperately, when every moment of the day I remember Tom?

She'd had to get away. That town was too full of memories. Streets where they'd walked together. A favourite restaurant. Even a radio playing a familiar tune in the background. Everything there held something of Tom. But Tom would never be part of her life again.

She swept the brush through her tawny hair, watching it spring back into heavy curls to rest on her shoulders. A swift flick of lipstick across her wide mouth. A touch of mascara to her still damp lashes. With a rueful smile she decided she'd present no competition for the lovely Astrid. Quickly she tucked her jade-green tee-shirt into her white cotton trousers and, taking a deep breath, opened the bedroom door.

A laughing group filled the hall. From their sun-bronzed limbs and sleek swim-suited figures, she realized that not all those at Penreath were the overweight clients she'd imagined.

'Ah, Bryony!' Astrid's husky tones filled the air and all heads turned to gaze with interest as she reached the bottom of the stairs.

'Another innocent lamb to the slaughter?' enquired a balding young man.

'Don't mention lamb, Charles,' groaned a dark-haired girl. 'The thought of meat makes my stomach go wild. How am I going to cope with a glass of spring water and dish of fruit salad?'

'I saw the way you were eyeing those limpets down there on the rocks, Jen,' the other man laughed back at her. 'Positively ravenous!'

'Bryony is to be our osteopath,' Astrid announced.

'Osteopath! That's a new trick for Gavin, isn't it?' the balding man drawled. 'A knee in your back and quick twist of the neck. Sounds like sheer agony to me.'

Bryony smiled wryly. Why did people always have the same idea? Surely by now everyone realized that osteopathy was a growing profession, requiring years of careful training, and that it wasn't merely concerned with back problems but every condition of the body as well. To qualify, she'd taken a four-year course.

Looking at him she could see from the way he stood

that one of his hips was a fraction higher than the other, and she guessed he would suffer with problems in the coming years, if he didn't already.

'Well, I'll let her give me an invigorating massage any day,' grinned the second, slightly shorter, man.

Bryony breathed deeply. That was another remark she had to contend with.

'I tell the kitchen you are ready for tea now,' Astrid interrupted, and picked up the phone on her desk.

'So you get real *food*, do you?' the dark-haired girl commented. 'Well, make sure you don't eat it anywhere near me then. I'll probably snatch it from your lips.'

'The lounge for staff,' Astrid said quickly, 'is through that door.'

With a grateful smile, Bryony went into a long-windowed room overlooking smooth lawns bordered by deep-red flowering fuchsia bushes and the pale blue lace of hydrangeas.

A tray was already placed on a polished round table and she smelt the spicy fragrance of bergamot as she poured Earl Grey tea into a delicate china cup. Two slices of paper-thin brown bread and butter were carefully arranged on a matching plate beside a cut-glass dish of home-made raspberry jam, while several nutty-looking biscuits filled another. Bryony picked up a tiny silver spoon and helped herself to the jam, settling into the straight-backed rose-velvet covered chair as she began to eat.

From here there was no view of the sea, only the sharp outline of the cliffs and lighthouse; its white walls catching the deep pink of the setting sun, making them glow like ... Bryony wouldn't let herself think of the word, feeling a prickle creep down her spine, her breath catching in her throat as she quickly turned her eyes away, taking in the wide vista of the garden.

The bushes had a look about them as though they had been swept by a heavy brush, their leaves scorched and brown on one side where they leaned away from the wind. And it must blow strongly here, she decided.

Where the garden ended and the cliffs continued on round the coast she could just see the tumbled walls of a building; windowless gaps yawning; ugly dark patches on the roof where tiles had fallen; and wondered what it was.

She tasted one of the nutty biscuits, savouring its flavour of rich treacle and dates, guessing how much the dark-haired girl would have enjoyed them, her mind slowly retracing the events of the day. The early start from her parents' home in the tiny castle-dominated town of Arundel; the motorway and roads jammed with endless lines of cars, exhaust fumes filling the humid air; the constantly changing countryside; and at last crossing the river dividing Devon from Cornwall where multi-patterned fields on the hills gave way to pale white mountains of china-clay waste around St Austell.

Then, seeing her first tall solitary chimney rise from a long-dead tin-mine; the bare square walls of a once-used engine-house; and finally the eerie line of huge round dishes above the satellite communications station on the flat, heather-covered downs of Goonhilly, before that narrow lane twisting its way to the very edge of the coast – and Penreath.

The door opened abruptly and a slender almond-eyed oriental girl came in, her black hair falling straight and sleek like polished jet around her rounded cheeks.

'Hi!' The girl's voice was low-pitched and soft. 'You must be Bryony. Gavin said you were due today. I'm Serena.'

Serena. It suits her perfectly, Bryony decided, Placid. Gentle.

'What do you do here?' she asked.

'I'm the most hated of the staff,' Serena laughed. 'Dietician. I work out what our victims may have, or more often, what they may *not*! If you study my back carefully, you'll see the embedded daggers!' She eyed Bryony thoughtfully. 'You need to step up on the iron, you know. That pallor isn't good. Have you been ill recently?'

Bryony shook her head. 'Not ill....' she said slowly.

The other girl's interest quickened. 'Something's wrong though, isn't it? No one has that kind of transparent look without a good reason. An emotional upset maybe?' she hazarded, then her face broke into a rueful smile. 'Sorry! The trouble with working here is that you study everyone professionally and making a snap judgement on their ills. After all, you're not a patient, are you?'

Maybe I should be, Bryony thought wryly.

'Gavin would be furious with me,' Serena continued, tucking her hands behind her thick hair as she relaxed against the back of her chair. 'I'm always doing the same thing whenever I meet people, and it annoys him intensely.'

'Have you had tea?' Bryony asked. 'If not, perhaps we could ask for another cup and saucer. There's still some left in the pot, and a couple of biscuits.'

Serena stood up and patted her flat stomach under her peach-coloured tracksuit. 'Don't tempt me! Having forced everyone to forgo such luxuries, they'd notice the slightest crumb and I'd be for the lynch-mob! Eat up quickly or they'll be in through the window. I'd better be off anyway. Two new patients arrived earlier this afternoon and I must check Gavin's assessments to decide on their evening meal – if any!'

'You don't really starve them, do you?' Bryony asked.

Serena opened her almond eyes wide and chuckled. 'Don't go down in the cellars, whatever you do. That's where we keep all the skeletons!'

When she'd gone, Bryony continued gazing through the window, seeing people begin to drift out on to the lawns. The activities for the day must be finished.

A path led across the grass and down the slope towards a white fence, and she guessed there must be a track along the cliff-top leading to the lighthouse when she saw several figures walk through a gate and begin to climb. Not a place to be on a dark night, she decided, rising to her feet and opening the French windows.

Only a huge crimson ball remained of the sun now, resting on the horizon, sending long fingers of colour across the gently undulating sea. A yacht, its straining white sails pink-tinged, meandered half a mile or so out, its pale wake rocking a tiny blue fishing-boat anchored nearby.

A light breeze blowing off the water made the sultry heat less intense, but looking at the dull brilliance of the sun, Bryony had the unpleasant feeling that a storm was in the offing. Here, it would be spectacular, she decided, with nothing to hide its fury.

When she reached the fence the tumble-down building was more obvious. A barn maybe? Or even an old cottage? Her curiosity roused, she followed the path through waist-high stems of dry grass and trailing brambles where fat berries were beginning to gleam darkly among the prickles, to view it more closely.

Once, she could tell from the narrow gaps where doors had been, this was a terrace of three old houses. Now, only walls outlined the rooms. Even the stairs were gone, leaving bedroom wallpaper to bloom with roses and ivy leaves that, years before, only its occupants had been privileged to see.

Three homes. Three families. Living there. Dying there. Bryony wondered who they'd been. Where they were now. Why they'd left. It was sad to see such dereliction.

She moved round to the gardens at the back, finding a clump of purple Michaelmas daisies abundant in one corner; a patch of marigolds glowing under one wall; a gnarled tree rosy with apples.

And she saw, too, a pile of new, sweetly-smelling wooden beams stacked at one end. Ready for what? she asked herself. Were the cottages to be rebuilt? Accommodation for some of the clients of the health farm, or staff maybe?

'Good evening.' The unexpected voice made her spin round, her body tensing.

A man stood almost filling one of the empty doorways, his fingers curled round the splintered wood of its frame, and she could see the golden hairs that sprinkled his arm glint in the evening sunshine. As she retreated quickly towards the path, her eyes took in the blue-check shirt, open at the neck, sleeves rolled above the elbows.

'I didn't mean to startle you.' A faintly discernible Cornish accent lengthened the words as he apologized. 'If you're interested, I'll give you a conducted tour of the place.'

He was moving towards her on long denim-clad legs and she shook her head. 'I'll be late for dinner if I do,' she said hastily, 'but thanks for the offer.'

He stood, towering over her, and she noticed that paler skin etched a wide line across the top of his deeply-tanned forehead, below the windswept thatch of his fair hair.

'Be careful how you go then. That path's not the safest one to be taken at high speed.'

Voices came from the small bar adjoining the hall as she

entered Penreath again and she could see through its open door a chattering group clutching tall glasses of what she could only imagine were fruit or vegetable juices.

'Bryony Scott? I'm Gavin Carthew, my dear.' A smoothly warm voice filled her ears and she turned to find a silver-haired man beside her. 'I'm so sorry I wasn't around to welcome you this afternoon. What will you have to drink?'

'What does one drink here?' she asked.

He laughed. 'I think we can find you something a little stronger than tomato juice unless, of course, you'd like it to disguise some vodka. How about white wine?' He indicated his own glass. 'I can thoroughly recommend it.'

'Thank you.'

Astrid, she noticed, now controlled the bar. Not so very different from the reception desk, Bryony reflected, watching the perfect features smile when she handed Gavin Carthew the wine.

'Let's sit outside.' His hand took her elbow, guiding her on to the paved terrace. Even there the humid air felt like a sauna. 'Sir Toby Balfour interviewed you in London, didn't he? The report I received from him was very complimentary.'

'It wasn't exactly an interview,' she explained. 'I was playing squash one evening. Someone on another court slipped badly. Being on the spot I gave him some treatment to relieve the intense pain he was suffering. It was only when he contacted me later that I discovered who he was. I treated him a couple more times, and several months after that he phoned to ask if I would consider working at Penreath.'

She hesitated, not wanting to admit that the offer couldn't have come at a better time, when her whole life was at a crossroads.

Gavin's grey eyes regarded her candidly. 'To be honest, I wasn't over-keen to have an osteopath here. I'm one of the old school, I'm afraid, my dear. Always been a bit suspicious about alternative forms of medicine. And some osteopaths do have a bad reputation.'

'Not registered ones,' she replied, her finger smoothing away a bead of moisture sliding down the glass. 'Anyone *can* set up in practice and call themselves an osteopath, but a sensible person would only consult one who's been fully trained and on the Register of Osteopaths.'

'But do the general public realize that?'

Bryony smiled ruefully. 'Probably not,' she admitted.

'Well, Sir Toby seems completely satisfied with you.' The grey eyes studied her shrewdly. 'That doesn't mean, of course, that our patients will.'

'Then I'll have to prove to them that I'm perfectly competent,' she retorted drily.

His hand closed over hers. 'I'm sure you will, my dear.'

She carefully eased away her fingers to pick up her glass again.

'You've certainly chosen a beautiful location for a health clinic.'

His mouth curved into a contented smile. Like a sleek cat, she thought. The Cheshire cat in *Alice*.

'That was Sir Toby again. He owns a lot of property throughout the country. Not all are clinics like this though. He likes to have a finger in several pies. Very profitable ones usually. Penreath was opened about five years ago and we do very well here. It is, as you say, a beautiful location. The Lizard is the most southerly point in the British Isles, you see. Apart from the occasional gale, the climate is very equable. And as you will have noted, there are no towns or industrial areas anywhere in the vicinity to create pollution. The helicopter base at Culdrose, just outside Helston, is about our only working area. Oh, and Goonhilly, of course, but neither could be termed industrial. We really live in our own select world here. Extremely pleasant.'

'And the clients – or do we call them patients?' she asked.

'Guests is preferable, my dear. A great many are Sir Toby's personal acquaintances. In his line of business, he meets a wide variety of people.' The smile deepened once more. 'All wealthy.'

'So Penreath is more of a holiday than a cure?'

'We like to combine the two. It would be an expensive holiday otherwise,' he replied smoothly. 'We can only accommodate twenty guests at a time but I'm quite sure they all return to their particular style of rat race completely restored to equilibrium again.'

'How about ages?'

'Mainly the over-thirties, although we do have a few youngsters every now and then. They tend to treat it as a bit of a lark. Get a little boisterous at times. Not to be encouraged. We did have some trouble....' His face darkened into a frown.

'What happened?' she probed.

'All over and forgotten now, my dear,' he said briskly.

'I noticed some ruined cottages further along the cliff. It looked as though some work was about to be done on them. Are they anything to do with Penreath?'

She saw his smiling mouth tighten into a thin line. 'Unfortunately no. They belong to a man called Veryan over at Coverack, a few miles round the coast. They'd have crumbled into a heap of rubble and been forgotten, but he's recently been granted planning permission to restore them.'

Dr Carthew finished the last of his wine and Bryony was surprised to see tension whiten his knuckles, curious as to why.

'It would be a pity to pull them down,' she commented mildly.

'All they're fit for,' he muttered, glaring across the garden. 'Conservation! It's progress we need in this part of the country, not stepping backwards into the past. Work is scheduled to begin any day now, I believe. But I shall be keeping a close eye on things. We've a right to privacy here – and peace and quiet. One atom of dust, one clatter of sound and I'll have that man out of there before he knows what's hit him. This is a health clinic not a blasted building site. Another drink?'

'No,' she said, rising to her feet, startled by such vehemence. 'I'd better get ready for dinner. Do we dress up or anything.'

'No tracksuits. That's the only rule. Everyone lives and dies in them all day.'

'Then I'll go and get changed.'

I suppose I am needed here, Bryony mused, slipping into bed later that night. Penreath appears to be far more like a luxury hotel than a clinic. At dinner, the food was beautifully presented. Slightly different from the two lettuce leaves and a grated carrot that people joked about when referring to health farms.

And there was a great deal of equipment. She'd been taken on a tour of the exercise rooms, saunas, jacuzzis, and seen both swimming pools – one indoor and one in the garden, surrounded by a wide patio with sunbeds, comfortable chairs and white wrought-iron tables.

Her treatment-room, although small, included every-thing that she'd requested, and the couch was a far better and much more expensive model than she'd had

in her own practice. For a moment her mind flickered
backwards, remembering, until she forced it to go on
again.

A cupboard held small snow-white pillows, paper-
sheets and towels, and everything else that she could
possibly need, while a venetian blind kept out the sun
and curious eyes. All she hoped now was that she would
have some chance to use it. Gavin Carthew hadn't
seemed all that encouraging, but maybe his guests, as he
liked to term them, would be more up-to-date in their
ideas.

TWO

Bryony wasn't sure whether it was the growing rumble of thunder or the brilliance of the lightning that woke her. The air was still humid, pressing down like a heavy damp blanket. Slipping her feet over the side of the bed, she went across the room to heave up the lower sash window. It wouldn't budge.

In the next dazzle of shimmering light she was puzzled to see a nail preventing its movement. Perhaps it was a safety measure to stop anyone falling out. The room was high: three storeys up. Astrid's words floated into her mind. *Too dangerous.*

She stretched up, tugging the upper window down a little further, looking out to where the darkness of the cliffs projected clearly against the quivering sky. The lightning made it like day.

Another crash of thunder tremored round her. She could feel the polished wood of the floor shake beneath her feet. A long finger of light beamed out from the lighthouse further along the headland, almost lost in the vividness of the surrounding sky. Heavy spots of rain were falling now, striking the window with a sound like small stones, and a gust of wind rattled the frame.

It looked as though tomorrow was going to be a bleak day.

* * *

The rain continued steadily all morning turning the sea a
dull grey that merged into the skyline without any apparent meeting. Bryony was surprised to see an appointment
firmly marked in her book when she opened it. *Charles
Morton*, she read. Wasn't he the balding young man she'd
seen in the hall yesterday afternoon? The one who was so
scathing about osteopaths?

'I need to take a few details first, before I examine you,'
she explained, studying the rather hunched shoulders
and forward thrust of his head. 'Your previous medical
history is very important.'

When she'd finished making her notes, she asked, 'Any
particular problems?'

'That's for you to decide, isn't it?'

'No,' she replied evenly, making him lean to one side.
'Without your guidance I can't begin to make a diagnosis,
or even treat you. It's fairly apparent that you work in
somewhat cramped conditions though. Your neck and
shoulders are very tense. Can you bend this way?' She
guided his head, holding his neck firmly between her
hands. 'Uncomfortable? Hop on the couch, please. Face
down. Hands by your sides.' With firm, but gentle
pressure her fingers moved the length of his spine,
sensing the problem areas as his body tensed slightly. 'Do
you use a computer, Mr Morton?'

His head lifted. 'Yes, but how on earth …?'

'How long do you spend at it each day?' Her hands
were smoothing lightly along his shoulders as she spoke.

'All day. It's my job.' His manner was abrupt.

'Any recurring headaches? Tiredness?' she
questioned.

'Yes,' he said reluctantly. 'Who doesn't in this day and
age?'

'Pins and needles?'

'In my fingers occasionally.'

'You should take a break every hour, for at least five minutes. Move completely away. Relax. Shrug your shoulders. Rotate your neck.'

'And look like a clown,' he retorted.

'It's far better to look like a clown than finish up with permanent damage to your upper spine, Mr Morton — which is precisely what you *are* doing. Your head's at a definite angle already.'

He jerked sideways, turning to stare up at her. 'You sound very alarmist.'

'I intend to be, Mr Morton. You're distorting your body. At the moment there's only minimal damage, but if you don't do something about it soon, the problems will increase.'

'So what do you recommend? Giving up my employment?' His tone was full of sarcasm.

'Of course not. Do what I've suggested. In the long run it'll save you a great deal of discomfort. There now, does that feel any better?'

He moved his shoulders cautiously and straightened his neck. 'I had a headache when I came in,' he admitted. 'The storm....'

She smiled at him encouragingly. 'And the headache's gone?'

'Yes,' he agreed reluctantly, 'but so has the stormy weather.'

'Then we'll have to see which returns first,' she commented drily. 'Another twenty minutes tomorrow should ease that shoulder too. Have you been playing tennis a great deal?'

'You're not a witch, are you?'

'Tomorrow, same time, Mr Morton?' she suggested, and watched him nod. Tomorrow, she decided, she'd mention that raised hip and recommend he wore a lift in one shoe to even it out.

By lunchtime she'd seen three more people, one of whom was Charles Morton's friend who, when removed from his companions, was a pleasant enough young man with a long neglected rugby injury to his lower back.

As there were no afternoon appointments and the rain had eased to a drizzle, Bryony pulled on her cagoule and ventured out, surprised by the soft salt smell of the air after its previous sultriness. The track along the edge of the cliff had been churned to thick mud and her feet slithered as she skirted deep puddles, the long beaten-down grass soaking her trousers as she struggled through.

Water dripped steadily from a broken drainpipe hanging halfway down the side of one of the deserted cottages and a bedraggled seagull perched on the gutter, watching her with beady eyes as she passed.

Where the path wound steeply up through twisted blackthorn bushes, chunks of rock made it easier to climb and when, slightly breathless, she reached the top, she could see the lighthouse only half a mile or so away. There and back will be enough for today, she decided, striding out, her hands tucked into the pockets of her jacket to keep warm.

Here, the wind was stronger, blowing in across the dull grey of the sea to whip her hair across her face and into her eyes, and she left the mud of the path and walked across the springy tufts of grass to where the cliff dropped raggedly away.

Below the tide was high, white foam-edged waves roaring in with a surge that rose to a column of spray as they met the rocks, then retreated again to reveal their cruel sharpness.

An elderly man passed her, silently raising his

walking-stick in greeting, a fat spaniel struggling along behind him on weary legs.

When she reached the white walls of the lighthouse, she could see further ahead a cluster of buildings and continued to walk, curious to discover what they were.

Wet and dejected holiday-makers, their soaking anoraks clinging in soggy layers to their bodies, peered at the contents of misty windows – lamps and novelties made of grey-green stone. An ice-cream sign flapped over a doorway. Rusting tables and chairs dripped emptily outside, where no one ate the advertised cream teas. A child wandered too near the cliff-edge and was seized and tugged away, wailing, to be strapped back into its buggy.

A smell of frying mingled with coffee hung in the air around the café door and Bryony suddenly felt hungry, reaching in her pocket for her purse before remembering that it was in her room at Penreath. The rain gathered force again, sending people hurrying to their cars.

It was driving straight into her face on the walk back, stinging her half-closed eyelids, trickling down the sides of her cheeks and under the edge of her cagoule hood. Her hands were icy, deep in her pockets, and the cotton of her trousers clung to her bare legs. Mud oozed under her feet with each step, making the path treacherous.

When she came to the tumble-down walls of the old cottages, she stopped. Blue sky edged the horizon. Any minute now the rain would cease. It seemed silly to struggle on against its force. No one would be working there on a day like this, she decided, and stepped in through an empty doorway. At least where the roof's undamaged, it'll be fairly dry, she told herself, untying the strings of her hood to shake out her confined hair.

Her shoe crunched on fallen slate, the sharp sound

shattering the silence, and a shape suddenly loomed in the dimness, making her jerk to a halt.

'It's all right – don't panic!' The command echoed round the hollow walls. 'Maybe this time you'll let me introduce myself – Adam Veryan.'

He was wearing a green Barbour jacket, dark cord trousers tucked into muddy wellington boots, his fair hair hidden by a low-brimmed hat, but she couldn't fail to recognize him. Veryan. That was the name Gavin Carthew had mentioned with such anger, she recalled.

'You are real, aren't you? Not a figment of my imagination?' Adam Veryan's tone was teasing now. 'Nor a long-lost spirit, who once lived here, doomed to haunt the ruins? Do you have a name?'

She couldn't prevent a smile as she said, 'Bryony Scott.'

'Bryony.' He repeated the word slowly, and made the name sound like music. 'Well, Miss Scott, as you're so very wet, may I suggest that I give you a lift home?'

'No, thank you, Mr Veryan. Penreath's only a short distance away.'

'Penreath?' The empty shell of the house had lightened as the rain died away, and she could see the amusement that curved his eyes and tugged at the corners of his mouth, deepening a cleft in his chin. 'You're one of Dr Carthew's pampered guests?'

'No,' she replied. 'I work there, and must be getting back before my queue of patients grows too long.'

'Am I really so terrifying that you have to run away whenever you see me?'

Bryony smiled, and began to slip and slide her way back along the path again, very aware that his gaze still followed her from the doorway of the ruined building until a dip hid her from his view.

When Charles Morton came for his second treatment the

following day, he was more relaxed, less abrasive towards her.

'How could you tell all those things yesterday?' he asked. 'That I worked on a computer. The headaches. My shoulder.'

Bryony laughed. 'It wasn't difficult. You'd be surprised what your spine can reveal. Every knob, as you'd term them, relates to a specific area of your body. A lesion on this one can affect the circulation to your legs and this, sinus or eye trouble. That's why I asked if you had any particular problems. It helps to be able to locate the correct area to work on.'

'Philip thinks you're fantastic.'

'Philip?'

'Old rugby injury. Had trouble for years. Used to be at school with him. Awfully athletic sort. Accounts for that bull-like neck. We come here every year.'

She noticed his body tense a little.

'Did that hurt?' she asked anxiously.

'Hurt? Not at all. Amazing what a difference you've made already. I didn't realize just how stiff that shoulder had become. No, I was just thinking about the gang of us who used to come here. Old Gavin didn't approve. Staid old blighter he is. Couldn't stand it when a few of us played around too much. Well, I suppose with the fees he charges having blokes like Tim Maxwell getting drunk doesn't go down too well. Not an hotel, is it?'

'Turn on to your side now. That's it.'

'Could still be floating around out there somewhere, I suppose. Creepy thought, isn't it? Wouldn't fancy old Tim suddenly nuzzling my foot when I'm down in the cove swimming.'

Bryony's hands stilled. 'What do you mean?'

'Tim Maxwell. Disappeared one night. Found his

dressing-gown and towel down there on the sand. Currents round here are pretty treacherous, you know. Obviously went for a midnight dip and that was that.'

'You mean he drowned?' she asked.

'Suppose so. Never found a corpse. All hushed up though. Gavin saw to that. Bad publicity. Not good for the place. Can't have your customers vanishing, can you?'

'How long ago was that?'

'Tim, you mean? Oh, two or three years back. Three, I think. Hey, mind what you do with that leg! It's still joined on. Another session tomorrow then?'

'By the end of the week I think we should have sorted out most of your problems, and I want you to wear this lift in your shoe.'

'Won't it make me a bit lopsided?'

Bryony smiled. 'You are already,' she said.

He paused in the doorway, looking back at her. 'What you were saying ... about osteopathy dealing with other problems, not just the back. Any good for migraine? Only Jen – you know, the dark-haired girl – they flatten her on occasions.'

'Might do.'

'OK if I send her along?' He stopped, his neck reddening. 'She and I ... we're sort of ... close, if you know what I mean.'

'You send her along, Charles, and I'll see if I can help.'

It was while she was swimming, leisurely counting the laps, in the warm water of the indoor pool that Bryony recalled her conversation with Gavin the previous evening. He didn't approve of young people at Penreath *larking around* as he called it. Was Tim Maxwell the reason? A mysterious disappearance, possibly a drowning, wouldn't be a good advertisement for the place. She rolled on to her back, stretching out her arms in a slow back-stroke, her mind drifting on. Those old cottages upset him too. And Adam Veryan?

From her room in the tower, as she dressed, she could see further along the cliff. One corner of the grey slate roof was visible, a ladder propped against it. After being cooped up in the treatment-room all morning, a little exercise is needed, she decided. A walk to the lighthouse and back.

'Going for a breath of fresh air?' Serena ran to join her as she reached the small gate in the fence. 'Mind if I come too?'

'Of course not,' Bryony lied. From the path she could see a green Range Rover parked beside the cottage walls.

'How are you settling in?'

'Oh, fine.' She could hear the sound of rending wood as they grew nearer. It could be anyone, she told herself firmly. Just because he owns the place doesn't mean....

'Good afternoon, Miss Scott.' The deep tones of his voice vibrated through her, tantalizing every nerve as she slowly raised her eyes.

Adam Veryan was perched astride the ridge of the roof where the slates were gone, an orange helmet covering his head, his leather-gloved hands pounding with a mallet at the decaying wooden structure. She gazed up, the breath catching in her throat, at his precarious position.

'Good afternoon, Mr Veryan.' Bryony quickened her pace.

'I didn't think you knew anyone round here,' Serena commented, adjusting her step to keep up.

'I don't. We just met in passing.'

'So why the heightened colour?' Serena chuckled.

'The path's steep,' Bryony replied swiftly. 'And with this wind blowing....'

'Remember what happened to Pinocchio?'

'Pinocchio?' Bryony demanded, turning to stare into the other girl's slanting eyes.

'His nose grew long when he told untruths,' Serena laughed. 'We'd better turn back now. I'd hate to miss tea and find everyone's taken advantage of my absence to tuck into the clotted cream.'

When they reached the cottages again, aware of Serena's interest Bryony deliberately averted her eyes, concentrating hard on a tanker far out to sea, but her ears were keenly tuned for Adam Veryan's voice.

When it didn't come, she glanced sideways, seeing the empty roof and her stomach gave a sudden lurch of anxiety.

Then, from behind the building she saw a length of wood rise in the air, guessing it was a replacement rafter, and with a sigh of relief she hurried on before the man carrying it appeared.

'How long have you been here, Serena?' she asked, opening the gate for the girl to go through.

'Just over four years. I came soon after Penreath was opened.'

'And Astrid?'

'About the same time. A little after me.'

'Charles Morton told me someone disappeared a few years back.'

'That's true,' Serena agreed.

'What happened?'

'His crowd were all a bit young and silly then. They shouldn't have been here at all. You know how strict Gavin is about keeping to regime. There's no point in coming to Penreath, if you don't. After all, it is a health farm. Charles and his friends brought in some scrumpy – the local cider. It's fairly potent stuff.' Serena began to lead the way up the stairs when they entered the house, continuing the conversation as she went. 'One of them – a boy called Tim Maxwell decided to go swimming. Stupid thing to do in the dark – and in that state. Gavin found his towel and things down in the cove the next morning.' She paused on the landing, before climbing the next flight. 'Gavin insisted it was nothing to make a fuss about. People do drown round this coast. There are strong currents. Tim Maxwell's body was never found though.'

Bryony stopped on the landing, outside her bedroom door.

'He had a room in this tower,' Serena ended.

The phone call surprised her.

'For you,' Astrid called, as Bryony was crossing the hallway to go into dinner that evening.

'Miss Scott?' The deep tones vibrated softly into her ear.

'Yes,' she replied hesitantly.

'It's Adam Veryan. May I take you for a drink later this evening?'

Astrid's wide blue eyes were watching her intently and Bryony wondered whether she could hear what he was saying.

'Miss Scott?'

'That's very kind of you,' she said slowly.

'Around half-past eight, or would that be too early?'

'No,' she replied. 'Half-past eight would be fine.'

Charles Morton's voice called to her across the dining-room as she entered, and she saw him beckoning from a table with Jen and Philip. 'Come and sit with us, Bryony. Promise we won't talk shop. Have that chair, next to Philip.'

'Charles says you have healing hands,' the dark-haired girl announced.

'Does he? I only wish I had,' Bryony answered with a smile.

'Well you've done marvels with my shoulder.'

'I only wish you hadn't,' Philip said, grinning at her. 'Charles beat me six-love in every set this afternoon.'

Bryony noticed Gavin Carthew frowning in her direction from the far side of the room where he was eating with one of the guests – a well-known and well-rounded lady-writer of somewhat raunchy novels. Sensing his disapproval, she smiled reassuringly back at him. After all, these youngsters were more in her generation than most of the people at Penreath, and if they wanted her to join them, why should he object?

'How will fiddling about with my back help migraine?' Jen questioned.

'It depends whether it's an allergic reaction or not,' Bryony replied. 'Have you had any tests?'

'Loads,' the girl sighed. 'Cheese. Eggs. Red wine. You name it, I've had it. Nothing works. The attacks just come on out of the blue. A horrible flicker in one eye that grows and grows until my whole vision's filled with one bright dazzle. Then the headache begins. It's agony. I can't do a thing. And sometimes I'm violently sick as well.'

'Oh, Jen! We did say no talking shop,' Philip reminded her.

'Come and see me tomorrow,' Bryony suggested as they finished eating. 'I have to rush now; I'm going out shortly.'

It wasn't quite 8.30 when she came downstairs as headlights swept across the windows of the hall. The air was mild when she stepped outside, the soft scent of roses mingling with the sharp tang of salt from the sea. Stars dotted the darkness of the sky and there was no moon.

Adam, a thick cream Aran sweater slung round his shoulders, was waiting to help her up into the Range

Rover, and his hand was firm under her elbow as he did so.

'I'm glad you came,' he said lightly. 'I wasn't sure you would.'

'It was kind of you to ask me.'

'Kind?' She could see the cleft in his chin deepen as he swung the vehicle round in a half-circle with a spatter of small stones, before heading out into the lane, and heard the hidden laughter in his voice. 'I thought we could go down to Helford, by the river, there's a pleasant old pub. Do you know the area?'

'I've never been to Cornwall before,' she admitted.

'Then you've been missing an awful lot.'

'Have you always lived here? You sound as if you have.'

'Sound?' he questioned.

'Your accent.'

'Have I got one?'

She laughed. 'Well, I think so.'

'A country bumpkin, is that it? Ooh arr, ooh arr.'

'Not *quite* like that.'

They were crossing Goonhilly Downs now, the Range Rover increasing speed, the huge satellite dishes in the distance pinpointed by lights.

'What exactly do those things do?' she enquired curiously.

'Telecommunications. They receive and transmit television pictures and telephone calls from all round the world. Quite eerie at night, aren't they?'

'Spectacular.'

'We go from the sublime to the ridiculous in Cornwall, you see. Modern equipment like that and Culdrose, the helicopter base further on, in contrast with the old tin-mines and their derelict engine-houses and solitary chimneys scattered everywhere. Then, of course, there are the standing stones and quoits on the moors, not to mention ancient castles. A mixture of the old and mysterious, and the new and incomprehensible. No wonder the Cornish are such a strange race. We're totally bemused.'

'Have you always lived on the Lizard?' she asked him again.

'Born and bred, as they say. My father and I have a place over at Coverack. You must come and meet him sometime.'

'I'd like that.'

'He's in a wheelchair.' There was a sudden flatness to his voice.

'What happened?'

They were turning into another of the lanes, waiting while a motorbike roared past.

'He was one of the Air Sea Rescue crew at Culdrose. They were rescuing a boy who'd lost his nerve climbing the cliffs. My father was being winched down when a gust of wind caught him, tossing him against the rock-face. He fractured his spine.'

'I'm sorry.' The words somehow sounded inadequate to her.

'Don't be,' he replied. 'He doesn't let it affect him too badly. Or hides it well. It amazes me how active he is. Puts the rest of us to shame.' There was a pause. 'What do you do at Penreath?'

'I'm an osteopath.'

'Oh.'

'You don't sound very impressed,' she said.

'You find a lot of charlatans in that line. We've met a few.'

'I can assure you, I'm not a charlatan,' she protested indignantly. 'It took me several years and a great deal of hard work to qualify.'

'I'm sorry.'

He was silent for a while, concentrating on the bends in the road before the Range Rover swung into a car-park on top of a hill, overlooking the pale gleam of water.

'It's very narrow and far easier if we stop here and walk down to the village,' he explained, switching off the engine. 'I should slip on your jacket. It'll be chilly by the river.'

The lane, crowded with old houses and cottages, led steeply downwards to a bridge. Bryony could smell the dank pungent odour of wet mud where the tide had retreated, before they began to climb again on the other side.

'So why Penreath?' he asked.

'Oh, it's a long story. Let's just say Penreath turned up at the right time for me. I needed to make a complete change.'

She could hear a slight breeze rattle ropes against the masts of moored yachts, making a tinny sound. A black cat slunk low across the lane in front of them, pausing for a moment to stare with yellow orbs, before vanishing, without a rustle, under a hedge. Pale silhouettes of flowerheads glowed in shadowed gardens.

With the opening of the pub door a roar of noise and heat burst forth, and Adam's arm guided her inside through the crush of bodies cramming the room. Cigarette smoke spiralled upwards, making her eyes smart after the sweetness of the air outside.

And then her limbs ceased to move; her body contracted; her throat suddenly filled with a terrible choking sensation; and her eyes stared in horror, before she turned blindly trying to fight her way back to the door, away from the crackle and spit of flame.

'Bryony!' Adam's hands were gripping her, his face sharp with anxiety. 'What's wrong?'

Her fists beat against his chest, compelling him to move, to let her escape. In the chill damp of the lane she leaned against a wall, resting her head against the lichened stone, eyes closed.

'Bryony,' he said urgently. 'For heaven's sake tell me what's the matter? Are you ill?'

Wearily she shook her head. 'Take me away from here. Please, Adam. Just take me away.'

THREE

The stars had vanished now, intensifying the night, only the muted glow of light behind curtained windows guided their climb up the hill to the Range Rover. Adam reached out and took her hand.

'What was wrong back there?' he asked gently. 'Too many people?'

She shook her head. 'No.'

'Then what?'

'There was a fire.' He had to lean sideways to catch the words, then wait for her to continue. 'I'm sorry, Adam.'

'We could try somewhere else,' he suggested.

'I'd rather go back to Penreath.'

'Another time maybe?'

'Maybe,' she answered.

'Why should a fire …?'

'Please, Adam. I don't want to talk about it.'

He sat quietly for a moment when they reached the car, looking down through the trees at the faint gleam of the river, then the engine revved and they were travelling the lanes again. The journey seemed far shorter this time. Perhaps he drove more quickly. Bryony wasn't sure. When she saw the beam of the lighthouse cutting across the sea, she knew their evening was over. A disaster. All her fault.

'Thank you,' she said, opening the door almost before

the car had stopped, and jumped down, stumbling as she landed on the gravel, quickly righting herself. 'Goodbye.'

'Goodbye?' She sensed the question in his voice, but didn't answer it, not looking back when she reached the house and went inside.

'You have returned so early?' Astrid's large eyes were regarding her in surprise.

'A headache,' she murmured, hurrying up the stairs, and saw the rearlights of the Range Rover illuminate the landing window when they reached the gate, then disappear.

Tom. His name whispered on her lips as she buried her face in the pillow and wept herself to sleep.

'Astrid tells me you were out last night with the Veryan man.'

Bryony looked up, startled by the anger in Gavin Carthew's tone. She was preparing her room for the first patient of the day and hadn't expected the door to open so forcefully.

'Yes,' she replied evenly. 'I was.'

'Please don't do so again.'

'I beg your pardon?' The ice of her words made them sound brittle.

'I would prefer you not to have any contact with him.'

'Dr Carthew,' she said quietly, 'whom I meet outside Penreath is entirely my business.'

'I'm afraid not, Miss Scott.' She couldn't believe the hostility in his grey eyes. 'While I am employing you....'

'But you don't employ me, Dr Carthew,' she interrupted swiftly. 'Sir Toby Balfour does that.'

The muscles of his face tightened. 'As you so correctly say, Miss Scott, but I would like you to take note of my feelings in this matter.'

'You have a reason, I hope.'

'Several reasons,' he snapped, 'the prime one being that while you are working here, you will behave in a suitable manner.'

'And going out for a drink with Adam Veryan is unsuitable behaviour?' Her scorn tipped every syllable.

'In my opinion, yes.'

'Then I'm afraid I can't agree with you,' she replied, and saw his fingers tighten round the handle of the door, while a pulse of anger flickered the corner of his eye.

Jen appeared in the corridor behind him, hesitating when she saw their faces.

'Come in, Jen,' Bryony smiled in welcome. 'Dr Carthew is just about to leave.'

'Did I interrupt something?' the girl asked, sitting down as Bryony opened her notebook after he'd gone.

'You came at a very opportune moment! Now, let's hear a little about you. When did these migraines begin?'

Her days were growing increasingly busy as people became more aware of what she was doing at Penreath, and others enthused about her. On Friday morning Bryony realized every hour was fully booked with patients wanting a last treatment session. I shall need a rest cure myself if this goes on, she reflected, removing a fresh pillow from the cupboard and closing the door.

She hadn't seen Adam Veryan again. Occasionally his Range Rover was parked up on the cliff-top near the cottages, but two older men were working there now. He probably has other work to supervise, she decided, although they'd never got round that fateful evening to discussing exactly what he did do. And no wonder, she thought. He must have imagined he was out with a raving lunatic!

When the phone rang in her room after she'd finished

working that evening she was in the shower and rushed out, clutching a towel, to answer it.

'I haven't caught you at an awkward moment, have I?'

She smiled at the sound of his voice, pushing back her damp hair to hold the receiver more closely to her ear. 'I was having a shower.'

'And Penreath's so well equipped it has phones in the bathroom too?'

'Not quite. I'm ruining a very expensive carpet.'

'Then I won't keep you dripping too long,' he laughed. 'Will you have dinner with me tomorrow? There's a good restaurant in Porthleven.' He paused, then went on gently, 'And no fires, I promise.'

'How can I refuse?'

'About seven?'

'Fine. And Adam,' she said with a rush, 'don't collect me from the house. I'll wait for you in the lane.'

'Can I ask why?'

'I'll explain when I see you.'

'Seven then.' The receiver gave a click and he was gone.

On Saturday, like an hotel, Penreath was a confusion of people arriving and departing. Bryony felt sad to see those she'd grown to know so well in the past few days leave. In the hallway Charles Morton, Philip and Jen crowded round her, all talking at once.

'See you next time. You will be here, won't you? And I'll remember what you said about the computer.'

'I'll write to let you know about the migraines, Bryony. That's a promise.'

'Any time you're in London, give me a buzz,' Philip grinned teasingly. 'I still could do with a little private treatment.'

Gavin Carthew stood in the porch waving away

various taxis, and welcoming the occupants of others, but during a quiet moment he turned to Bryony and said, 'I'd like to have a word with you in my office, if you don't mind,' and led the way along the corridor.

She followed apprehensively. Since their argument, she'd purposefully avoided him as much as possible. Now there seemed no way to escape.

'Sit down, Bryony.' He moved a comfortable black leather chair to face her. 'I must say first that, contrary to my own reservations, our guests appear to be very complimentary about your treatment of them. I feel, however, that you may have concentrated rather excessively on some of the younger group, but from the number of appointments in your book that doesn't appear to have prevented you spending a reasonable amount of time with our more respected clients.'

How pompous and snobbish can he be? Bryony fumed. 'Everyone who asked for an appointment, had one,' she pointed out.

'Yes, I realize that, and I also appreciate that you are still fairly young and need the companionship of your peers but, as I mentioned before, I would prefer you to confine your current friendships to people under this roof.'

'And not Adam Veryan?'

He picked up a delicately engraved little silver paper-knife and poised it between his two hands, studying it thoughtfully, before he raised his eyes to hers again. 'Maybe I was a little hasty with you the other day,' he smiled.

The Cheshire cat again, she thought.

'You see, I do have my reasons for not liking the man. Those cottages up on the cliff are an interesting feature – as ruins – but once restored and inhabited, they will completely overlook the grounds of Penreath.'

'Does that matter?'

'Matter? Of course it does. Their rebuilding means noise, dust and dirt. My guests come here for rest and privacy, Miss Scott, not to be gawped at by all and sundry.'

'I doubt anyone will do that,' she reasoned.

'We frequently have important names staying here.' He placed the paper-knife beside the stand of a matching silver inkwell, then carefully straightened it. 'The Veryans and I have been in opposition about the future of those cottages for several months now. Unfortunately, I'm not a Cornishman, so they were granted planning permission to renovate and restore them to their former state.'

'Which will be a considerable improvement,' she said.

'It's completely unnecessary and I don't want it to happen.'

'But it will,' she replied, 'so it seems rather pointless for you to keep up your objections. The work won't take very long, and as it's during the winter months people won't be in the grounds very often, will they? I'm sure you're making a mountain out of a molehill, Dr Carthew.'

'As a close friend of young Veryan, you would be biased, Miss Scott.'

'I scarcely know him, Dr Carthew.'

She saw the cat-like smile reappear. 'I rather jumped to a different conclusion. My apologies.' He rose to his feet and walked across the deep carpet to the door, opening it for her. 'Then I take it you won't be seeing him again.'

Bryony went quickly into the corridor, and gave no answer.

After the sultry heat of the previous weekend, ending in a storm, the weather had settled down to the gentle balminess of autumn. It was October and already leaves were beginning to yellow and float down from the trees and bushes overshadowing the high banks of the lane. There was a slight nip in the evening air and Bryony wished she'd worn a skirt and jumper instead of a silky dress. It was the only rather special one she had, purchased hurriedly before she came down to Penreath, after the fire had destroyed everything she possessed.

The sound of a car engine grew closer and she stepped back against the grass bank as Adam's dark-green Range Rover came into view.

'I'll have to turn in the gates,' he said, leaning across her lap to slam the door when she had settled into the seat beside him. 'The road's too narrow.'

As he did so, Bryony was dismayed to see Gavin Carthew's red Porsche heading out behind them, and knew the doctor couldn't help catching sight of her. Oh well, she thought resignedly, I didn't actually *say* I wouldn't see Adam Veryan again.

The Range Rover increased speed, twisting expertly round the sharp bends, the Porsche closely following. Leaning her head sideways to glance up into the rearview mirror, Bryony could just make out the taut lines of Gavin's face, the red glow of the rearlights giving it a sinister hue.

'He would decide to go out now,' she groaned.

'Dr Carthew?'

She nodded. 'I've been warned off you,' she said with a slight smile.

'Warned off!' Adam's laughter echoed round her.

'I gather you've been fighting a bitter battle over the cottages.'

'He did raise some opposition,' Adam admitted. 'I really can't think why. My father bought them a few years back and has been trying to get permission to restore them ever since. It means an access road by-passing Penreath and that's been one of the problems.'

'How did the people who lived there in the past go to and fro?' Bryony asked.

'Originally the three cottages were part of the Penreath estate, used by people working there, and their families. A track led across from the main entrance. However, when the owner died, his heir – a remote Cumbrian nephew – didn't move here and dismissed most of the staff, leaving the cottages empty.'

As they reached the main road, the Porsche shot past with a blare of its horn and disappeared into the distance.

'The house and cottages were sold in two separate lots to meet death duties when the nephew eventually died, and my father bought the three cottages to convert into one large house where he and my mother would live.' Adam's voice hardened. 'Things didn't work out as planned.'

'The accident?' she said softly.

'The accident ... and other things.'

'So why didn't Sir Toby buy the whole estate, I wonder?'

'He didn't buy anything at that time. The person who purchased did it for a quick profit, and sold Penreath to Sir Toby Balfour at around twice the price almost a year later.'

'Couldn't your father have done the same with the cottages?'

She saw his teeth gleam in the darkness of the car as he smiled. 'You have yet to meet my father, Bryony. When he couldn't live there himself, he decided to convert them into sheltered accommodation for retired Cornish people. It's an ideal spot with a very mild climate.'

'Which is why the health farm is there.'

'Exactly,' Adam agreed. 'My father's bought quite a

few derelict properties round here since he had to give up flying, and we've restored and converted them. He sells only to the Cornish, at low prices, mainly young couples starting out in life or those retiring to live on a pension.' He pointed to his right. 'That's Culdrose — where my father was stationed before the accident.'

Bryony watched the long perimeter fence and the lights of the open hangars recede while Adam continued.

'Property value has soared in the last decade with people moving down here from other parts of the country, and the average Cornishman can't afford such exorbitant prices, so they're being forced to leave.'

'And you obviously feel quite strongly about it,' she said.

'Wouldn't you?' he challenged. 'It's our heritage. We've fought to exist and scrape a living from the sea, or the tin and copper mines, for centuries. No way are we going to be driven out by those too wealthy to care about what happens.'

The road twisted and rose and dipped between dark hedges and open countryside until it finally descended another winding hill, and Bryony saw the outline of masts above the low harbour wall.

'We'll park here,' Adam told her, jumping out, and coming round to help her down.

They crossed the road at the bottom of the hill, and he guided her past windows that revealed the shadow out-lines of candlelit tables, and in through the low doorway.

'That colour suits you,' he said, taking her jacket, and she looked down at the soft blue of her dress. 'It matches your eyes — like harebells on a summer's day,' he ended softly.

'Do you work for your father?' Startled by his unexpec-ted compliment, her voice sounded sharp.

'In a way. I began as a constructional engineer, but

somehow I've deviated into the restoration business. It's far more satisfying to see something that's been neglected revert back to how it was intended to be. At first it was more of a hobby, but now it's grown until I feel as strongly about conservation as my father.'

'And your mother – how does she fit in with all this?'

His fingers tightened round the stem of his wineglass. 'She doesn't,' he gritted. 'My mother walked out a month after my father's accident. He was still in hospital. One of his friends at the base was going to Canada. She couldn't face up to life with a cripple, and went with him. They're married now.'

'I'm sorry. It must have been a terrible shock for her though....'

'For her?' She saw the bitterness that made his eyes like stone. 'And what about my father? Can you imagine how he felt losing his mobility, his job ... and his wife?'

The waitress hovered beside them.

'Let's change the subject, shall we?' he suggested tightly. 'Or else I'm going to spoil your meal.'

'I shouldn't have been so inquisitive.'

'No,' he smiled, some of the pain leaving his eyes, 'but now it's my turn for the questions. You haven't told me anything about yourself; where you're from; your family; how you came to be at Penreath.'

She looked down at the heaped dish in front of her, dipping her spoon into the prawns. 'This looks delicious.'

'Bryony,' he warned, spreading pâté on to a slice of toast, 'don't be evasive.'

'I don't want to bore you.'

'You could never bore me,' he replied, and the colour flared into her skin at the note in his voice.

'What can I tell you then? I come from Sussex. A small town called Arundel. It's a few miles from the coast. My parents still live there. I've one brother, three years older, married, living near London.' She paused as the waitress removed her empty dish. 'How I came here was quite by chance. I gave Sir Toby Balfour some osteopathic treatment after he fell playing squash. Then, a short while later he offered me a job at Penreath. And that's about it.'

Adam's blue eyes were regarding her gravely. 'Is it?'

'There's nothing else that would interest you,' she replied, glancing away from him to pick up her knife and fork and slice into the delicate meat of a rainbow trout.

'No man in your life, Bryony?'

She kept her gaze fixed on her plate, refusing to meet his. 'No. Not any more.'

'But there was?' he persisted.

'There was,' she replied slowly.

The room blurred as her eyes brimmed and she bit her lip, compelling it not to quiver. Adam poured wine into her glass and she drank deeply, blinking away the tears.

'And it still hurts?' His voice was gentle.

Looking back at him across the table, seeing the sympathy in his blue eyes, she nodded, not trusting herself to speak.

'One day will you tell me?' he asked, and she nodded again.

'So how do you like living amongst the wealthy and famous?' he enquired, clearly making an effort to divert her mind.

She lifted her chin, meeting his gaze levelly again. 'Some of them are quite fun,' she said. 'It's a pity they have to leave when you've just got to know them. When I had my own practice, at least I was able to keep in touch with most of my patients.'

'You had your own practice? Where was that? In Arundel?'

Bryony shook her head. 'No, I was working just outside London. Harrow. Quite near to where my brother and his family live in Pinner. I'd stayed with them when I was training at the British School of Osteopathy.' And Tom was my brother's best friend, she wanted to add, but somehow her mouth couldn't form his name.

She spooned more courgettes on to her plate from the dish by her side, making herself concentrate on the action.

'So you left all that to come to Cornwall?'

'Sir Toby offered me a job.'

'And you gave up a practice of your own to work here?'

'Yes.' The word came out loudly and abruptly, like a pistol shot.

The middle-aged couple at the next table looked across and she saw surprise reflected on their faces.

'Can we talk about something else?' she requested.

'Of course.' Adam leaned back in his chair and studied her quizzically. 'What shall it be? The weather? That should be a fairly innocuous subject from your point of view, shouldn't it?'

'Now you're being unkind.'

'Am I? Then I'm sorry, but it is rather difficult to hold a conversation when you clam up so easily. It gives me the impression that you have a dark and mysterious past, and yet to look at you....'

The blue of his gaze intensified, challenging hers. 'One day I hope you'll trust me enough to confide. Now, what will you have for a sweet?'

She pulled her jacket closely round her, the wind cutting in from the sea when they reached the harbourside again.

'Can we walk to the end of the jetty?' she asked.

'Certainly,' he said, taking her arm.

The sea was high and Bryony could taste its salt upon her lips and hear the thud of waves at the base of the wall.

'There's a freshwater lake a short way along the coast at Loe Bar,' Adam told her as they stood, watching columns of spray rise up the cliffs. 'It's quite a strange phenomenon, with a long bank of shingle, dividing it from the sea. We could walk over there one day. The path's been eroded badly in places, but it's safe enough if you take care.'

'How are the cottages progressing?' she asked, as they turned back towards the car.

'We've hardly started yet,' Adam replied, falling into step beside her. 'There's a great deal to be cleared away first. Last winter's gales had a disastrous effect and the roof suffered. I had hoped to save most of the slates, but a lot were lifted and shattered. The rafters need replacing too, and the upper floors are a bit shaky.'

'All the effort's going to be worthwhile though?' she questioned.

'Yes,' he said softly. 'All the effort's going to be worthwhile.'

When they reached the gates of Penreath, Adam stopped the engine, and she sat in the sudden silence, conscious of the closeness of his shoulder beside her head, the strong column of his neck rising to meet his thick smooth hair where it curled behind his ears.

She heard the movement as his head turned. Slowly he bent towards her and she felt the warmth of his lips brush her skin before the door opened and his voice said quietly, 'You're home, Bryony.'

It was a moment before she registered the meaning of his words and then her limbs stretched, her feet touching the gravel of the drive. She saw the pale outline of his face behind the glass as the door closed, heard the car crunching backwards as it turned, then was gone, leaving her with a sense of desolation.

Gavin Carthew's red Porsche was lined with the others. She wondered where he'd gone earlier that evening and whether, tomorrow, she would have to face his renewed anger. What does it matter? she thought bleakly. Adam is unlikely to ask me to go out with him again.

And if he did.... Oh, Tom, why do I still love you so much?

It was Sunday. The new guests settling in. Rather like being back at school, Bryony thought. A fresh term. There were still a few left from the previous week. One was Jill, the novelist. Bryony had already treated her on a couple of occasions; a lower back problem, aggravated by long hours hunched over a word processor.

Since then Bryony had been trying to persuade her that regular exercise would help. Swimming in particular. Jill wasn't convinced.

'I'll swim with you, if it helps,' Bryony suggested. 'Just until you get your confidence back. It really is a good form of exercise. There's no stress on your back at all. The water will support you.'

'Just look at me,' Jill grimaced wryly. 'Fourteen stone of lard. I'd swamp the place like a stricken whale.'

'Nonsense,' Bryony laughed. 'We have dozens far larger than you staying here. Besides no one's going to take any notice.'

Today, at last, she'd succeeded in getting her into the water.

'I haven't swum for years,' Jill groaned, striking out gingerly.

'No one forgets,' Bryony comforted.

'Like elephants? I should be all right then.'

'Take it slowly until your muscles get more supple. There now, what did I tell you? It's quite easy after all.'

Through the window Bryony could just see the corner of the headland, and as she looked the green Range Rover was bumping its way over the springy grass. Adam was at the cottages.

'I feel fantastic,' Jill said, heaving herself out of the pool. 'Let's follow that up with some of your healing treatment. My back's been so much easier since you worked on it yesterday. I only wish I'd come to you before. But, I've still a week left. We'll make the most of it while I'm here.'

'How about this afternoon?' Bryony suggested, her eyes on the disappearing vehicle.

'No time like the present,' Jill insisted. 'Besides, this afternoon I'm booked for a sauna. Last week I lost over six pounds. This week I intend to make it another half stone at least. And now that my back's less painful, I shall be trying one of the aerobic classes as well.'

Reluctantly Bryony opened up her treatment-room, and ushered Jill in, hoping Adam would still be at the cottages once the session was over. There would be just enough time for a walk before lunch.

As she slipped through the gates, she kept her fingers crossed that Serena wouldn't join her this time, and began to stride swiftly up the narrow cliff track.

She could hear the sound of whistling above the noise of a hammer before she pushed her way through the tangle of long grass around the empty doorway, almost bumping her head on an orange helmet dangling from a nail over it. Adam should be wearing that, she frowned.

He was working on the upper floor, at the far end of

the building, where the roof was badly shattered. She could see the long lines of his jean-clad legs braced against the rungs of the ladder as he stretched upwards, battering away at the timbers.

He hasn't heard me, so I won't call out in case it startles him, she decided, watching the rhythmic movement of his tanned arm move backwards and forwards, the muscles of his neck tensing.

Shafts of sunshine filtered through the broken floorboards above her, tiny flecks of sawdust floating down, whirling and twisting. A musty smell of damp and decay filled her nostrils. She could hear the slight creak as the ladder shook with the force of his blows.

And then, as she stared upwards, the boards seemed to move in slow motion like an action replay on film, splintering into long jagged fingers of wood, the ladder falling sideways.

She heard the sound of Adam's cry echoing round her, heard the rending rush of noise as the upper floor disintegrated beneath him; then the sickening thud as he hurtled through the gap to land on the ground, only yards from her.

Her body propelled itself forward, each limb straining as if held back by a heavy weight; and she knew the scream reverberating in the air amid the shrill of seagulls was her own.

FOUR

Bryony's mind became a blank, as if to shut out all the horror. One thought only was there. *I mustn't move him.* Adam needed expert attention. In the shadows of the empty house she could see his face. Even his lips were white.

She dragged her arms from the sleeves of her jacket and laid it over him, hardly daring to touch the stillness of his body. *What shall I do?* The words pounded in her brain, but she didn't know the answer. Fear caught at her throat. *If I leave him …?* He was unconscious now, but if he woke …? She must stay.

Fearfully her fingers touched his throat, feeling for a pulse, and the chill of his skin terrified her. Shock, she told herself, trying to stay calm. It had that effect. He was alive. He had to be.

The murmur of voices filtered into her hearing. She raised her head, listening. Someone was on the path. Swiftly she stood up, running outside. A man and woman were passing, a lively terrier tugging them on.

'Help me,' she pleaded.

They stopped, the dog barking in excitement as it leaped around her legs.

'Down, Fred,' bellowed the man.

'There's been an accident,' she faltered. 'Please fetch Dr Carthew … Penreath … the big house over there....'

The couple looked at each other doubtfully.

'Please,' she implored. 'Adam's badly hurt.'

'I'll go.' The man turned and was running now, the dog trying to follow, jerking at the lead the woman held.

'I'll tie Fred to a bush, dear. Gets a bit boisterous sometimes. This breed do, you know. Excitable little creatures. Now, you tell me what's happened. You're as white as a sheet.'

Bryony led the way back into the ruins of the cottage, silently indicating Adam's twisted body in the debris of the floor, and heard the woman's intake of breath. 'Oh, poor lad! We can't leave him in a heap like that. Here, you take his legs.'

'No!' Bryony heard her voice cry out in a shrill protest of sound. 'Don't touch him!'

'But he's all twisted up,' protested the woman.

'If he's damaged his back, he mustn't be moved. Wait until the doctor comes. He'll know what to do.'

Why can't I? she asked herself. *All I have to do is probe those limbs, his spine, his neck. All I have to do.* But it was as if she'd been turned to wood. Too frightened of the outcome to dare to make the lightest move, knowing that if Adam had injured his spine or neck, the slightest jarring could cause permanent damage, even paralysis.

'Let me tuck my jumper under his head then. Make him comfortable.'

'No!' She caught at the woman's arm, digging her fingers deep.

'There's no need to act like that!'

'I'm sorry,' Bryony said, releasing her grip, 'but it could be dangerous.'

The dog was going frantic now, jumping around outside in a frenzy of high-pitched yapping. Footsteps came thundering along the path; the sound of rapid breathing as the man appeared in the doorway, breathless with exertion, his large round face red and sweating. 'Helicopter,' he gasped out. 'Doctor couldn't come.' Or was it *wouldn't come*? Bryony couldn't be quite sure of his correct words.

He bent down beside Adam, his hand reaching out.

'No,' his wife said, with a warning glance at Bryony. 'We mustn't touch him.'

'But …?' the man began.

'Could do damage,' his wife explained. 'So she says.'

A flutter of sound trembled in the air, sending the dog into even greater agitation.

'Here they come,' the man said in a satisfied voice, rising to his feet and going outside. 'I'll give them a wave.'

The roar of noise vibrated round them, sending the dust rising, blinding their eyes. Bryony felt herself begin to choke, cupping her hands above Adam's face in an attempt to stop it from being covered. Grass stems and bushes flattened, and the dog suddenly hurtled in, the broken end of its lead trailing, heading straight for Adam's prone body.

With one unexpectedly lithe movement the woman scooped it up, hugging it to her, kissing its wet nose, making crooning noises, comforting it.

'Poor little love,' she soothed, rubbing her chin against its head. 'Did a nasty airplane make 'oo frightened then?'

Bryony heard the scrabble of feet on the rough ground at the back of the building, saw a tall, broad figure appear, and a wave of intense relief flooded over her. Now Adam was safe.

'He fell.' Her voice was a thin imitation of itself as she pointed upwards to the splintered ceiling.

'We haven't touched him,' the woman butted in. 'Thought it best. Could have done himself a nasty injury in a fall like that.'

Another of the rescue crew joined them, crouching

down beside Adam, his competent hands moving lightly over the still body.

'It's Veryan's son, isn't it?' he asked, turning to Bryony.

She nodded bleakly.

'Remember that guy who smashed himself up over at Manacle Point?' he enquired of his companion. 'Looks like there's two of them now.' Her eyes pleaded with his, wanting him to be wrong. Adam's father had broken his back, confining him to a wheelchair. 'Someone must let the man know. Will you?'

Silently she nodded again, watching as they slid Adam on to a stretcher, padding his limbs, strapping him carefully. She followed their cautious progress over the uneven ground to where the helicopter blades beat the air, seeing their backs bend under its rotating arms, and raise the stretcher. And then the noise was tearing into her, filling her head, resounding in her ears, shaking the earth under her feet, twisting her hair into a vicious tangle around her face.

Her eyes desolately observed its progress as it swung away in a wide arc, rising higher into a sky where clouds were gathering in grey clusters like trailing smoke, and watched it grow smaller and smaller with distance.

'Will you be all right now?' The woman's hand on her arm made her jump.

'Yes,' she answered, trying to smile. 'And thank you.'

'Looked bad, didn't it?' the man commented, shaking his head mournfully. 'Wouldn't like to rate his chances,' and then he stopped, his eyes flicking away as the woman nudged him with a warning nod in Bryony's direction.

'Going back along the path, are you, dear? We'll just make sure you get there safely. Shook you up a bit, I dare say. Boyfriend, was he?'

Bryony stared blankly at the woman, hardly catching her words. Why hadn't Gavin Carthew come? He couldn't know it was Adam. He was a doctor. There to save life. So why didn't he come?

Her car was parked near the edge of the garden and as she crossed the lawn she felt in the pocket of her jacket for the keys, wondering when she'd put it on again.

Coverack. That was where Adam lived. They'd passed it on a signpost somewhere. The car jerked out into the lane. She drove automatically, changing gear, rounding bends, her mind detached. All she could see was the pale outline of his face; eyes tightly closed, lips bloodless, slightly parted, only the faint whisper of his breath telling her that he was still alive.

Still alive. But for how long?

At a junction in the road, she saw the sign again — Coverack — and followed its direction, descending swiftly to the sea-wall. It was only a tiny fishing village; stone-built houses and whitewashed cottages lined above the horseshoe of a harbour where boats swayed at anchor. She slowed the car, not knowing where to go. The sea was calm, lapping gently at the rock-scattered sand of the shore. It made no sound. Sandlings and turnstones dabbled their beaks along the water's edge.

She saw a shop, cabbages heaped on a bench outside; bundles of firewood stacked below the window; a sack of daffodil bulbs yawning sideways. Postcards hung in long straight rows around the door. She went inside.

'Hullo, m'dear, and what can I do for you?'

'Veryan. Adam Veryan.' Even the sound of his name caught at her throat. 'I need to find his father.'

'Matthew Veryan, you'll be wanting then.' The woman came out into the road and pointed further on up the hill. 'That turning there,' she said. 'Bungalow at the far end. Bright blue paint. Can't miss it.'

'Will he be there?'

'Should be. 'Tis lunchtime. Try the garden, m'dear.'

Bryony climbed back into the car and followed the road indicated, dropping to a low gear as the hill steepened, entering open gates. A ramp led up to the front door. No one answered the bell and Bryony remembered the woman's words, finding her way round to the back of the bungalow where the garden stretched away to the surrounding fields.

A man sat by a reed-edged pond, head back, eyes closed, the sunshine glinting on the large metal wheels of his chair. Bryony hesitated about waking him.

'What's wrong?' Flint-grey eyes were probing deeply into her.

'It's Adam,' she said.

'Sit down before you fall down.' The order was sharp, his hand indicating the flat stone bench beside the water. Gratefully she sank on to it. 'Now then, what's happened? You look like a ghost. Out with it then.'

'He fell....'

'Done much damage, has he?'

'I don't know ... Someone called the helicopter. They took him away.' She realized she didn't know where.

The man's voice softened as he looked at her. 'You're the girl up at Penreath, aren't you? He's mentioned you.' A slight smile tugged at the corners of his lips reminding her of Adam. 'Quite frequently.' The wheelchair spun round, heading towards the bungalow. 'Come on. Don't just sit there wraithlike. We'll give them a buzz.'

Obediently she followed into the dimness of a kitchen where pale blue blinds part-shaded the windows, making it cool. The chair moved rapidly into a lounge, scattered with books and newspapers, and for a moment Bryony could picture Adam there, fair head bent as he read.

His father was dialling a number. She listened while his

voice spoke authoritatively. A man used to being in command, she decided. Even now.

His likeness to Adam was quite striking. Both had the same strongly boned face, the square chin, the wide mouth. Only their eyes were different. Both compelling. But Matthew's were a pale smoke-grey in contrast to Adam's almost sapphire-blue gaze. And their hair. Matthew's was iron-flecked. Still a handsome man though, despite....

Her eyes travelled from the broad shoulders in their faded navy sweat-shirt to the lifeless legs clad in the same kind of denim jeans that his son so often wore. Was Adam now to be like his father in every way?

'Don't look so scared!' She blinked, raising her eyes to his face, realizing he'd put the phone down. 'Still unconscious. They're doing tests. Fracture to the left wrist. Multiple bruising. Always said that boy had a thick skull!' The chair rattled across the polished boards of the floor. 'Going over there to see him now. Want to come?'

'Can I?' she said, still bewildered by his briskness.

'Why not? My car. Trust my driving, will you?' The steely eyes bored into her, daring her to refuse, and once again she could see Adam in his challenging gaze. 'That's better. So you can smile. Don't hang about then.'

She watched as he levered himself into the driving seat, deftly folding the wheelchair and placing it behind him, knowing instinctively she must make no attempt to help. It was a practised movement, carried out countless times, and taken for granted.

He drove at a speed similar to his son. Another likeness, she reflected, trying to relax as the hedges whisked past, conscious that every so often his eyes glanced in her direction.

'Should have given you a brandy. You won't faint on me, will you? Not sure I could cope with that.'

She smiled, trying to reassure him. 'No,' she said, 'I won't faint,' and hoped she wasn't proved wrong.

As they passed Culdrose a helicopter spluttered, then rose into the air, heading out to sea, and she saw his head turn, his grey eyes suddenly filled with an intense longing, then his concentration was on the road again, the fleeting expression gone.

How must he feel, she wondered, knowing that once that, too, was his life? His whole life. What must it be like to perform such a hazardous job? A job that must test a person to the very limits of endurance; where you controlled life and death by a tenuous thread. And then to have it all end; finally, abruptly. Horrendously.

'They've taken him to Truro.' Matthew's words interrupted her thoughts. 'Quite a way. I was there myself – before I went to Stoke.' Cold fear ebbed over her again. What was he trying to tell her? 'Adam'll be all right, don't you worry. Take more than falling off a roof to restrain my son.'

Is he trying to convince himself? she wondered.

She hated the smell of hospitals. It seemed to linger, losing itself in one's clothes to reappear later, persistently clinging. Her hands clenched into fists against her sides, fighting back memories.

They were sitting in a long corridor, a constant stream of people moving past. Brisk nurses in their stiffly rustling uniforms. Anxious visitors, fixing their smiles and composing themselves before entering a ward. An occasional child, wailing, or running excitedly, enjoying the sound of its echo.

Bryony watched them all, trying to guess their lives. The shuffling old man so obviously visiting a wife. The tearful young girl, wedding ring still bright, carrying a small baby. The couple, middle-aged, the lines on their worried faces growing deeper with each passing moment, holding each other's hand for comfort.

Beside her Matthew was silent. He's been through all this before, she remembered, only then it was for him everyone worried. She let her mind travel slowly over the time she and Adam had spent together. So little time. She'd been drawn to him, as if by an invisible bond, from the first second; frightened by the feelings he aroused in her. She still loved Tom.

When he'd asked her out for a drink, she hadn't been able to refuse. But when she did – she'd retreated. Unable to tell him her fear. And yet, he'd asked her again. She remembered his probing questions as they ate in that little restaurant in Porthleven. Why couldn't she reveal to him that she loved Tom so much? Still did love him. She couldn't love anyone else. It wasn't possible to feel the same way about another man. Not the *same* way.

But Adam was different. Adam wasn't Tom.

And Tom was dead. She had to face up to that. Couldn't go on grieving for him. Mustn't. Life had to go on. Everyone told her that. *Life has to go on.* Tom's life was ended. But not her own.

Once she'd been so sure it was. That she couldn't exist without Tom. Once. But now ... Was it possible to love again? She felt like a traitor even to think such a thing. Was this love? This heart-rending torturing agony of whether another person lived or died? Someone she hardly knew. Someone she'd spent hours, not days, or months, or years, with. Was this love?

Matthew touched her arm. A nurse was bending over him, speaking softly. Bryony tried to bring her mind into focus. Matthew's wheelchair began to move away down the corridor. He twisted his grey head, looking back at her, and smiled, raising one finger to beckon.

'Push my chair, will you,' he instructed. 'I told her I
needed you with me. Thinks you're my daughter. Didn't
enlighten her. You do want to see him?'

'Please,' she breathed.

Adam's head was turned away from them, his hair
smooth and silky as if freshly brushed against the whiteness of the pillow. Bryony realized she'd never seen it
look like that before. There'd always been a sea breeze
wherever they met, ruffling it over his forehead. She
moved closer.

His features were clearly defined – and characterless;
his eyes closed, their lashes dark against his skin. Eyes
reveal so much, she thought. The whole expression of a
face. Without them, it's as if there's no one there. As if
he'd gone and left an empty mask behind.

In repose his mouth was not as wide, but then she'd
always seen it smiling, his lips curving upwards, deep
lines curling into his cheeks. Even the cleft in his square
chin was lost. His whole body lay still; straight under the
covers. Only the faint movement of his breath disturbed
it.

'Looks like a bloody corpse,' she heard his father
mutter, sensing that the words were to hide his shocked
emotions. 'Come on, son. Come on,' and she saw him bite
hard on his lower lip.

'Any change and we'll let you know.' The nurse had
followed them into the room. 'His pulse rate is good.
Tough guy, your son. He'll be OK. Don't worry. Why
don't you go and have a cup of tea?'

Bryony reached out to touch Adam's cheek, feeling the
graze of rough stubble, needing him to know she was
there, and then turned away to push Matthew's wheelchair from the room.

'Tea! I could do with something stronger,' he burst out,
once they were outside, and she saw that his hands were

trembling on the wheels.

'Coffee then? Good and black,' she smiled, in an attempt to cheer him up.

'I'm scared, Bryony,' he said quietly, stilling the chair in the corridor. 'Seeing him like that ... it brought back so much. Same room I was in, would you believe? You don't think ...?'

'They'd have told you,' she comforted, placing her hand over his shaking fingers, wanting to believe it too.

'Huh! Treat everyone as if they were daft. Everything hush-hush. Never consider it's your flesh and blood. Always so much damned secrecy.'

'I'll find a doctor. You can ask him. Someone must know. The nurse did say though....'

'Nurse! What do damned nurses know? The patient's quite comfortable,' he mimicked. 'And all the time the patient's in bloody agony.'

'Stay there. I'll see who I can find, and tea, if there is any.'

'Stay?' he roared. 'Where else do you think I'll bloody well go?'

She found the nurse in a side room, chatting to another. They both looked up, smiling when she entered.

'Mr Veryan ... he's very worried. Is there anyone he can talk to? A doctor maybe. Someone who knows what's happening.'

'They'll be just starting the rounds, but I'll go and catch them if I can.'

One girl left the room. The other looked keenly at Bryony. 'He is going to be OK,' she smiled. 'It's probably only concussion. By tomorrow morning he'll be chasing us round the wards like the rest of them,' she added with a twinkle.

'He fell so heavily.'

'Don't worry. Some people can trip over the cat and do far more damage. This one's a fit young specimen. He'll come up smiling again.'

Footsteps echoed down the corridor and Bryony went out to see a grey-haired woman hurrying down the corridor with the nurse.

'This is Dr Pentland,' the girl explained. 'I've told her Mr Veryan would like to see her.'

'Good grief, it's you!' Matthew declared with a start of recognition. 'Keep her away from me, Bryony. That's the monster who kept me pinned to that bed in there.'

'I knew it was going to be you,' the doctor laughed. 'Well, I'm pleased to say Adam isn't going to end up in one of these contraptions, not that it seems to impede your progress very much, Matthew, but that was only to be expected.'

'Come on now, Penny, my dear. No paddling about. I want the truth. If anyone knows what I can take, it's you.'

The doctor's face grew serious. 'We've done some tests, and when he's conscious we can do more. Until then, there's not a great deal I can say. The scan showed no damage to his spine, if that's what's worrying you. He's going to have some nasty bruising, and a lot of stiffness to begin with, but that'll wear off. Once he's out of shock and fully round again, we can do some neurological tests. The wrist fracture is quite straightforward. It will annoy him, if he's as impatient as you, but time will cure that. Come back tomorrow. We'll know more then. Now, I must start on my rounds. Nice to see you again, Matthew.'

'Great girl, that. Trust her with anyone's life, I would, and there's not many you can say that about, Bryony. We'd best be off home. No point in hanging round this morgue any longer.'

Bryony stayed at the bungalow for a cup of tea, refusing

the whisky he offered her.

'Put a bit of colour back into those cheeks,' he declared, but she shook her head, wondering even so how she was going to manage the drive back to Penreath.

'Let me have your number. I'll give you a buzz if anything crops up,' he said, handing her a pad. 'Dare say Adam knows it by heart, only he's not around to ask.'

'Is there someone ...?' to cope, she wanted to ask, hating to leave him alone.

'I'm perfectly capable, you know, even if I do look like a total wreck.'

'That's not what I mean,' she faltered.

'Don't need a wet-nurse, if that's what you do mean.'

'Would you like me to stay? Make you a meal?'

'Stop fussing! I'm perfectly able to cope. This isn't anything new, my dear. After nearly ten years, I'm quite used to the defects. At first ... it took time to come to terms with a body that exists in part only.' There was a sudden bleakness to his face, ageing it, and she knew in that moment what Adam would be like as an old man. 'I couldn't bear it if my son had to cope with this though. And I'm not sure whether he could either.'

'He won't have to,' she murmured, bending to kiss his forehead.

'Watch out, young lady! I'm not as defective as all that! Be off with you now, before I give young Adam a run for his money.'

Carefully she reversed her car and went through the gate, seeing his hand raise and wave, before the wheelchair turned towards the garden.

'And where do you think you've been all afternoon?' Gavin Carthew's chill tones met her as she slipped wearily in through the front door.

'I'm sorry, Dr Carthew. There was an accident, up at the cottages. Adam Veryan....'

'Ah yes.' His voice was like silk. 'Adam Veryan.'

'Presumably you know because someone came here for your help,' she retorted frostily, 'which you declined to give.'

'As it happens, I was out,' he replied. 'I gather Astrid telephoned the correct authorities to deal with the matter. The man should have realized what an unstable condition that building is in. It's supposed to be his job.'

No enquiry as to how Adam is, she noticed.

'That doesn't explain where you have been though.'

'Someone had to inform his father,' she answered.

'Oh yes,' he said, almost maliciously. 'The man's a cripple.'

'Matthew Veryan is confined to a wheelchair,' she replied.

'And when you'd told him?'

'We went to Truro. Adam's in the hospital there.'

'The father can't drive, I suppose?' Without waiting for her reply Gavin pulled back the sleeve of his immaculate dark suit and looked at the slim gold watch on his wrist. 'It's now past six. Once you've tidied yourself and had dinner, I think you should be able to manage at least five of your missed appointments. I'll let the guests know you'll be expecting them.'

'So what was all the excitement up there on the cliff?' Jill joined Bryony for dinner, eyeing her well-filled plate with a sigh. 'I've forgotten what it's like to eat a meal like that – yet you stay so slim. How on earth do you manage it? I exist on thin air and look at me!'

She raised her spoon and dipped into a small cut-glass dish of fresh fruit and yoghurt. 'This is my lot for tonight and I'll still be lucky to have shed an ounce by tomorrow. Now, tell me about the accident and take my mind off my stomach. There've been so many rumours flitting around all afternoon, but you were on the scene, Astrid said. Someone working there, wasn't it?'

Bryony nodded, her whole body aching with tiredness. 'He fell through the upper floorboards.'

'And?'

'He was still unconscious when we left the hospital.'

'Friend of mine came a cropper on a horse. Or off a horse, I should say. Out like a light for three days and nights. Never the same. Bit doolally ever since. Falls like that can have a ghastly effect. Did this chap break anything? Every bone in his body, according to the grape-vine here.'

'He fractured his wrist.'

'Was that all?' Jill sounded disappointed. 'Probably have after-effects though. Usually do. Think everything's all fine and dandy, then a couple of years later, all sorts of complications begin. You should know, Bryony, being an osteopath. Half your cases must be the result of past accidents.'

'Sometimes,' she agreed wearily. 'Look, I'll have to go. Dr Carthew wants me to catch up on the appointments I missed.'

'Can you fit me in as well? You really are doing wonders for my back, you know. I actually *climbed* the path to that lighthouse this afternoon. First time I've walked anywhere for yonks.'

'I'm sorry, Jill. You are booked in for ten tomorrow morning, aren't you?'

The woman's plump cheeks pouted. 'That's tomorrow, darling. I really could do with a good night's sleep, and those hands of yours send me into oblivion within seconds.'

'I really can't fit in any more this evening. It's going to

be past ten before I finish.'

As she went out into the hall, Astrid was striding towards her. 'Oh, Bryony. It is a telephone call for you. I was coming to find you. Matthew Veryan. Very urgent that he speak with you. Shall I put it through to your bedroom?'

Bryony's heart gave a lurch of fear, her feet stumbling as she ran up the stairs, reaching the top floor, hesitating outside her door to find the key. Inside she could hear the trill of the phone.

'Matthew!' she gasped breathlessly, sinking on to the end of her bed as she clutched the phone close to her ear. 'What's wrong?'

'Don't get in a panic, my dear! Penny just rang from the hospital. Nice girl that. Always was very considerate.'

'What did she say, Matthew?' Bryony tried desperately to keep her voice on an even note.

'Adam came round about half an hour ago. She's going to start the tests straight away. Thought you'd like to know. Put your mind at rest, I dare say. I'm on my way over there now.'

'But aren't you tired, Matthew?'

'I'll cat-nap when I get there. Never sleep that well in any case.'

'Would you like me to come with you?'

'Heavens no! Nothing you can do. Nothing either of us can do. Thought I'd like to be there though, just in case....' His voice died away. 'Won't delay you, my dear. Dare say you've lots to do. Keep you posted anyway. Bye now.'

'Bye, Matthew, and thank you.'

She remembered the orange helmet dangling by its strap from that wall, and wondered whether it was still there.

FIVE

Bryony slept fitfully that night, her dreams re-echoing the horror of the day, and finally she woke to see a thick mist hanging over the bay, completely hiding the cliffs and lighthouse from view. It was as if an impenetrable layer of gauze separated Penreath from the rest of the world. The air was chill. Cobwebs starred with tiny beads of moisture covered every bush, stretching from twig to twig of trees to catch wetly at unsuspecting faces as they passed. All sound was muffled.

Even the guests were subdued, talking in quiet voices as they ate their breakfasts before beginning the events of the day. Bryony was joined by a sprightly Jill, her hair still dripping from an early morning swim, her plump cheeks glowing with excitement.

'It's done the trick!' she announced, delving into a bowl of muesli with enthusiasm. 'Blown! Completely gone.'

'What is?' Bryony asked, her mind unable to concentrate.

'My writer's block! I haven't been able to produce a coherent sentence for weeks and then, last night, wow! I was off. Haven't slept a wink, but I feel bloody marvellous.'

'So what do you think started you writing again?'

'Who knows? Freedom from pain maybe. That back

of mine's been murder. In fact that's what the new book's going to be about.'

'Backs or murder?' Bryony enquired, wondering whether it was too early to phone the hospital.

'Both!' Jill exclaimed triumphantly. 'I've been wanting to break away from my usual run of things. Everything's been getting so predictable, but then when you've produced over twenty romantic novels, it's not surprising. No, this time it's going to be a whodunit! Set in a health farm! What do you think?'

Bryony was only half-listening. 'Should be fantastic,' she replied, hoping that was the right answer.

'Fantastic! It's going to be more than that! There's so much scope here. Even better than an Agatha Christie! A bunch of people all confined to one place, seething with pent-up emotions. I'd scarcely put my head on the pillow last night, when zoink! Thank goodness I always carry a couple of notepads around in my bag.'

She poured a glass of fruit juice and came back to the table.

'I'm going to have a word with Gavin about using the word processor he has in his office. It's completely wasted on him. By the end of the week I can have at least a couple of chapters and complete synopsis ready for my agent when I get back home.'

'But you're supposed to be here for a rest, Jill,' Bryony warned.

'Rest! What do I need with rest? This'll do me far more good.' She gave a deep sigh. 'Oh, Bryony! If you only knew the relief! I'd begun to think I was over the hill. That I'd penned my last word. Burned out. It's been getting me down for weeks. But now ... *the leetle grey cells*, as Hercule Poirot would say, are functioning again! And not only that, but I feel really great too. Can we skip today's treatment session? I can't wait to get my fingers on a keyboard again.'

'It would be silly to stop, when we're making such progress with your back, Jill. Is half an hour really going to make all that difference to your book?'

Jill smiled at her, her eyes glowing. 'No,' she agreed. 'You're right. It would be stupid. After all, that's what I'm here for, isn't it? And at the rate Gavin charges.... Look, I must go and have a word with him about that word processor. See you around ten.'

Bryony watched her weave her way across the room between the tables, rather like a huge pink elephant in her glowing tracksuit, and begin a rapid conversation with Gavin, her hands demonstrating in the air as her enthusiasm grew. From the look on Gavin Carthew's face, Jill was going to have difficulty in convincing him. His office was his sanctum. Bryony couldn't see him being too keen to have his privacy invaded.

She rose to her feet with a quick glance at her watch. There was time to phone before her first appointment. She'd try Matthew Veryan's number. The hospital wouldn't reveal much to an outsider. When there was no reply, she guessed he must still be in Truro, but whether that was good news or bad, she couldn't decide.

For the rest of the morning she had no time to phone again, and it was midday before she had a breathing space between appointments. Outside she could see the mist still obscuring the landscape, cloaking it in an eerie silence. Even the gulls had ceased to cry.

Matthew's voice sounded exhausted and she was worried she'd woken him, but he assured her she hadn't.

'Only just got back,' he said. 'Was going to ring when I'd had some coffee. Thought you might be busy. Didn't want to upset Carthew. You don't want to hear all this though, do you? Adam's going to be fine.'

Bryony felt her shoulders untense and her grip relax a

little on the receiver.

'Sitting up and talking now,' Matthew went on. 'Well, not so much talking as complaining bitterly about being kept in bed! Looks a bit of a mess though. One or two bruises coming out. Arm in a sling, although from the way he was chucking it about, I can't see that staying on for long. Asked after you.'

Bryony smiled to herself, guessing just how impatient Adam would be at being restricted.

'Had a chat to Penny. No beating about the bush with that girl. Straight talker. Know where you stand with her. Assured me everything's all right. Given him a good going over. All in working order. Should be home in a few days.' He gave a short laugh. 'If they can tie him down for that long.'

'It's amazing he's come off so lightly,' she said.

'Did a bit of parachuting a year or so back. Charity do. Learnt how to fall then. May have helped. You'll have to ask him. Had a word with Penny. You can pop in any time.'

Bryony hesitated. She'd already annoyed Gavin Carthew by not being there the previous afternoon.

'Why don't you go over this evening?' Matthew suggested. 'Old Carthew probably keeps your nose to the grindstone during the day. He's that kind of blighter. I'll give it a miss tonight. Poor boy's seen enough of me for one day.'

'Are you sure?'

'Run out of conversation if I visit too often,' she heard him chuckle. 'Besides, I'm sure he'd much prefer to see a pretty girl like you. Take care on the road though. This mist's diabolical.'

'OK then. Now you'd better get some sleep.'

'Yes,' he replied quietly. 'I'll be able to now I know everything'll be all right.'

Poor man, she thought. He must have been going through agonies. The whole episode would have brought back the events which caused him to be in that wheelchair. Only this time, it would have been twice as bad.

Her first appointment of the afternoon wasn't until 2.30. Bryony decided to fill in the time with a swim, but discovered everyone else had the same idea and the indoor pool was too crowded for comfort. She gazed out of the window, staring at the grey oblivion, feeling restless. It would be muddy along the cliff-path, but the walk up to the lighthouse was becoming routine now. She'd chance it anyway.

The mist beaded her lashes and made her hair cling limply to the sides of her face, prickling the air as she breathed. Momentarily it reminded her of smoke, but she swiftly pushed the thought away. It was strange how silent the sea had become. Almost as if it wasn't there. Her ears strained, listening.

The path trailed on ahead, looming up, section by section, to vanish instantly behind her. It was like walking in a vacuum. Pale walls of invisibility closing her in on either side. Leaves hung, unmoving, on wet bushes as she passed. Not a bird sang or fluttered among the thin twiggy branches.

At the cottages, she stopped, crossing the small expanse of ground to stand in the empty doorway, staring into the gloom. The murmur of voices startled her, and she heard a car door slam, the sound reverberating eerily. Two figures appeared out of the mist from the back of the building, then halted abruptly.

'Gave us quite a turn, you did, standing there,' one declared. 'Like a little ghost, you were.'

She smiled, recognizing them as the men who were working on the building during the week.

'Sorry,' she said, 'but I didn't expect anyone to be around on a day like this.'

'Don't make much difference to us,' the other said. 'Walls is walls, whatever the weather. Just had a bite to eat. Got to get on now.' He gave Bryony a searching look. 'Aren't you the young lady from Penreath as found young Adam?'

She nodded.

'Nasty do, that,' he continued, wiping his hand across his mouth as he frowned. 'Someone's been playing around here.'

'Playing around?' she queried.

'Those boards up there've been part sawed through. Weakened them, you see. Anyone working up there would've gone through, given time. Could have been Arthur here, or even me.'

Only it was Adam, she thought, working there at the weekend.

'But why should anyone do such a thing? Were they trying to steal the wood?'

'Wouldn't be much use, apart from kindling. And 'tis going to a lot of trouble just for that. Plenty gets washed up on the shore, though 'tis true does smell a bit when you burn it.'

'Nasty sort of trick to play,' the first man growled, shaking his head. 'Could have killed a body.'

'But you're sure it was deliberate?' she persisted.

'Take a look for yourself, m'dear.' He picked up a section of board and held it out to her, and she could see the clean cut before it had broken jaggedly. 'Careful bit of work, that. And took time. Just enough to hold them steady until a bit of weight put pressure on them.'

'Young Adam's a bit lighter than we are,' his companion added. 'Probably worked away for an hour or so before they finally gave. Lucky you was passing and noticed him.'

Not exactly passing, she thought wryly. But it was true. If she hadn't been there when he fell, he could have lain for hours, with people walking along the path only yards away.

'He likes to come over of a Saturday and Sunday to check what we'm been up to in the week, and do a bit himself. Not afraid of getting his hands dirty is young Adam. Does a job as good as anyone, too.'

'I'll be seeing him this evening. Shall I tell him what you've said?' she asked.

'You do that, m'dear. We'll all need to take a bit of extra care while there's a joker like this around. Give him our regards, won't you? Look forward to seeing him back, we'll be. Watch your step on that path. 'Tis treacherous in a sea fret like this.'

So someone had deliberately weakened the upper floor, knowing that it could cause a bad accident, even a death. But why? she mused, picking her way back along the track to Penreath. There were always vandals around wherever you went, only this seemed such a calculated thing to do, not a sudden mindless impulse. Someone had gone up to those cottages with a saw and spent several hours on the task.

Someone who wanted to impede the renovation work. And the only person she knew who objected to that was Gavin Carthew. But would he do such a thing? It really seemed absurd. Gavin was much too suave to skulk around in the dead of night, sawing through floorboards. Besides, why bother? It would only make the work take far longer. Something Gavin wouldn't want to happen. He disliked the idea of Penreath's privacy being invaded by what he considered to be prying eyes and noise.

Adam was sitting up in bed doing a newspaper crossword

when she arrived but tossed it aside, his mouth breaking into a smile of welcome.

'Bryony!' No one else could make her name sound like that.

'I didn't know what to bring you,' she said, putting a box of fudge on the locker beside him. 'I don't know what you like.'

'Seeing you!' he grinned. 'Instant cure. Far better than all the jollop those nurses keep pouring down me.'

'You don't look too bad, whatever they've given you,' she smiled, recalling the way he'd been when she last saw him, lying there on the pillows, as if he'd never move again.

'Won't let me get out of bed and walk about though,' he grumbled. 'Heaven knows why. I feel fine.'

'But probably not when you start moving around again,' she warned. 'Why on earth you're not in a dozen pieces, I shall never know. You came through that floor like a ton of bricks!'

'Dad said you were there. What happened? It's all rather a blur. I remember being up the ladder, then nothing until I woke up here.'

Bryony looked at him doubtfully, wondering whether he really was in a fit state to be told all the details. A dark bruise was growing on his left cheek and she could see another on his shoulder above the plaster concealing his fractured wrist.

'Come on! Out with it.'

'What do you mean?' she asked.

'There's something bothering you, isn't there? I know I should have been wearing a helmet, but it gets pretty hot in one of those. Something must have gone wrong though. Come on, Bryony, what did I do?'

'You didn't do anything wrong,' she said slowly, and hesitated before continuing. 'I met two of the workmen up there today.'

'Joe and Arthur.'

'Probably,' she replied. 'And one of them said the boards of the upper floor in the cottage had been partly sawn through.'

She saw his brow pucker into a frown.

'Sawn? They couldn't be.'

'It's true,' she said. 'He showed me one. It was quite definitely cleanly cut with a saw. And, Adam, if you remember, yesterday was brilliantly sunny.'

He nodded. 'Yes, I do remember that. It was why I didn't wear my helmet. Under that corner of the roof it was like an oven.'

'Well, when I stood there, looking up at you, the sun was beaming down through cracks in the ceiling. Broad rays of light, dazzling my eyes. And I noticed, without thinking about it, that they were filled with floating sawdust. It settled all over my dark jacket in tiny specks and I tried to brush them off. My mother always used to talk about "fairies dancing on a sunbeam" when I was a child and saw motes of dust swirling in them. It made me think of that.'

Adam's gaze was fixed on hers.

'You're sure it wasn't just dust from where I was hammering.'

'Some was, but that was gritty, not the same at all. I looked at my jacket again when I was talking to them. There were still specks in the creases and under the collar. I'd put it over you when you were lying on the floor. It was both grit and sawdust.' She bit her lip. 'Someone wanted you or one of the men to have an accident, Adam. I immediately thought of Gavin Carthew. He's the only one who would want to prevent the project, but somehow it seems rather out of keeping with a man like that, don't you think?'

'We do get problems with vandalism,' Adam mused, his brow wrinkling.

'This is more than vandalism, Adam.'

'Have you mentioned it to my father?'

Bryony shook her head. 'I haven't had a chance. I've been working all afternoon. Why? Don't you want him to know?'

'I don't want to worry him any more than's necessary. He's got enough to contend with.' Adam looked enquiringly at her. 'What do you think of him, now that you've met him? He was certainly bowled over by you — and women don't rate all that highly on his list, I'm afraid, after the way my mother treated him.'

'I liked him. You're both very similar, you know.'

'Are we now?' he grinned. 'So can I take it from that remark that you like me too?'

She smiled back at him without replying.

'And this does give me an excuse to have you visit me,' he teased. 'I bet it would have taken weeks to get you sitting on my bed.'

'Be serious!'

'Is that an invitation? Because I could become extremely serious, if you'd only give me half a chance.' His fingers caught her hand in his, refusing to let go as she tried to pull away. 'What is it about me that frightens you? Why do you constantly hold back? What's happened in your life to make you like this, Bryony? I want to know.'

She stood upright, staring into his eyes. Eyes that held her gaze as closely as his hand was holding hers.

'You were in love,' he said gently. 'You've a fragile, haunted look that hides a damaged soul. Maybe you're still in love. If so, then I shall have to understand. But I want to know, Bryony.'

'Tom and I were engaged.'

'Were?' he echoed the word.

'Tom died.'

It was as if a dam was cracking and bursting inside of her, all the pent-up emotions ready to rush out and be freed. Sentences formed in her head, waiting to be spoken. Adam's hand was like a lifeline bridging the gap between them. All she had to do now was step across.

With a burst of sound, the door opened behind her. A wheelchair rattled towards the bed, propelled by a rosy-faced little nurse. 'They want you down in X-ray, then it's a dollop more plaster on that wrist.'

Bryony snatched her fingers from his grasp, stepping away from him, retreating to the door, seeing the desperate appeal in his blue eyes.

She watched as the nurse eased him into the wheelchair, his lean muscular body moving awkwardly. For a moment he sat, looking back at her before the chair began to move. And in that brief second, Bryony saw the image of his father sitting there. That, she remembered, could have been Adam's fate as well.

'Come back soon,' he whispered.

The mist was beginning to clear as she drove to Penreath, dense only near the sea and when she crossed Goonhilly Down, making her slow the car. It had a ghostly, eerie sort of quality taking her back to times long gone, when wreckers had gathered on lonely shores on nights like this, eager for a floundering ship to hit the rocks.

She could almost hear the creak of harness and soft padding of muffled hooves as donkeys and ponies followed the winding paths, loaded with bales and bundles to be stowed in a secret hidey-hole or cellar away from curious eyes.

Had Penreath once been the destination for such

smuggled goods? It was an ideal spot. The tiny cove below. The open cliffs. No one to see. Except the inhabitants of those cottages, maybe. And they were probably part of a wicked group who scavenged the rocks for plunder.

For a fraction of a second the road ahead cleared, the mist thinning to swirling wisps. She could see a distorted shape held there. Her foot slammed on to the brake, shuddering the car to a halt, but it was only a strand of old man's beard trailing down from the hedge, to catch against the window as she passed. And yet, for that moment, it could so easily have been a shaggy-headed face peering in. Jill ought to be with me, she thought. She's the one with an active imagination.

It was a relief to see the gateposts of Penreath waver through the gloom and hear the familiar crunch of gravel beneath the wheels as the car crept along the drive. Lights gleamed dimly from all corners of the house, creating a welcome. A chatter of voices came from the little bar as she ran up the stairs, the air pleasantly warm after the dampness.

Shall I phone Matthew, she wondered, or will he be asleep? It must have been a long and exhausting day for him. Maybe it was better to let him rest. Her own bed lured her. And it was Adam's face that lingered in her memory, not Tom's, that night when she fell asleep.

After the mist came drizzle, blowing in thinly from the sea, barely strong enough to soak anyone's clothes, but coldly unpleasant. Autumn seemed to be hurrying on, after a glorious summer, and the leaves were changing rapidly. One gale would bare the trees completely.

Bryony shivered as she stared through her bedroom window, glad that she hadn't bothered to ask Gavin to have the nail removed from the lower sash window.

There wasn't any need now, until next spring.

She looked at it thoughtfully, running her finger over the flat metal head. It had been driven in and bent with considerable force. The paint surrounding it was gone in large flakes. The whole thing had probably rattled in the wind, driving the occupant frantic, she decided. No wonder such ferocious blows had been used. But it was odd really, when the rest of the house was kept so immaculately.

Had this once been a guest room? The other tower rooms were all used by guests. She was the only member of staff who slept there. And the view was awe-inspiring, every window set at a different angle. It was like being on a pinnacle.

Penreath must be quite old. Bryony wished she knew a little more about architecture and could recognize the style of old buildings. Maybe Adam or Matthew would know. The cottages must have been built around the same time.

A smile curved her mouth. Would Adam be returning home soon? All the tests had proved negative. There was no reason for him to stay in hospital for long, and she could guess that he was impatient to leave.

Jill descended on her during breakfast. It had become a habit now. She's a strange woman, Bryony thought. Rather like an unmade bed with her baggy tracksuit and untidy shock of wild hair. No one would ever imagine her to be a best-selling author with an income that probably ran into many thousands.

'How's the novel?'

'Fantastic! I've just done the first murder. Loads of gore! Gavin's been absolutely marvellous supplying me with gruesome details. He worked in forensic medicine years back. Did you know that? He's a mine of information. I've booked in for another two weeks. This is a superb place to work, you know. Nothing to distract me — apart from all the pampering, of course, and I shall let that tail off a little.' She hitched the sleeves of her tracksuit a little higher above her elbows. 'You'll never guess what, but since I began on the book I've lost weight without even trying! It's miraculous! Weeks of dieting to no effect, then eureka! A complete stone since I arrived. Do you think it's the swimming? I couldn't do that before I came here because of my back.'

'Well, it would tighten up your muscles a little, but I doubt it would have all that effect. A whole stone in weight? I should think it's because you're more active in general. You've been trotting up to the lighthouse and back on occasions, haven't you?'

'Ah, now, there's a reason for that!' Jill laughed. 'Murder number two will be over the cliff-edge. I need to taste the atmosphere for that and sitting indoors doesn't provide the right setting. I want the actual feel of the wind, the roughness of the ground underfoot, the snatch of brambles round my ankles, the sounds and sights. Oh, this time I've really cracked it, Bryony. I've had best-sellers before, but not like this is going to be.'

'Well, I'm glad everything's working out so well.'

'And it's mainly thanks to you. That back of mine's been crucifying me for yonks. I don't know about water wearing away a stone, but nagging pain certainly has a destructive effect on the brain. And now, I feel as though I've been reborn. It's fantastic. I'm telling everyone about you. Penreath won't know what's hit it when I get back to London. I should ask Gavin for twenty-five per cent commission! He'll be up to his eyes in gold-dust.'

'Don't get too carried away, Jill,' Bryony laughed. 'I've only got one pair of hands and a certain number of hours in one day.'

'How would you feel about working in London? I could keep you supplied with patients by the score. You'd be on a golden trail too, instead of helping to keep Gavin's pockets filled.'

Bryony shook her head ruefully. 'I tried that once, Jill. And once was enough.'

'Well, don't forget, darling. If you ever need a helping hand, it's my turn to do you a favour. I owe you an awful lot, you know, and I shall be eternally grateful.'

'That's what I'm here for,' Bryony smiled, beginning to feel embarrassed by so much gushing praise. 'And if I don't get going soon, Gavin will be chasing my tail.'

'Oh, don't you worry about Gavin! He's an absolute sweetie when you get to know him. Hidden depths and all that. The darling moved his word processor up to my room. Just think of that! Wouldn't hear of me having to share the office with him. Ruining my muse, he said. Wasn't that kind? So now I can play away with it day and night. And I must admit, I get some of my best ideas in the witching hours. This place is teeming with vibes. Am I holding you up, darling? Sorry!'

Bryony shot down the corridor to her treatment room in time to catch the first patient of the day, hearing Gavin Carthew emerge from his office after she'd passed. Now what have I done? she wondered, as his footsteps fell softly behind her and his voice called her name.

'I was curious to know the latest news of the Veryan man,' he said, when she turned to meet him.

'Adam? He should be out of hospital some time this week, I think.'

'As soon as that?' His silvery eyebrows rose.

'He was very lucky, Dr Carthew. The accident could have been fatal. I should imagine the police are dealing with it by now.'

'The police?'

'Yes. You see, someone had sawn part-way through the boards of the floor his ladder was standing on. It was only by chance he wasn't killed. Then, we'd have had a murder enquiry hanging over Penreath, wouldn't we?'

She met his eyes, searching them for any guilt, but all she could see was a faint gleam of sardonic humour.

SIX

Bryony couldn't believe it was November already. She'd been at Penreath for just over a month and the time had flown by. Every day seemed to be busier than the one before, and she was beginning to feel that Gavin Carthew would have to take on a second osteopath, if her workload didn't decrease a little. Even her evenings were booked now, and although there was the occasional spare hour during the day, she found it wasn't long enough for her to go anywhere or do anything, apart from a short walk, or swim or sauna at the house.

Jill was her most regular patient and, sometimes, Bryony wished she wasn't. The writer was so full of praise for the way her back problems had been eased that she greeted all newcomers with the details, and enthusiastically recommended they try a session for themselves.

The new novel was progressing rapidly, and Bryony could frequently hear the print-out of the word processor whirring away for hours into the night as Jill's room was directly below her own in the tower.

Gavin was proving to be a fantastic help, Jill ecstatically told everyone. It surprised Bryony that he had worked in forensic medicine. No one, it appeared, knew very much about his earlier life, so she was curious to discover what else Jill would learn.

When the new month began, other news worried
Bryony. Gavin had decided on a Guy Fawkes firework
display for the guests. Preparations commenced that
week when a number of trees were drastically pruned,
the wood being heaped ready for a bonfire. The pile
had grown daily until now it was over ten feet high and
almost as wide, with empty boxes and household waste
constantly added.

Bryony eyed it with dread, knowing she couldn't face
such a celebration. Even the thought of it terrified her.
And here, on the bleak bareness of the cliff, there would
be nowhere to escape the brilliant flare of flame, or its
accompanying hiss and crackle.

Matthew phoned to tell her when Adam returned
home, but she had so many appointments already
booked that it was the following evening before she
could go to see him.

'He's through there, in the lounge,' Matthew
announced when he opened the door. 'And so restless,
he's driving me mad! That hospital must've been
thankful to see the back of him. Keep him amused, will
you, my dear, while I go and make some coffee.'

Bryony pushed open the lounge door. The bruises
had passed through their colourful stage and were
beginning to fade, but her experienced eyes could tell
from the way Adam moved that his body was still
painful and she guessed he'd torn muscles or ligaments
in the fall.

'I thought you were never going to come, Bryony.' His
voice held a note of reproach.

'Did you?' she said, thinking how like a petulant child
he looked with that frown. 'Then I'm sorry, but now that
the weather's so much colder everyone at Penreath's
given up outside activities like croquet and tennis and

bowling to stay indoors, so I've been kept busy. I have thought about you though,' she added softly.

'Have you?' he smiled, the cleft in his chin intensifying. 'That sounds most interesting. What exactly were you thinking?'

The kitchen door swung forward and Matthew's wheelchair rattled through, a tray of mugs and plate of biscuits resting across his lap.

'Have you succeeded in quietening him down a little, Bryony?'

Colour burned in her cheeks as Adam gave a throaty laugh. Hastily, she bent her head to take the coffee from Matthew as he said, 'Arthur brought one of those floorboards over to show me a day or so ago. He was quite right. It had been partly sawn through.'

'Did you let the police know?' she asked.

'There's not much point,' Adam observed. 'Without being around to see it happen, there's not a lot they can do. Anyone could have been up there. We don't even know when it was done.'

'It *was* deliberate,' she protested. 'You might have been killed.'

'But I wasn't,' he replied.

'That doesn't make any difference!'

'To me, it does.'

'You should take it more seriously,' she warned.

'I dare say someone was just playing around,' he soothed.

'I'm not so sure, Adam,' his father said. 'It would have taken a great deal of care and precision to cut them like that. Just enough to weaken them, but not enough for any to break there and then. And only one section of the floor, under the roof where the next part of the work was to be carried out. There was nothing random about it.'

'Well, I think you should tell the police,' Bryony insisted.

'She's right, Adam.'

'What good would it do? After what happened, I doubt anyone's going to play the same trick again.'

'It might be something different next time,' Bryony murmured.

'There won't be a next time,' Adam retorted firmly. 'Now, let's change the subject and not dwell on the past. How about taking me for a drive tomorrow?'

'Me?' she said.

'Who else?' he grinned, waving his plastered arm at her. 'Surely Gavin Carthew doesn't expect you to work every day – it is Saturday.'

'I could manage the afternoon,' she suggested. 'Everyone rushes for a final appointment in the morning, before they leave, and then it's a bit slack until the new group arrive and get settled in.'

'The afternoon it shall be then,' Adam replied. 'And don't forget to bring a couple of nice soft cushions!'

'Are you still in a lot of pain?' she sympathized, noticing how any sudden movement made him wince, although he tried to hide it.

'My musculo-skeletal system *has* suffered trauma,' he teased. 'Why? Are you about to volunteer to restore its harmony and balance with a few high velocity thrusts and some gentle massage?' He gave her a wicked smile. 'You see, I did listen to that dissertation on osteopathy you were giving me the other day, when I was totally helpless and couldn't escape from my hospital bed. To be quite honest, I hoped you were going to put it into practice there and then, but unfortunately nurses always seem to appear at the most inopportune time.'

'The hospital gave you physiotherapy, didn't they?' she said, deliberately ignoring his teasing.

'Yes,' he replied drily, 'but I think the physiotherapist was a throw-back from medieval days when the rack and thumb-screw were in vogue. I'm sure your soothing hands would be much more effective.'

'Wait and see what a drive in the fresh air does for you tomorrow,' she observed.

'Tomorrow then,' he sighed.

It was one of those crisp November days that occasionally happen in autumn. There'd been a hard frost on the ground when she woke, converting the landscape into a dream-world of sharp contrasts. Every twig and stalk was rimed with a delicate coating that sparkled in the fast growing sunshine. The lawns stretched away to meet the long grass of the cliff in smooth perfection, their whiteness only marred by tiny etched footprints where a bird had skittered across searching for some interesting morsel of food. Bryony breathed in the brittle air, hoping the sun would last for their drive.

Jill was leaving that morning, and had booked in for one final treatment before her taxi arrived. Even in the few weeks she'd been there, Bryony could detect a difference in the texture of her skin, the muscles tightened now by exercise and swimming, instead of pain.

'Quite sure I can't persuade you to come back to London and work?'

Bryony shook her head.

'You'd make a fortune once I spread the word,' Jill coaxed.

'I doubt it,' Bryony smiled.

'But in a couple of days I'll be doubled-up again.'

'Not if you follow those exercises I gave you. Ten minutes a day, that's all they'll take. But you must do them regularly.'

Jill sighed. 'How about learning to type, then I could

employ you as my permanent secretary? You could live in, all expenses paid.' She screwed up her face in a grimace. 'No, I suppose even a luxury flat in dockland is no comparison with living in a place like this on the edge of the sea. I'm in two minds about moving to Cornwall myself, only it would mean giving up an enjoyable social life. I'd write more though.'

'You'd be bored stiff after a while,' Bryony laughed.

'I dare say you're right. I could become a bit hermit-like down here, especially in the winter. This stretch of coast must be bleak then, with gales blowing straight in from the Atlantic and not even a tree for protection.'

'How long before you finish the book?' Bryony asked, bending Jill's knee and rotating her hip joint.

'First draft should take up to Christmas. I always go flat out on that. Need to get the whole story down on paper, and know exactly where I'm going. Then the hard graft begins. Rewriting, and rewriting, until I reach what I hope is perfection. That takes months.'

'So I won't be reading it on my summer holiday then?'

Jill shook her head. 'Not next summer anyway. It might be out by Christmas twelve-month, if I'm lucky. My agent's reading the first three chapters and synopsis at the moment. He was the guy who came down last weekend.' She chuckled. 'Needs at least six months here to get rid of some of that surplus weight. I always tell him he lives off the fat of the land, although it's really all the authors he has slaving away. Still, without him, I wouldn't have got very far.'

'What did he say about you changing from romance to murder?'

'He was a little wary. Why change when you're on a winning streak, was his way of putting it. Bit of a gamble, he thought. But I reckon my name should carry me. It's really up to the reviewers. They can make or break sales.' She gave a rueful laugh. 'If they all damned it, it would probably be my greatest hit yet. It's amazing how a critical review can send sales rocketing.'

'Is Gavin still being useful?'

'He'd have made a fantastic murderer! He knows such detail. Would you believe that the police can tell exactly the angle a knife struck by how and where the blood spatters a wall or other surface? There was even one case he was telling me about where they caught a murderer from the bite marks in a sandwich. Built up a replica of his teeth and jaw, and from that they were able to make a sketch of his actual face.'

'That's it then,' Bryony said, moving away from the couch. 'Don't forget those exercises, will you? They should make a difference.'

Jill slipped back into her pink tracksuit and bent to tie up the laces of her trainers. 'One thing he did say intrigued me – about the perfect murder,' she mused. 'It's happening all the time, but because it is the *perfect* murder, no one knows. That really did make me think.'

The sides of the lane were deep in leaves when Bryony drove out through the gates that afternoon, crunching crisply under her wheels and swirling up as the car increased speed. She'd carefully fixed a special back-rest on to the passenger seat and was rather apprehensive about what Adam's reaction would be when he saw it. She didn't have long to wait.

'I'm not an infant,' he roared, glaring at it.

'It'll make you far more comfortable, Adam. Much better than cushions. This will support your back correctly. You can adjust it into a suitable position.'

With a few more grumbles, he settled in and she realized how small her Fiesta had become, filled by his presence. His head almost touched the roof, his knees were bent, and she could feel the pressure of his shoulder against her own.

'Well, where are you taking me?' he enquired as she put the car into gear and they began to descend the hill from the bungalow towards Coverack harbour where a few boats swung at anchor.

'You're the native guide,' she replied. 'I'm only the driver.'

'Right then,' he instructed. 'We'll go out past Helston, across to Redruth and over to St Agnes. That's old mining country. Quite spectacular. Then we'll take the coast road back round Hayle to St Ives. Has your lord and master at Penreath given orders for when you're to be back?'

She shook her head. 'I'm in no hurry. There's a Guy Fawkes party this evening, so the further I'm away from that, the better.'

His head turned sharply. 'What is it about fires, Bryony? Why do they scare you?'

Her fingers tightened on the steering wheel. 'I don't like them. That's all.' She didn't want to be reminded. Even the thought of seeing those bonfire flames rise high into the night, terrified her.

'You must have a reason,' he said gently.

She glanced sideways out of the window at the open countryside, hedges and fields stretching on either side of the car. Here she was safe. Here there were no walls to confine her. Constricting her. Preventing her escape.

'Wouldn't it help if you talked about it, Bryony? You can't go on fighting against something like that for ever.'

Her body tensed as she took a deep breath. 'Once I was caught in a fire.' The words came in a rush.

'Long ago?' he asked.

'Two years. Please, Adam, let's change the subject. Is

that muscular stiffness easing a little? Does the seat help?'

'Bryony,' he said quietly. 'You need to talk. I saw you that evening when we were in Helford. A log-fire in a grate, that's all it was, and yet you went nearly berserk. Tell me what happened. I want to help. Please let me.'

The car slowed at a crossroads. Automatically Bryony's head turned side to side. Her foot pressed down on the accelerator again. In a flat, toneless sound, her voice began to speak. Jerkily. Reluctantly.

'After I qualified, I set up my own practice near London. A flat. Only small. Over a shop. A newsagents. It was noisy at times. Early opening. Paperboys and girls. People constantly in and out. The flat was nice though. Tom and I did it up.'

'And Tom was your fiancé?'

She nodded, her eyes staring fixedly ahead. 'I'd known him for years. Ever since I was a child. He was a friend of my brother's. Like a second brother in a way. I loved him.' Her voice trembled on the words, and she took another deep breath before continuing. 'Tom was an airline pilot. Heathrow wasn't all that far away. We were going to live in the flat once we were married a couple of weeks later. I was staying with my brother and his wife in Pinner, but had already moved a lot of my clothes and belongings over there.'

Tall, lonely chimneys appeared, dotting the horizon, and every so often the square stone walls of a ruined engine-house. Bryony watched them pass, her face tight and drawn.

'I was tired that evening. It had been a busy day. People were starting to hear about me and came from quite a wide area. Some of Tom's friends. Flying can be a back-destroying business. There's a great deal of tension too. I knew quite a few of them.'

She watched smoke curl from a garden bonfire, twisting and spiralling up into the clear blue sky, and gave a faint shudder.

'Tom was on a three-day flight. One out, one there, one back. I made a cup of coffee and sat down to drink it, while I went over the notes of the last patient. A motorbike accident had left multiple fractures. They'd mended, but the patient still suffered a great deal of pain. I had a feeling a lot of it was psychosomatic, but I couldn't be sure. He was a courier, taking parcels and packets around London. His job depended on being able to ride a motorbike. And he was scared. The mind is a tricky subject. These things are hard to define though.'

Her eyes glanced sideways at Adam, but his face was impassive.

'I was reading through them, trying to remember everything he'd said. People reveal a lot as they relax. Quite irrelevant things at times, but often they let slip some tiny point.... It was a while before I became aware of the smoke. Seeping insidiously under the door. Suddenly I couldn't breathe. It was like hands squeezing my throat, closing it, choking me.' Her voice quivered slightly. 'Then I heard the noise. At first I couldn't understand what it was. I suppose my brain was confused, not functioning properly. A tremendous roar of sound. Fires crackle and sputter, gaining hold. This one must have been burning for a while. At the back of the shop bundles of papers and magazines were stored. Cartons of cigarettes. Plastic jars and boxes of sweets and chocolates. Someone had pushed lighted petrol-soaked rags through the rear door.'

Adam's fingers lightly soothed the back of her hand as it clenched round the steering wheel.

'I went out on to the landing. It was like an inferno.

Tongues of flame shooting up the stairs, sparks flying. I still couldn't believe that terrible noise. I remembered reading somewhere that you should always keep near the ground. Smoke is the killer. Smoke rises. Crawl to safety. But there was nowhere for me to crawl. Nowhere at all. I was up there, with no escape.' Mechanically she steered the car off the main road towards St Agnes, her concentration fixed intently, only her lips moved. 'I went back into the flat. Slammed the door, trying to keep it out. It was impossible. Then I heard Tom shouting to me. He was standing in the road amongst a growing crowd of people. I could see him from the window, staring up, the flames casting shadows on his face. I remember wondering why he was there. He should have been on that flight. Not returning home until the following day.

'I could hear his voice quite plainly. Telling me to jump. All I had to do was open the window. Open the window.... I couldn't move. Couldn't raise one hand. Couldn't reach out to undo the catch. All I could do was stand there, looking down at him. Then he was gone. I heard the sirens. Police cars; a fire-engine weaving its way through vehicles parked on both sides along the road; the gleaming white of an ambulance, lights flashing. Everything outside became one confusion.

'Then I fainted. Or maybe it was the effect of the smoke. When I opened my eyes, someone was carrying me down a ladder. A fireman, I suppose. It had to be, didn't it? Something smothered my nose and mouth, making me fight. All I wanted was Tom. And he wasn't there.'

'Park the car here,' Adam directed her quietly, and she carried out his instruction as if a wound-up robotic toy, guiding it off the road on to a stony patch of ground used as a car-park.

A breeze from the sea stirred brown stumps of heather and gorse. Her eyes gazed sightlessly to where surf roared in the distance towards the cliffs. 'Tom was dead.'

Adam's arm curved round her shoulders, pulling her head against his, his lips softly feathering her hair.

'Tom burned to death in that building. And it was all my fault.' A tear brimmed and then began a straight course to her chin, to be followed by another and another, finally released. 'My fault.'

His arm tightened round her, holding her close, letting the pent-up torrent of emotion flood away until it was over, her face wet against his cheek, her body shaking. Then he lifted her chin with one hand and gazed deeply into her eyes. 'It wasn't your fault, Bryony. Whoever started that fire was to blame. Did the police find out?'

She shook her head, her hair misting his eyes. 'The shop was owned by an Indian family. There was often trouble in the area. They decided that was the reason.'

'What did you do after everything was over?' he questioned gently.

'I went back to my family in Sussex. I wanted to forget.' She turned her head to stare up at him. 'But how could I? I knew that Tom would still be alive if I'd done as he told me. There wasn't any need for him to come into that inferno. No need at all.'

'Except that he loved you, Bryony. As I do.' Adam's lips gently met hers with a touch like a butterfly's wing, and then were gone again.

There was a sense of peace surrounding her. Only the faint surge of the sea disturbed the quietness. Above, where clouds drifted slowly across the blue of the sky, she could hear a lark sing, the sound of its music spiralling down to her in a paean. Adam's arm held her close and she could feel the rhythmic beat of his heart against her cheek through the soft warmth of his Aran sweater.

Once Tom had held her like this. Tom. Quickly she lifted her head and pulled away. 'So now you know why I can't bear to be near flames, Adam,' she said, and her voice was hard and abrupt.

'Yes,' he agreed. 'Now I know and understand.' He undid the catch on the car door and swung his long legs out. 'Let's go for a walk.'

His fingers curled round hers, leading her along tiny tracks that criss-crossed the heathland like a complicated maze to where ruined mine buildings were gathered in a slight dip near the cliff-edge.

'Mind where you tread,' he warned. 'Most of the old shafts have been capped, but you sometimes come across the occasional unmarked hole that can shatter an ankle.'

The horizon was beginning to fade now, growing blurred as the afternoon wore on, and the sun slipped down to meet the sea, losing its warmth. Nearer the cliffs huge waves surged in, hitting the granite in a foam of whiteness, filling the air with drifting salt.

'That's Towanroath shaft-head,' he said, pointing to a chimney and roofless engine-house walls rising as if from the ocean itself.

She followed as he began the descent, her mind still far away, her feet slipping on loose stones so that his grip tightened round her hand. Dried pale-brown heads fluttered in soft cushions of thrift beside the path as it widened again, one still pink hiding low against the short wind-flattened grass. The thunder of the sea was louder now and, looking sideways, she was uncomfortably aware of the sheer, straight drop to where it moved relentlessly back and forth.

'The engine was housed here to pump out the shafts up at Wheel Coates mine,' Adam explained when they reached the rough stone building and stood by the base of its tall tapering rounded chimney, looking up at the stark squareness of the empty-windowed walls. 'Some of the deeper workings were prone to flooding.'

'What a desolate place to work,' she said.

He smiled at her, leaning his long back against the sun-dappled wall. 'There wasn't a great deal of choice centuries ago. It was the tin and copper mines, or the sea. Both were hard lives. Miners would walk eight or nine miles along these cliffs, then climb five hundred feet or more down ladders into the shafts to work. And at the end of a long day they'd reverse the process for their trek home again. You can imagine what these tracks were like in the dark with a gale blowing. Not a life I'd relish.'

'Perching on roofs appeals far more?' she said, with a faint smile.

He laughed. 'Or falling off,' he said ruefully, glancing down at the plaster encasing his fingers below the sleeve of his jumper. 'I'm glad to see you smile again. I was afraid I'd dredged too deeply and brought back too many horrors.' He lowered his head to gaze into her eyes. 'But they have to be faced, Bryony. Tom is dead. That part of your life is over. Would he have wanted you to grieve for ever?'

She turned away, staring out to sea, seeing through tear-hazed eyes the deep scarlet of the sun begin to sink below the edge of the horizon.

'Would he have mourned for you like this?' The question was only a whisper from Adam's lips.

She could picture Tom. His crisp black hair cut short. Deep-set dark-brown eyes. Short, straight nose almost too small for the length of his face. The generous fullness of his mouth. The firm caress of his touch. The strength of his body. The sound of his laughter echoed in her ears. Tom was always laughing. Always the centre of a noisy chattering group. Where Tom went, others gathered. Sometimes it upset her. She wanted him to herself at times, not to share. Just to be the two of them. And when he was away....

He'd taunted her with being jealous, not understanding what his presence meant to her, or her need to be assured of his love.

If she had been the one to die in that fire, would he have mourned like this? Her eyes turned back to Adam, and she shook her head, bewildered. It was a question she had never asked herself. Never thought about. Why should she? Tom was the one who'd died.

But would he have mourned for her? He had loved her. What better proof than that he'd died trying to save her? He had loved her. He must have done. A shiver trembled her body.

'You're getting cold. Let's go back.' Adam's hand took hers again, warming its chill, and she was glad to leave such a bleak and lonely spot, climbing the path, seeing the cluster of buildings that had once been part of an active mining community, now fallen into desolation.

Why did life have to change? Why was nothing safe, secure? Why?

They took the coast road to St Ives, past Porthtowan and Portreath, then Godrevy Point, until it swung away towards Hayle, and she could see high dunes of sand hiding the far shore. Towans, they were called, Adam told her, and she thought what a strange name. Towans.

The road wound on until they reached the top of the hill, looking down at St Ives harbour and the town that curved its edge. Adam directed her to the narrow jetty and she parked beneath the sea wall, a seagull flapping heavily away to perch on the mast of a small boat, its wings outstretched in uneasy balance as it wavered there.

Beyond the harbour the sun still tinted the flat sea with rosy colour, leaving shops by the waterside in shadow. A few late holiday-makers strolled between houses that almost touched each other across tiny streets that twisted away into confusion.

Bryony ate spicy currant-rich toasted teacakes, steeped in butter, while she looked out from the upper window of a café, seeing lights begin to blink and the scene fade in the growing twilight, footsteps echoing along the pavement with a sharp sound that foretold a frosty night to come.

'No cream teas,' Adam rued, biting into a teacake. 'I was forgetting the tourist season is over. Next spring we'll come again.'

Next spring. Bryony wondered whether she'd still be at Penreath then. What did the future hold? She seemed to live from day to day, finding the weeks and months, disappear. Soon it would be Christmas.

The thought seared into her. Last Christmas she and Tom had bought the ring. She glanced down at her hand, every finger bare. Remembering how over a week after the fire a policeman had phoned to say they'd found the stones while sifting the ashes for evidence. Diamonds don't burn. She hadn't been wearing her ring that day, not while treating a patient, so it had been in a little china dish on the bathroom shelf. A dish with blue forget-me-nots patterning the edge.

With a whoosh of sound a rocket soared into the sky, stars of crimson and gold radiating from it to shimmer down and fade above the sea, followed by another, then another until the heavens were ablaze with sparkling light. Her teacup chinked against its saucer as she lifted it. She was aware of Adam's blue eyes watching her, concern mirrored in their depths.

When they stepped back into the street the acrid smell of smoke tinged the air, losing itself when they reached the jetty and climbed back into the car.

'Are you all right to drive?'

She nodded, glad to concentrate her mind again, and they wound their way out of the town for the journey home.

SEVEN

Only glowing embers remained of the bonfire when Bryony drove in through the gates of Penreath late that evening. From the tower window of her bedroom she could see the dull red of its ashes glow as the wind stirred them, scattering like fireflies across the lawn, but the air was still heavy with smoke.

She could feel it catch at her throat and for a brief moment closed her eyes, fighting off a growing sense of terror, her ears tuned for that unforgettable roar of sound that once had filled them. Her fingers flattened against the cold glass of the window as if trying to force their way through; her whole body rigid. The walls seemed to be closing in on her. The door too far away.

It won't happen again, she told herself desperately. It can't happen again. Not here.

The telephone on her bedside table shrilled into life, its sound vibrating through every nerve ending. She stared at it, unable to move. Slowly she forced her hand to reach out and lift the receiver.

'Bryony!'

The breath released itself from her stiffened body in one long sigh.

'Adam.'

'I was worried about you. Today of all days. I wish I could have driven you home. Is the bonfire over?'

'Almost.'

'But you can still see it?'

She nodded, her eyes fixed on the window, then remembering he couldn't see her, whispered yes.

'Pull the curtains.' Obediently she shut out the sullen glow. 'You're quite safe, Bryony. Nothing's going to happen to you.'

She sank down on to the edge of her bed, her fingers gripping the phone, winding the wire around her wrist as if it would join her with Adam, bringing him closer. His voice talked to her gently, and she felt his calmness soothe into her.

And when he said, 'I love you, Bryony,' she listened to the words without comprehending them, only the quiet timbre of his voice drifting over her, giving her peace. It was only later in the darkness of the night that, sleepily, she remembered them. *I love you.* Tom had said that so many times before. Tom. The image of his face blurred in her mind. Only the clear blue of Adam's laughing eyes was there.

Serena joined her for breakfast next morning, her straight black hair falling into a gleaming waterfall around her cheeks. 'Where were you last night? You missed a fantastic evening. Gavin had really gone to town on that display. It lit up the whole cliff-side.'

'I took Adam Veryan out for a drive.'

'*You* took *him*? Oh, I was forgetting his fractured wrist. How is he now? He really did have a lucky escape.'

Bryony opened her mouth to answer, then stopped, transfixed. Across the room, at a table by the window, two girls sat eating. As if aware of her stare, one raised her eyes, and she saw the surprise that filled them as the girl nudged her companion.

'What's up?' Serena turned in her chair to follow the

direction of Bryony's gaze. 'Someone you know?'

Bryony nodded, her mind beginning to dart away. That auburn-haired girl. What was her name? Carol? Karen? Cathy. That was it. Cathy. And the other? The fair one. Bryony frowned in concentration. It began with an R. Rose? Rosemary? Rosalind. Both of them were air-hostesses. She'd met them at several parties. Everyone seemed to have parties. Nearly every week there was one. And those two girls were always there. Part of the same crowd. Tom's crowd.

At the end of the meal, she went across. There was no way she could avoid talking to them. Here, at Penreath, they had to meet.

Their faces were wary. She could guess why. Death affects some people like that. Embarrassment. Not knowing quite what to say. Or what reaction their words will provoke.

'Cathy. Rosalind. Nice to see you again. You must have arrived yesterday afternoon when I was out.' Someone had to make the first move. Their expressions relaxed a little.

'Bryony. Fancy seeing you here.' It was Cathy who spoke. A rather husky voice that Bryony now recalled.

'I work here,' Bryony explained. 'An osteopath.'

'Oh yes,' the red-headed girl replied, wrinkling her forehead slightly. 'I remember Tom saying that's what you did....' She paused, and looked away quickly.

'We were so sorry,' Rosalind's soft Welsh voice broke in. 'It was a terrible thing to happen. A dreadful shock. For all of us.'

'How long are you here?' Bryony asked abruptly. Seeing them had already brought back too many memories. She wasn't sure she could take any more.

'A fortnight,' Cathy said. 'It was Penreath or the Canary Islands and we go there so often, it's become a bore.'

'What a nice way of being bored,' Bryony commented drily. This girl had always provoked antagonism in her. It annoyed Tom.

'We decided we knew so very little about England, and Cornwall in particular, that we really ought to spend a holiday here,' Rosalind put in hurriedly. 'Only at this time of year, what is there? And then someone suggested a health farm. It seemed ideal. A good way to tone up and lose a few pounds.'

'Not that I really need to,' Cathy added, straightening her slim shoulders. 'But it was something different and anything different has to be experienced, don't you agree?'

Why does this girl infuriate me so much? Bryony wondered. Right from the very first time she'd met her at a party on a river-boat somewhere on the Thames, it had been the same. They hadn't even spoken and yet, somehow, the air between them was suddenly taut. Tom introduced them, one arm lightly round Cathy's shoulders, drawing her forward. Maybe it was that cascade of beautiful red hair tumbling in a confusion of glowing curls over the shoulders of her jade-green dress. She'd certainly looked very striking, and seeing the way the girl laughed up into Tom's eyes, Bryony felt a flame of anger. Or was it jealousy?

Afterwards she'd found herself watching them whenever they were together. But why Cathy? Tom acted in exactly the same flirtatious way with every girl he met. She felt Cathy's reaction to her was the same. A wariness. A caution. Now she was here at Penreath, releasing a store of long-forgotten memories.

'I must try some osteopathy while we're here,' Rosalind smiled.

'Well, watch out,' Cathy advised. 'You could end up

crippled for life.'

'I think that's very unlikely,' Serena interrupted, joining them. 'Bryony can work magic, as many of our guests will tell you. Now, ladies, I need to go over your diets for the next few days. Would you like to join me in my office?'

When Bryony escaped into the grounds after lunch, she could still smell the bonfire. Deliberately she pointed her footsteps in that direction, forcing herself to stand looking down at the charred ends of branches lying there amid the pale grey ash. A scurry of wind blew across the lawn, fluttering flakes of blackened paper near her foot and she stirred them gingerly with the toe of her shoe, watching them crumble. She'd never gone back to see what was left of the flat, but it must have been rather like this. Fine grey ash and charred black wood. A tiny curl of smoke twisted upwards and she retreated hastily, seeing a smouldering red gleam among what once had been the pages of a magazine or book.

The thud of a hammer reverberated the still air and she glanced across to the cliff-top. Surely it couldn't be Adam? Not so soon after he'd left the hospital. Not with that plastered arm. There was a car tucked round the back of the building. She could just see the top of its roof. Too small for Adam's Range Rover. Maybe it was Matthew. Adam had most likely persuaded his father to take him up there. Bryony smiled to herself. Knowing Adam's persistence, perhaps persuaded wasn't quite the right word. There was just about time to walk there before the afternoon sessions began.

It was Matthew's car, she discovered, and he was sitting in it, reading, a pile of Sunday papers on the seat beside him. She tapped on the window, and he looked up with a smile, then wound it down.

'He couldn't keep away,' he told her wryly. 'Had to be

up here, investigating what happened. Trying to assess just how long it will take to get the work finished. No good Arthur and Joe telling him. Had to come and see for himself. At least he's put a helmet on this time.'

She caught a glimpse of shiny orange in the gloom of one of the cottages and left Matthew, to find Adam bending over a pile of debris.

'If that's what I landed on, no wonder I didn't do much harm,' he remarked, when she entered. 'A couple of old tarpaulins. Probably been here for years.' His eyes darkened almost to black as he looked at her. 'I hoped I'd see you.'

'You're not proposing to do any work here, are you?' she queried. 'If you do, you're asking for trouble. You must give those ligaments a chance to recover.'

'I feel fine,' he assured her. 'That tour of ours yesterday worked wonders. The question is, how are you?'

In the shadows she could see the pale outline of his face and guessed the concern filling his eyes. She'd seen it so often now. He was such a caring man. So different from Tom. 'Thanks for your phone call,' she said softly.

'Did it help?'

'A great deal.' Just knowing he was there, thinking of her.

His hand reached out to touch her cheek, his fingers warm on her skin.

'I must be getting back,' she said hastily, moving sideways.

'Why do you always run away?' he asked.

She didn't answer, couldn't answer, but turned to wave to Matthew as she passed the car and hurried on down the track towards Penreath. Two figures, one dark, the other with flowing auburn hair, were coming from the direction of the lighthouse. Looking back when she reached the garden gate, she saw them stop by the ruins of the cottages and a twinge of unease probed at her.

Cathy, she saw from the appointment book, was due to see her before tea. When she arrived, the girl was scathing. 'I can't think why I bothered. Ros talked me into it. I doubt there's anything you can do.'

'About your knee?' Bryony questioned.

Cathy's eyebrows shot up. 'How did you guess?'

'I've watched you walk. There's obviously a stiffness. What did you do to it? A fall, maybe?'

'I'm not really sure. It's been getting more painful for weeks now. Not a sudden thing.'

Bryony was examining the knee carefully while Cathy spoke, her fingers gently probing, waiting for any sign of tension or resistance.

'Turn on to your tummy so that I can check your back.'

'It's my knee that's painful!' Cathy snapped.

'I know.'

'Jiggling about with my back isn't going to have any effect on it.'

Bryony smiled. 'My jiggling about, as you put it, should have some effect on that. If you come back for more treatment, you'll probably notice a difference in a day or so.'

'Huh! By the way, who's that guy working on the cottages? Ros and I saw you talking to him. Tall. Hunky. Wearing a sort of crash helmet.'

Bryony's body stiffened slightly. 'Adam Veryan. He's doing some work up there.'

'One of your patients, is he? I noticed the plastered arm.'

'He had an accident there,' Bryony replied. 'The floor gave way when he was repairing the roof.'

Cathy gave a slow smile. 'I wish I'd been there to catch him then. He certainly improves the scenery around here. I was finding it a little boring. A house full of overweight Romeos isn't my idea of a holiday. I meet enough of those.'

Among the new guests that week were a band-leader popular in the late 1950s, his singer wife and three of their group. They still toured the country in the summer months, visiting towns where the not-so-young chose to holiday.

Gavin suggested that he organize a dance at Penreath during their stay, which they accepted eagerly, and once the plan got underway, it was decided to sell tickets outside the health clinic to make it a bigger event. The main hall of the house had been designed for this purpose and it would be fun to use it in that way again.

As the days went by, excitement grew and Bryony realized the occasion was to be formal enough to wear a long dress – something she hadn't possessed since the fire. Serena suggested they make a trip to Truro where the precinct had a selection of the more popular shops, including a Laura Ashley, and with Christmas only weeks away, a late-night shopping evening gave them the opportunity.

'What colour are you going for?' Serena asked as Bryony parked the car down near the river and they walked back into the town.

'I haven't a clue,' Bryony frowned, screwing up her face in a grimace. 'I usually rely on finding the proverbial little black dress.'

'Not this time!' Serena chuckled. 'Adam Veryan can't be wasted on anything so mundane.'

Bryony had already begun to wish that Adam wasn't going. It could cause trouble when Gavin discovered him there, although as the dance was open to the general public, she didn't see how he could object. Tickets were on sale throughout the Lizard. It would have been difficult to keep him away, once he learned of the fact. Tentatively she suggested that perhaps a plastered arm should be kept to a less crowded place, but Adam swiftly rejected the idea.

'It doesn't stop me doing anything else, so it's certainly not going to prevent me jumping at the chance to hold you close for a whole evening,' he'd observed with a mischievous smile.

'We'll tour every shop first,' Serena announced, 'then go back to those with the best choice.'

'It's all right for you,' Bryony protested as the evening wore on, watching the oriental girl slip into yet another jewel-bright dress. 'With that dark hair and those eyes, you can wear any colour. With this nondescript mop, I just look washed out.'

'Nonsense!' Serena declared firmly. 'Maybe strong shades aren't for you, but we'll find something. Now, which of these do you think looks best. The crimson taffeta or this metallic goldy one? They're both gorgeous.' She stepped away from the mirror, her small face pouting.

'The red fits better,' Bryony advised. 'That other puckered when you fastened the belt. Try it again and you'll see what I mean.'

While Serena did so, Bryony looked at the collection of dresses, wrinkling her nose. In none of them did she feel right and as the shops would close in half an hour, it would have to be the little black dress in the first store they'd visited after all. Dejectedly she slid out of the cubicle to hand them back to the assistant, as someone else did the same.

'Too small,' she heard her say, and looked at the mist of

blue the woman was holding out.

'Could I ...?'

The material draped itself delicately over Bryony's arm as she carried it in through the curtains. Serena was studying herself critically, head craned over one shoulder.

'Stand still, and look into that mirror behind you. You're twisting the dress out of all recognition,' Bryony scolded. 'Now, do you see what I mean? Maybe if you loosen the belt a notch. The colour's beautiful on you.'

'Hmm,' Serena mused, not convinced. 'Tell you what, I'll take them both. After all, Christmas is coming and there's bound to be loads of parties, so I'm going to need more than one dress, aren't I? Where did you find that one. It looks fantastic.'

The chiffony material clung in soft folds from a straight neckline, enhancing every contour of Bryony's body, before it fell in a series of tiny pleats to the floor. Its colour was hard to define, one minute the hidden depths of the sea, the next the mist of bluebells in the spring, and a myriad shades in between, constantly changing as she moved. Serena picked up the price tag and gave a low whistle.

'No wonder it looks good.'

But Bryony had already made up her mind.

Surprisingly, Cathy returned for more treatment, not quite so condemning in her manner the second time.

'I remembered I did have a fall,' she admitted, stretching out her long slender limbs on the couch. 'It was so long ago, I'd forgotten. On one of the Greek islands. There was a stony track. A heavily-laden donkey coming the other way. The wretched man in charge allowed it to take up all the room. I was forced to one side and slipped.' Her eyes met Bryony's defiantly. 'It wasn't my knee though.'

'You sat down hard, which produced a sharp pain in your back?'

Cathy moved her head slowly in agreement.

'That could have caused it.'

'My knee!'

'Yes,' Bryony replied, letting her fingers begin their gentle pressure. 'Your knee.'

'All sounds a bit far-fetched to me.'

'Well, that's how it works, I'm afraid.'

'It was a terrible way to die.' Cathy's abrupt statement startled Bryony and her hands ceased their movement for a brief moment, before continuing to manipulate the girl's spine.

'Yes.' Her voice was low, knowing instantly who Cathy meant.

'And all because of you.'

'It's something I can never forgive myself for. Never will.'

'Did you love him?' Cathy's voice was harsh.

'There'd never been anyone else. I'd loved Tom since I was a child. He was my brother's friend. We'd grown up together. He was always there. Someone to look up to and admire. I can't remember when I didn't love him.'

'It wasn't the same for Tom, you know.'

'I realize that,' Bryony answered, 'but then I was only his best friend's little sister. It was a long while before he even noticed me. A long time before I grew up. He'd been a pilot for several years.'

'And enjoyed life,' Cathy said. 'Tom was that sort of guy.'

'Had you known him for long?' Bryony asked.

'Long enough.'

For what? Bryony wondered sharply. Had her instinct

been correct? Was that why she'd always disliked this girl?

'Flying can be a lonely sort of existence. In a strange country you need companionship. It passes the time. He talked a lot about you though,' Cathy remarked grudgingly.

'We were engaged,' Bryony answered tautly.

'He'd been engaged before. Did you know that?'

'Yes, but it was over a long while before we started going out together. Tom never spoke of it.'

Cathy gave a short laugh. 'I bet he didn't. Off with the old, and on with the new. That was Tom all right.'

Was it? Bryony thought. It made him sound like a snake, shedding one skin for a newer, brighter one. And she wondered why such an analogy should occur to her.

'Did you imagine marriage would change him?' Cathy's voice persisted.

'Change him? I loved him as he was.'

'You wouldn't have done if you'd known what he was really like.'

'I did know him!'

'You think?' It was almost a sneer.

'How can *you* judge?' Bryony asked.

'Oh, I can judge all right.' Cathy laughed. 'My eyes weren't misted with star-dust.'

'You've had enough for today,' Bryony said tightly, moving away from the couch. 'Do you want to come back for a further session?'

'Why not. I find it all most enlightening. And, you never know, you might just do something for my knee as well.'

She's my patient, Bryony reminded herself. Someone I'm trying to cure. I won't let her annoy me. I don't have to listen. But she had listened already. And Cathy's words were disturbing.

Tom did love her. That was why he'd gone into a blazing building.

On the evening of the dance, she could hear music floating from the hall below. By now she should be there too, but the tiny buttons at the back of her dress were proving difficult, especially one midway down. I'll need an osteopath myself if I'm not careful, she decided, twisting her neck to peer into the mirror and find its location. Twice already she'd caught hold of the loop, only to lose it again.

Serena burst through the door, looking radiant in the crimson dress.

'So you finally decided on that one,' Bryony laughed.

'The other makes me look like a festive parcel, so I'll save it for Christmas,' Serena chuckled, reaching out to fasten the button for her. 'Now for goodness sake hurry up. Everyone's arriving. You'll find Adam clasped in someone else's arms if you're not careful.'

Cathy's face floated unwillingly into Bryony's mind as she bent to flick some colour across her lips.

'Is *that* all the make-up you're going to wear?' Serena shook her head in despair. 'We'll stop off in my room on the way and add a bit more glamour. Surely Adam's worth more than a touch of blushing rose or whatever that pallid stuff's called?'

Protesting, Bryony found herself dragged through Serena's door into what looked like a jumble sale, with garments scattered everywhere.

'Don't you ever tidy up?' she asked.

Serena's slanting dark eyes regarded her with surprise. 'I have,' she protested. 'Things sort of get distributed. Now, sit down and stop telling me off. I'll drape this blouse round your neck.'

She rummaged through a collection of cosmetics

covering the top of her dressing-table and set to work on Bryony, emphasizing her blue eyes until they widened and enlarged, illuminating her whole face. Her skilful fingers brushed a soft wave of colour lightly across Bryony's cheekbones to meet her temples, then she outlined the curve of her lips and darkened them slightly. Finally, she stood back with a smile.

'Now, what do you think?'

Bryony regarded herself dubiously in the mirror. 'It's not too much, is it?'

'Of course not! The light from the chandelier is all they've got down there. We can't have you merging into the wallpaper, can we? Just wait until Adam sees you! He'll be completely bedazzled. You go first down the stairs. I haven't got anyone to impress.'

He probably hasn't arrived yet, Bryony decided. Or worse, maybe Gavin's barred him at the entrance. From the top of the curving staircase she gazed into the swirl of couples below moving rhythmically in time to the music. It was like a romantic fairytale, the hall transformed back to a bygone age, the carpet removed to reveal polished boards, the chandelier glittering like a thousand captured stars.

She could see Gavin's silver head bow as he greeted a group of new arrivals. Was Adam with them? How would the pair react? Surely on an occasion like this there could be no aggression? Familiar faces began slowly to emerge from the crowd. People from the surrounding district she recognized. All the guests. Astrid in a sheath of silver that made her even more a Nordic ice-maiden.

A couple moved from the shadows at the side of the room, drifting towards its centre. She saw Adam's fair head, his face turned to that of his partner. Bryony's fingers tightened round the smooth polished wood of the banister and her foot wavered on the stair.

The girl he was dancing with swung into view, her long auburn hair pinned into a rich confusion on top of her head.

Cathy had already marked out her conquest for the evening.

EIGHT

Memories came flooding back to Bryony. Finding her way along a dark corridor on a river-boat. The noise of laughter and voices from the party in the background. Tom appearing from the shadows. And the girl, her auburn curls cascading in an untidy tumble round her shoulders, caught in the circle of his arm.

'You haven't met Cathy, have you, Bryony?' She could recall the ease with which Tom had said those words. Now her eyes were watching Adam dancing with the same girl.

'What's the matter?' Serena was nudging her on. Reluctantly Bryony began to move again. One of the guests stepped forward as she reached the bottom of the stairs, his pudgy little face wreathed in smiles.

'Such a beautiful lady needs someone to dance with,' he beamed, and she felt the damp warmth of his hand on her spine, guiding her into the crush of people. Mechanically her feet followed his steps, her gaze still fixed on the fair head towering above the others in the room. 'My wife speaks highly of your treatment, Miss Scott. She's been troubled with arthritis for many years now. Such pain is very wearing.'

Bryony stared at him blankly, trying to work out exactly who his wife could be. There were so many elderly people this week. Most had some form of rheumatic problem.

'Her hip replacement made some difference, but now her wrists and hands....' His voice continued, but she was only half-listening, watching the movement of Cathy's fiery head, noticing how the girl's hand had slipped from Adam's shoulder to the back of his neck as they danced, feathers of hair brushing his cheek with her closeness.

Why should I care? she asked herself. Adam Veryan can dance with anyone he likes. Why should it matter? But however much she tried, her gaze wouldn't be distracted; nor her mind.

'She has tried hot wax baths, to no effect. What do you consider would be best? I wish so much to ease her suffering, Miss Scott.' The little man's face stared up at her with troubled eyes.

'It's difficult to say,' Bryony answered, wishing she could remember which of the patients was his wife. 'Has Dr Carthew given any advice?'

'Many doctors have given advice, Miss Scott, but no positive help. Sir Toby spoke highly of you. I had hoped ... we both hoped ... I would so like poor Gwen to find some relief. She rarely complains, but just to see her growing more and more infirm, it breaks my heart. We will stay here for as long as we can afford, if it will help her. Money cannot buy health, I know, but it can assist in giving comfort.'

Gwen. Gwen Mason. Bryony could visualize her now. A fragile little woman badly affected by arthritis. Nothing could be done to cure her condition, but Bryony knew the pain could be eased and mobility improved, and that she was trying to do.

The woman had been very nervous on her first visit, frightened that the treatment would consist of twisting and cracking her joints, so was both surprised and relieved at the gentleness she received. Serena was also concentrating on her diet and Bryony knew that, too, could play an important part in alleviating the pain and stiffness of arthritis.

The music ended with a resounding roll of drums, and the little man gave a deep bow, then hurried back to where his wife was sitting.

'So you've decided to be an old man's darling, rather than a young man's slave.' Adam's lips brushed her cheek as he spoke.

'I thought you were preoccupied,' she parried, wondering what had happened to Cathy.

'Snatched into the jaws of a red-headed man-eater, is that what you mean? I was petrified!'

'You didn't look it,' she retorted drily.

'Transfixed by terror, that's why. She descended on me before I could escape. Does Women's Lib mean that young ladies don't wait to be asked to dance any more? That one scooped me up and virtually dragged me on to the floor. When I saw you coming down the stairs, I thought I was about to be saved. Why didn't you come and fight for me?'

Bryony smiled. 'Pistols at dawn, you mean?'

'Nothing less,' he grinned. 'After all, it's only fair if we're going to have all this role reversal stuff. Now, do I have to wait for you ask me to dance or may I request that pleasure myself? We Cornish folk aren't up to the ways of you sophisticated Londoners.'

'What about your arm?' she said, noticing how the sleeve of his dinner jacket had been eased to allow the plastered wrist to emerge.

'Ah yes, my arm,' he mused, his eyes regarding her quizzically. 'Well, holding it up in the air clasped round your hand would be far too painful, so the only way to relieve it is to put it round your waist, like this, to meet the other one. It would make it far more comfortable, of course, if you'd link both your arms round my neck. I'd hate us to overbalance and fall over in the middle of the floor.'

'And all those stiff muscles, how are they going to survive?'

He gave a mock sigh. 'Now those make it quite impossible for me to leap about as one should while dancing, so all I can do is hold you even closer, like this, and sway in time to the music. We're in for a very dull evening, I'm afraid.'

'I didn't notice you experiencing this problem when you were dancing with Cathy.'

'That's true,' he said thoughtfully. 'We could call that episode useful research. Without it I'd never have sorted everything out before I found you, and we'd have wasted valuable time experimenting until we reached such a satisfactory conclusion.'

'Are you ever serious?' she asked him.

He leaned away slightly, his blue eyes looking down into hers. 'With you,' he said, 'very serious.'

'What's been happening to the cottages up on the cliff?' she asked quickly, her cheeks beginning to flame.

'Now that, of course, is a very serious question,' he replied, studying her mockingly. 'Arthur and Joe are making good progress with them – unfortunately, without my help. They've removed all the rotten wood and made a start on repairing the roof. You've probably noticed another chap's been working on the walls. If we can get the outside finished before the bad weather sets in, it'll make everything easier.'

'So when do you think they'll be completed?'

'Hopefully, early spring. It all depends on what kind of winter we have – and how soon I can get back there. Dad's ferrying me around at the moment, but once I've softened this wretched plaster a little I intend to be back in the driving-seat.'

'You mustn't,' she protested. 'For goodness' sake give that wrist a chance to mend properly. All sorts of problems could set in later, if you don't.'

'Then I shall come to you to make them better,' he retorted.

'Do be sensible, Adam. You really could do a great deal of harm if you try to rush things.'

'Rest and warmth, is that what it needs?'

She nodded. 'And to flex your fingers to keep them active.'

His arms moved more closely round her waist and she saw his mouth twitch at the corners. 'Then this must be what the doctor ordered.'

'Did you have any problem with Gavin Carthew when you arrived?'

'How your mind travels,' he observed wryly. 'From one doctor to another. No. There were several other people coming in at the same time. He merely glowered and shook my hand. I have a feeling, from the look in his eye, that he would have preferred it to be the other one, so that he could have crumbled the plaster to dust, my hand included. There wasn't very much he could do though. My ticket was obviously in order. I did wonder if he would cry out, "Do not darken my doorstep again," but no such luck. Besides, the building work is going ahead, however much he dislikes it. Have you had any more trouble with him?'

Bryony shook her head.

'I'll be up there in the morning with a load of window-frames. How about meeting me for a pub lunch later? Will the good doctor permit that? You did say Saturdays were pretty slack, after the old set of guests had gone and the new lot were settling in.'

'I'd like that,' she smiled, then frowned slightly. 'And talking about windows, I must get somebody to look at the one in my room. There's a huge nail stopping it from opening. It probably rattled and whoever was staying there, hammered it in.'

'A sash window?'

She nodded.

'Well, be careful. They can be dangerous if the cord's old and frayed. Do you want me to check it for you?'

'I doubt Gavin would approve of that,' she laughed. 'No, I'd better ask the odd-job man here. It's just that I keep forgetting until I want to open it, but that's not very likely now with the winter coming on.'

She remembered Astrid's uneasiness about the tower room. And that Serena had mentioned the missing boy – Tim whatever his name was – had slept in one of them.

'Do you recall a drowning a few years ago?' she asked Adam. Adam raised his head from where it was resting against her cheek, and sighed heavily. 'This is a night for romance, Bryony, not death and disaster.'

'But do you?' she persisted.

'People are always getting drowned round this coast. Mainly visitors who don't, or won't, accept how treacherous the currents are.'

'But do you remember one here, at Penreath?'

'There was a lot of gossip about a missing boy once. The son of a wealthy financier, I think he was. A whole crowd of yuppies used to stay here on occasions. Still do, I gather. Went a bit wild at times. There was some trouble with a group of them down in Helston. Drugs. All hushed up, but it caused quite a lot of anger amongst the locals. We can do without that kind of thing.'

'Was the boy one of them?'

Adam wrinkled his forehead. 'It was quite a while back, Bryony. A boy did go missing, that's all I know.

And he was staying here. A towel and some of his clothes were discovered on the beach down in the cove. I think it was Dr Carthew who found them. No body turned up though. What made you suddenly ask about him?'

'I wondered whether he used my room.'

'*Your* room? You've not been suffering from a dank and dripping ghost, have you?' he teased.

'No, it was just that Astrid made a comment about not liking the room on the day I arrived, and then Serena said something about the missing boy having one of the tower rooms.'

'And so you instantly decided it was yours! Oh, Bryony, you do have an active imagination. That's called putting two and two together and making five, you know. Now, for goodness' sake let's get off such a morbid subject and enjoy the dancing.'

She was enjoying the dancing. Rather too much, she decided, drawing slightly away from Adam's close embrace, as his grip tightened.

'Did you deliberately choose a dress to match your eyes so perfectly?' he murmured. 'Harebells on a summer's day.' She remembered he'd used the same description once before. 'They grow up near the lighthouse, you know. Delicate and fragile, half-hidden in the grass, among pale pink clumps of thrift in early summer. Quite beautiful.'

His lips hovered across her skin as he spoke, and paused near the corner of her mouth. All she had to do was turn her head a fraction to meet them.

The tempo of the music changed from a slow waltz to a faster beat, quickening their steps, and the chubby little band-leader's voice blared through the microphone in a crackle of sound, 'Now, ladies and gentlemen, for some spot prizes!'

People began to surge on to the floor, pushing their way nearer the raised platform.

'Shall we sit this one out?' Bryony suggested, conscious that Adam's arm was in danger of being jostled.

He raised his eyebrows at her. 'No letting me be the first gentleman to arrive at the front with a pair of lady's tights over his arm, or a picture of the Queen? What a spoilsport you are, Bryony.'

'I was thinking about your arm,' she said. 'Shall we eat now, while the buffet's fairly empty, before the crush begins?'

'At least I'll have you all to myself in there. Oh no! That liberated woman's back again.'

Cathy was advancing purposefully towards them.

'Do staff have privileges the guests aren't allowed ...' Her voice lingered on the word *staff* as she eyed Bryony before turning her sultry gaze to Adam. '... in commandeering the best-looking man in the room?'

'I thought I saw you concentrating your talents on Dr Carthew.'

Cathy smiled slightly at the barb in Adam's tone. 'Ageing men don't have quite the same ...' She paused, leaning against his shoulder as she reached across the table to fill her plate '... appeal.'

'I doubt Dr Carthew would like to hear that,' Adam replied, moving away from her, balancing his glass and plate awkwardly in one hand.

Cathy ran a crimson fingernail lightly over the back of the plaster, but her eyes were fixed on Bryony. 'You do seem to have a jinx-like effect on the men in your life, don't you, Bryony? I should take care if I were you, Adam, her last boyfriend ended up charred to a cinder.'

Bryony swung away, pushing blindly through a group of people filling the doorway, to run along the corridor and through the nearest door. The faint gleam of water stopped her, tiny patches of brightness reflected from the surface of the swimming-pool to dance on the shadowy walls as she stood in the darkness, staring down into it, tears blurring her eyes.

Footsteps echoed behind her and then Adam was there, his arms turning her towards him, his mouth seeking hers.

The kiss was a balm, a solace. Nothing more.

Softly his lips moved to feather her hair, her eyes, following the curve of her cheek, along the smooth line of her jaw, down to the hollow of her neck, before they reached her lips again, enchanting her, bewitching her until her fingers slid fiercely upwards to curl round his head, drawing him closer.

Time ceased to exist. And for her, at last, Tom ceased to exist.

Only Adam.

The fire came back to her when she dreamed that night. She could hear the sound of its fury thundering in her ears; feel its blistering heat; smell the choke of smoke biting into her throat; see again Tom standing there in the road outside, his face turned up to her, flames flickering, changing its contours; his betrayed eyes dark with pleading. She wanted to call out to him, tell him she still loved him, but her voice was trapped deep inside her, caught as if in a web.

Her throat ached with pain when she woke to hear waves pound against the rocks in the cove and rain beat the window-panes. The room was dark and its darkness smothered her like a heavy cloak.

Tom. Tears scalded her cheeks.

In the morning the rain had died away leaving only the dampness of wet grass and rotting leaves. A leaden sky met a sullen sea. Saturday. Departing guests huddled in the hallway, waiting for taxis, eyes heavy after the previous night's festivities. Their voices were subdued as though weary from so much exertion. Bryony watched them go, wishing that Cathy was one of them.

A small red truck was bumping along the track beside Penreath from the lane and she wondered whether it was the window-frames that Adam had mentioned were arriving that day. She would walk up to the cottages later and meet him, ready for their lunch together.

Her final appointment that morning was for Rosalind, Cathy's friend. They were so unalike that their friendship surprised Bryony. Ros, as she preferred to be called, was quiet, almost shy, and seemed to follow in Cathy's shadow. Maybe that's the only way she can enjoy a similar sort of life, Bryony thought. They'd always appeared together at parties in the past, although Cathy rarely left with her.

The girl complained of discomfort in her arms and shoulders, especially after a flight when she'd had to bend over passengers a great deal. Bryony questioned her carefully and discovered that several months before she'd been involved in a minor car crash. At the time there had been no apparent injury, but the discomfort had appeared shortly afterwards.

'I think you suffered a slight whiplash – your head probably jerked backwards and forwards rapidly during the impact.'

'Nothing showed on the X-rays.'

'Maybe not, but there could be nerve damage. If I work on your spine, it will release any minor compressions of the joints and you'll probably notice a difference.'

Ros began to relax as Bryony's fingers moved rhythmically.

'It must have upset you quite a bit when we arrived

here,' the girl said thoughtfully. 'Of all the health farms to choose!'

'These things happen,' Bryony replied.

'Even so I expect it brought back a few memories.'

'Yes,' Bryony admitted.

'We were all crazy about Tom, you know. He was a great guy. Always the life and soul of the party wherever we went. It must have been a dreadful shock for you. How long had you been engaged?'

'Only a few months, but I'd known him for most of my life.'

'Well, as you say, these things happen,' Ros said. 'It couldn't have been easy for you though. Was that why you came down here?'

'It seemed a good distance.'

'And has it made a difference?' the girl persisted. 'Time's a great healer, so they say, not that I've ever lost anyone close.'

'I haven't been here long enough to know the answer myself,' Bryony replied, wishing the conversation would end.

'To have us, of all people, turn up must have been terrible.'

'It did bring back things I was trying to forget.'

'I bet! Cathy *is* attractive though, isn't she? You can see why all the guys go wild over her, and she makes her intentions quite blatant.'

Had Ros noticed Cathy's pursuit of Adam last night? Bryony wondered. It was fairly plain for all to see.

'I think I could improve that neck with a few more treatments, if you'd like me to.'

Ros looked doubtful. 'I'll see what happens after this. I only came because you've worked such magic on Cathy's knee. We walked miles along the cliffs the other day. It didn't bother her at all.'

'I'm glad,' Bryony observed drily. 'She hasn't mentioned it to me.'

Ros smiled ruefully. 'No, she wouldn't. Cathy's like that. Hot on the complaints, but not so good with the compliments.'

'I'm glad it had an effect though. Let's hope I can do the same with you.'

As she walked up the track towards the cottages, Bryony could see the red truck parked with Adam's Range Rover on some rough ground nearby. He's really asking for trouble, driving that, she thought, her heart beginning to beat faster as she went in through the doorway and saw the arch of his back leaning against one of the inner walls while he talked to Joe.

His eyes darkened into deep pools of warmth when he saw her, and a smile that made her pulse quicken spread over his face.

'You shouldn't be driving.' It wasn't the greeting she'd intended, but the horror of what he could do to his arm worried her.

'I'm not.'

'But your car's outside.'

'Yes,' he agreed, 'but that doesn't mean I drove it here.'

Joe's weather-beaten face grinned back at her. 'That's right, m'dear. I brought the gaffer up, though 'twas a mite difficult to persuade him, that's for sure.'

'Some friend!' Adam muttered.

'So who's going to drive it back?' she demanded.

'You are,' he teased.

'Me! I can't drive a monstrosity like that.'

'What an admission! How are we going out to eat then?'

Joe stood listening to them with a twinkle in his eye.

'Go and give Arthur a hand with shifting that pile of slates for the end roof, instead of standing there ear-wigging,' Adam growled. 'I'd do it myself only madam here will lecture me even worse. Whoever delivered that load left them right in front of the wall George's starting on next week. It'll save him a bit of time on Monday if you shift them now.'

With a wink at Bryony, the man plodded out and she could hear his voice murmuring to Arthur, obviously telling him the tale, and the throaty chuckle of their laughter.

'Now look what you've done,' Adam told her. 'Inciting mutiny.'

'It really would be silly if you tried to drive, you know, Adam. If that plaster cracks or bends, it's not going to do much good for your wrist. You don't want to finish up with it permanently weak, do you?'

'Not if it stops me doing this,' he said, reaching out to draw her close. 'Come here and give me a kiss, instead of lecturing.'

There was a sudden yell and Arthur's voice shouted an oath, then Joe came running inside. 'You'd best come quickly, gaffer. He's bleeding fair bad.'

'What happened?' Adam questioned, as they hurried round to the back of the building.

'A great shaft of glass sticking up through the middle of they slates. Neither of us saw it, until it caught Arthur's arm. Torn it pretty bad, I'd say,' Joe gabbled.

Arthur was standing, his face drawn, eyes wide, staring down at where blood was soaking into the sleeve of his grey woollen jumper, and trickling down his hand to drip through his fingers.

'There's a first-aid kit in the Range Rover,' Adam ordered. 'Under the dashboard.'

Joe raced across the grass towards the car, while

Bryony gingerly rolled back Arthur's sleeve, catching her breath when she saw the gash. 'You'll need some stitches,' she told him, 'and a tetanus jab. Can we get him to a hospital quickly, Adam? He's losing a lot of blood.'

Together they guided him over to the Range Rover and sat him on the seat, while Bryony bound his arm tightly, trying to slow the bleeding.

'I'm afraid you'll have to drive again, Joe,' Adam instructed. 'Don't worry about the speed limit. I'll deal with it if anyone stops us.'

'What about Penreath, gaffer?' Joe questioned. 'Couldn't we take Arthur there?'

'No use,' said Bryony. 'Arthur needs stitches. Dr Carthew couldn't do that at Penreath. It's only a health farm and he doesn't have those facilities. There's no point in wasting time by stopping there. It's got to be a hospital, and I do think we'd better hurry.'

The bleeding was worrying her. Even with pressure on the artery, it was continuing to flow. Adam helped Arthur into the back seat beside her and joined Joe in the front, the Range Rover jolting backwards, then bumping off down the track towards the lane.

'Can you cope with him like that, Bryony?' Adam asked, turning anxious eyes to look at her.

'We're fine, aren't we, Arthur?' she said, feeling the weight of the older man slump against her shoulder as they met yet another rut.

'Fine,' he echoed weakly.

For once, Bryony wished it was Adam who was driving. Joe took each corner cautiously, slowing the journey, but eventually, when they met the main road, he speeded up a little. She could see from the rigid set of Adam's shoulders that their progress irked him and guessed he must be cursing his plastered arm. Arthur sat, eyes closed, beside her, blood darkening the pad of bandage she tried to hold steadily pressed to the wound, and the miles seemed longer than she'd ever known.

'How do you think the glass got there?' she asked while they waited on a seat in the Casualty Department for Arthur's return.

'Fair puzzles me,' Joe commented, rubbing a muddy hand over his chin. 'Like a dagger, it was. Sticking right out from between two piles of slates. As Arthur lifted them away, the danged thing sliced right into him.'

'But surely the man delivering them would have noticed?' she mused.

'There's no way it could have been there then,' Adam said. 'If it had, it would have been shattered by the journey along that track.'

She stared at him with dawning horror. 'You mean someone deliberately put it there later?'

'It looks very much like it.'

Her mind went back to when Adam fell through the upper floor. Boards that had been part-sawn through. Someone had wanted an accident to happen. Was that same person responsible for this as well? Adam's fall had delayed work on the building. With Arthur injured, it would be delayed even more. So what was the point? Why slow it down?

The cottages were to provide retirement homes for local people. No one was going to object to those. And the acts were far too devious and clever to be sheer vandalism. Someone had given them careful thought. On both occasions it was the people working there who had been injured. Was the malice directed only at them? Had Joe, or Arthur, or even Adam, enemies? But it was far too random for that. If one of them was the intended victim, then the acts had to be specific. And these had been done by someone who didn't care which of them was hurt.

'When were the slates delivered?' she asked.

'Yesterday dinner, some time,' Joe told her. 'Me and Arthur'd walked up to the pub like we do on a Friday. Found them when we got back. Said to Arthur, I did, 'twas stupid to stack them by that wall. George'll be fair moaning 'bout that, I said. All have to be shifted before he can get working. Bit of a lad brought them, I dare say. No thought only to get them dumped quickly and off again. Even left the delivery note stuffed under a bit of stone. Lucky it didn't blow away.'

'And you and Arthur went home about four, when it got dark?'

''Bout then, Miss. Can only do short days at this time of year.'

'It wouldn't take long to slip a piece of glass in amongst them,' Adam observed. 'Anyone walking past could have done, I suppose.'

'But who goes for a walk with a long sliver of glass in their hand?' Bryony reasoned. 'And it's not the kind of thing you'd find walking along the cliff path, is it?'

'Probably came from an old window or greenhouse,' Adam said. 'People do dump rubbish out on the cliffs, but it seems a bit unlikely.'

'Someone obviously did it quite deliberately, Adam. Wanting to hurt one of you. But why? And who?'

Arthur emerged, rather unsteadily, from behind a curtain and Adam went to meet him, taking the older man's arm and helping him along.

'This makes us a matching pair,' he grinned, looking down at Arthur's sling.

'Seven stitches, I had,' Arthur announced proudly, beginning to perk up a little. 'Though that tetanus injection hurt a mite more than they did. Rest it a while, the doctor told me. I'm sorry, gaffer, but 'tis going to mean having a few days off. Just when we're about to finish the roof and start on the inside work too.'

'Don't worry yourself about that. You have as long as it takes to get it right again, Arthur,' Adam replied. 'I'll bring one of the lads working over at Ruan Minor to give Joe a hand. They've nearly finished on that barn conversion.'

It was past three in the afternoon after they'd dropped Arthur at his home, and Joe collected the truck again. Too late for their pub lunch. Adam suggested they went back to Coverack. It meant Bryony having to drive the Range Rover, but after some rather dramatic jerking while she got used to it, she soon settled down and they finally made it up the steep hill to the bungalow.

'Will a bowl of soup and beans on toast do you?' Adam enquired, producing a couple of tins from one of the kitchen cupboards. 'Dad's gone off to Truro, so you'll have to make do with my poor cuisine.'

'Sounds fine,' she smiled. 'Can I help?'

'Well, after that leap-frogging journey home, I'm loath to put you in charge of the toaster. Mechanical objects don't seem to be quite in your line. How about stirring the soup? Can you use a wooden spoon?'

'It'll make a good weapon if you don't stop being rude!' she warned, making a grab at it, only to find herself caught firmly in his arms.

'This is far more enjoyable than a pub lunch,' he murmured softly. 'Are you quite sure you want to bother to eat at all?'

NINE

'Where's your father gone?' Bryony asked a while later.

'All very mysterious,' Adam replied, 'but I did notice he'd sprinkled himself liberally with my aftershave. It wouldn't surprise me if he's meeting Dr Pentland. They seemed to get on very well when I was in hospital, and he does know her from way back when he had his own accident and was there for a while.'

'Well he certainly has a very high opinion of her,' Bryony said, remembering Matthew's comments about Penny, as he called her.

'We *could* make it a double wedding, of course,' Adam observed casually.

'Who mentioned anything about weddings?' she retorted, and saw his mouth widen into a smile that sent her heart somersaulting.

'Are you suggesting we live in sin then?' he teased. 'You do shock me, Miss Scott!'

'Is this a devious way of proposing?'

'Do I need to?' he asked. 'I thought I'd made my intentions perfectly clear. All I'd like to do now, is make them honourable.'

'Then shouldn't you be down on one knee?'

'I would, if you weren't sitting on it.'

'Shall I stand up then?' she suggested sweetly.

'I prefer you where you are,' he answered, leaning

back into the deep armchair, taking her with him.

Everything's moving much too fast, Bryony warned herself. I need time to stop and think. She was being swept along at an overwhelming pace in a torrent of emotions – and reason wasn't one of them.

Adam was so different from Tom. And yet she loved Tom. Still loved him. Tom had been her whole life. She'd never thought of anyone else. Until she met Adam. But I still love Tom. Because of me, he died. How can I break such a bond?

'So when's it to be then?'

Her eyes stared blankly into Adam's blue gaze.

'The wedding,' he smiled. 'How about Monday? The vicar's otherwise engaged tomorrow. Sunday is his busy day.'

'Be serious,' she warned.

'I am,' he protested. 'The sooner, the better – although it would be nice to get this plaster off first and be able to put both my arms around you properly.'

'That'll be December.'

'So how about a Christmas wedding?'

Matthew returned later that evening to be greeted with the announcement.

'We did consider making it a double wedding,' Adam said, laughing at the startled look that appeared on his father's face. 'You and Penny.'

'How the hell …?' Matthew began, and then saw their amusement.

'So it *was* Dr Pentland you've been visiting in Truro,' Adam declared triumphantly.

'We did meet up,' his father admitted grudgingly.

'And?' Adam demanded.

'You concentrate on your own love-life, and I'll look after mine!'

'Note the word love-life, Bryony,' Adam murmured. 'Write that down and we'll use it in evidence against him at a later date.'

'Don't tease!' Bryony reproved. 'Not everyone's as blatant as you when it comes to the art of courting.'

'Faint heart never won fair lady,' he retorted, catching her round the waist and giving her a kiss. 'Come on, Dad. Tell us all about it.'

'There's nothing to tell,' Matthew protested. 'Penny and I hit it off pretty well when I was in hospital all those years back. Straightforward kind of girl. The sort you can trust. Seeing her again reminded me of that. We lost contact after I went to Stoke. Besides ... there were other things happening.'

'Like Mother,' Adam said softly.

'Yes,' Matthew agreed. 'Like your mother.'

'But that's a long time ago now, Dad.'

'It needed time, Adam. Lots of time. I felt rejected then. There was a lot of pain. And not just bodily pain either.'

'But now that pain has healed,' Bryony suggested.

'Is healing,' Matthew replied. 'Do you want me to drive you back to Penreath? I take it you had to drive Adam's Range Rover here.'

'Don't rush him,' she warned Adam when Matthew had gone out to his car. 'Your father was badly hurt, physically and mentally. Let him take things gently.'

'All I want is for him to be happy again, Bryony,' Adam replied quietly. 'As happy as I am.'

Bryony was having a quick break between appointments, strolling round the lawns at Penreath when she saw the odd-job man carrying a box of flower-pots towards the greenhouses by the side of the house.

'Mr Jenner,' she called out. 'Could I have a word?'

The man stopped and smiled at her. 'Several words, if you like, m'dear,' he replied. 'Come on into the greenhouse. It's a sight warmer there, out of the wind.'

She followed him inside, while he lowered the awkward box on to the slatted bench.

'It's one of the windows in my room,' she explained. 'There's a nail holding it down. I wonder if you could remove it some time.'

The man looked at her, puzzled. 'Nail?'

She nodded. 'The lower window. It looks as though it's been there for some time. I don't open the windows all that often at this time of year, but it annoys me when I forget and try to with that one.'

'Come along now if you want me to. Can't see why anyone should put a nail in though. Dr Carthew wouldn't be any too pleased about that.'

'Are you going to transplant some of your geranium cuttings into these pots?' she asked, looking at the plants overcrowding the adjoining greenhouse.

'Not for a day or so. Still waiting for a bit of glass to do that pane at the end. Let the frost in, that will.'

Bryony glanced to where he was pointing and saw a shattered pane in one corner, near the ground. 'What happened?' she asked, thoughtfully studying the jagged gap.

'Somebody being a bit clever with some of those croquet balls in the shed t'other day. Having a game of bowls with them, the chap said. Caught that corner smack on. Now, I'll just go and fetch my box of tools, and then I'll be up to look at that nail for you.'

'It's the tower room on the top floor, Mr Jenner. On the west side of the house.'

She looked down at the broken pane of glass again. One long pointed section was missing, shaped rather like a dagger.

* * *

Mr Jenner regarded the bent nail with some puzzlement. 'Can't think who'd make a bodge-up like that. Been there some time, I should say. Nicely wedged in, that is.' He ran his finger up to the top of the window-frame. 'Can't see why they did it though. That bit of cord's quite safe. Not frayed at all. No danger of the window coming down in a hurry, once it's opened. That's the problem with this sort, you see. Cord goes. Down crashes the window. Smashed. Or they that be looking out of it, maybe.'

'Perhaps it rattled and disturbed whoever was sleeping in this room. There were some fierce gales last winter,' Bryony suggested.

Mr Jenner shook his head. 'This room's not been used for a couple of years. Not since that young lad slept in here. Dr Carthew wouldn't let no one use it. Until you came, that is. Didn't want to waste one of the guest rooms by putting you in, I dare say. Lose him a bit of money, that would. Proper old tight-fist, that one is.'

'What lad was that, Mr Jenner?'

'Young chap that went missing. Lot of trouble there'd been with him and a few others. Still come back they do. The rest of them, not that boy. Here a few weeks back. Quietened down a lot now they have. Only youngsters then. Never did know what happened to that lad though. Strange that was. Vanished clean off the face of the earth. Went in the sea, they reckon. Never washed up though. Still, there's lobsters round this way. And the occasional shark. They aren't choosy about their dinners.'

Bryony shuddered.

'Don't think I can get that out without a deal of trouble, m'dear. Hammered right down it's been. Might split the wood. Dr Carthew wouldn't like that. A new window like this would be a bit costly. Best have a word with him, m'dear. Let him make the decision.'

Nobody had used the room until now, Bryony reflected. Not since Tim Maxwell slept there and disappeared. Did somebody fear his ghost would haunt it? If so, he hadn't troubled her yet. But was he dead? Everyone said he'd caused trouble. Perhaps it had been a good way to start again elsewhere – like that man in a series she'd once watched on television. What was his name? Perrin? Reginald Perrin. He'd left a pile of clothes on the beach and disappeared. It was the sort of thing that might appeal to a youngster.

But Charles Morton was a close friend. Surely Tim Maxwell would have contacted him in some way. And Charles seemed very sure that Tim had never returned. It was all very odd, she decided.

Cathy hadn't returned for any more treatment on her knee, but from what Ros said, it appeared to be much better, although Bryony did feel the girl herself might have mentioned it. Knowing when something was improved gave an insight into dealing with other cases.

She'd received a long letter from Jen only the day before, saying that since her return to London she hadn't had a single migraine, and also that a long weekend at Penreath was planned for December. Charles and Phil would be joining her. Maybe then I can ask more about Tim Maxwell, Bryony decided.

The Welsh girl, Ros, did continue with her treatment though, and during the sessions she talked quite a lot. Cathy featured strongly in most of the conversations and Bryony could tell that Ros was impressed by everything she did, following along in her shadow as if she hoped the gloss and glamour would brush off. They certainly hit some high-spots but Bryony realized that travelling around the world so easily, everything, for them, soon became a bore. They needed something extra to add a little zest to living. In a way she felt sorry for them. They could never be satisfied. Every peak achieved had to be surpassed. She wondered what would happen when it all ended. Contentment was a rare gift.

Tom's name cropped up frequently in their conversations as well. At first it had irked Bryony. Ros seemed to know far more about him than she herself did. Working together for the same airline, they'd led a shared life. No wonder Bryony had never felt at ease when she met his friends. They lived in another world. At times she'd feared that Tom was growing away from her in some way. Listening to Ros, she realized just how much their lives had differed. How dull he must have thought her. And yet he had chosen her to marry. Maybe that's what he'd needed. A safe base to return to.

'Did you know the girl Tom was engaged to before?' she asked Ros casually. She'd often wondered about her.

Ros stared at her in surprise. 'Of course I do. It was Cathy.'

Shock jolted through Bryony, her mind darting back to that evening on the river-boat. Seeing them together. No wonder she'd felt such instant antagonism. Cathy. Tom had been engaged to her. Why had he never mentioned it? She'd met the other girl frequently. Cathy was part of the same group. Part of Tom's crew on many occasions.

'Didn't you know?'

Bryony shook her head, feeling suddenly sick.

'He was the one to break off the engagement,' Ros went on. 'It really gut-blasted Cathy. Not that it made a lot of difference.'

'What do you mean?' Bryony could sense Ros's back tense.

'Nothing. Tom's dead now. I don't want to upset you more.'

'How do you mean – upset me?'

'Well, Tom wasn't a saint. You must have realized that.'

'So everyone keeps telling me,' Bryony replied stiffly.

'He certainly enjoyed life. I always felt a bit sorry for you when I saw you at those parties but then, you must have known.'

'Known what?'

'The way he played around.'

Bryony's fingers stilled in their movement. 'No,' she said in a whisper. 'I didn't know.'

'I'm sorry. Let's change the subject, shall we? You don't want all this dragged up. Besides, you've got a new boyfriend now, haven't you? Tom's in the past.'

'I'd like to know,' Bryony insisted.

'Cathy never really let him go,' Ros said thoughtfully. 'She couldn't believe he'd chosen someone like you. I don't mean that unkindly, Bryony, but you two are different, aren't you? Like chalk and cheese. I mean, who could compare with Cathy?' She paused awkwardly. 'That sounds awful, doesn't it? I'm sorry. Anyway, they still saw a lot of each other. And, when we were away....' Her voice trailed off. 'He always came back to you though, didn't he? And that really got up Cathy's nose. In the end she gave him an ultimatum. He had to make a choice – her or you.'

Bryony stood as if turned to stone, waiting for Ros to go on.

'It was that day ... when he died. We'd been away on a two-night stint.'

'Two-night?' interrupted Bryony sharply. 'He told me he'd be away for three. I didn't expect him back until the following evening. That's why I was so surprised to see him.'

'No, it was two,' Ros said. 'I suppose he was spending the third with Cathy....' Her voice died away again. 'Look, shall I stop now? You must be hating all this.'

'Go on,' Bryony ordered bleakly.

'Cathy and Tom had a blazing row just after we got back from the flight. That's when she told him. He had to make a decision. There and then. And he did. He chose Cathy. I'm sorry, Bryony, but you did want to know. Don't blame him too much, though. He'd never really got her out of his system. Cathy made quite sure of that. But he said he must tell you himself, straight away. It wasn't fair to go on two-timing you as he had done. He cared a lot for you, you know.'

'But not enough to marry me,' Bryony said flatly.

'He'd only have made you unhappy in the end. Leopards don't change their spots. Cathy would always have been there.'

'So that was what he was coming to tell me. That everything was over between us. What a pity he bothered! Another few minutes and I would have been nicely out of his life.'

'Don't be bitter,' Ros pleaded.

'What else can I be?'

'I shouldn't have told you.'

'I'm glad that you did,' Bryony said quietly. 'At least now I'm under no illusions.' She sat silently for a minute or two. Her mind running back to that evening. Seeing Tom standing there outside in the flicker from the flames. Hearing him call out to her above the roar of the fire. And then, losing sight of him. 'And yet he still tried to save me. He ran into the shop to find me.'

'Yes,' Ros mused slowly. 'Perhaps he wasn't such a rotter after all.'

What with Christmas and the wedding, the preceding

weeks flew by. Bryony decided to marry in Cornwall. It would be far easier for Matthew, rather than an arduous day's journey up to Sussex, and she wanted to please him as well.

Besides Adam was a Cornishman. He'd been born there. It was only right he married there. The church in Coverack was small. She wanted it to be a quiet family affair.

A hotel nearby would do the reception, and guests could stay overnight. Serena and Astrid were delighted too. Bryony asked them both to be her bridesmaids. She would have preferred just to have Serena, but it wouldn't have been fair to leave out Astrid. Gavin Carthew was the only one to raise any objection. A disruption to the everyday routine, he complained, until Bryony suggested that the publicity in the local paper could be advantageous to Penreath.

It was a slack time for the health farm in any case. After the long summer and autumn rush, few came again until the new year when resolutions determined a slender and healthy figure. Several of the rooms were in the process of redecoration, including those in the tower. An all-pervading smell of paint hung in the air.

It did, however, mean that Bryony had more time to spare, and she spent that with Adam. The cottages on the cliff were progressing quickly. All outside work had now been completed and the men had started on the interior. Water and drainage had yet to be installed, but trenches were being dug to connect from the lane outside Penreath.

'How did the people who originally lived there manage?' Bryony asked Adam.

'It was lanterns and candles then, with a shared well for water. For safety, my father had it filled in when he bought the cottages years back,' he said, 'so that will now have to come from the mains supply. The water authority have got on pretty fast, but annoyingly we've been held up with the bathroom and kitchen fittings. They were only delivered today. It means that Joe and I'll be working late for the next few days, installing them before the pipes are connected.'

'Gavin was furious when he came back from a trip to London and saw those trenches everywhere,' Bryony chuckled.

'He's lucky we've not had much rain,' Adam retorted. 'That would've made the area muddy with the lorries and vans travelling to and fro. Anyway, I thought it was pretty quiet up at Penreath at the moment.'

'It has been but there's quite a crowd coming in next weekend – not that it pleases Gavin. It's Charles Morton and his friends. They're all fairly young and "lark around" as he puts it. He prefers the older wealthy set, preferably those with a wide circle of business acquaintances who'll come down on their recommendation,' she said. 'Still, at least Charles's lot aren't likely to complain about the smell of paint. Guests are having to be housed in the north and east wings. The tower where I am is being decorated now, so I'm the only one left.'

'You can always move over to Coverack and stay with us,' Adam suggested.

'Not really, Gavin's a bit fussy about staff being on hand to entertain the guests when there are so few of them around. It would look a bit bleak if we all disappeared.'

'Pity,' Adam smiled. 'What's he going to do when we're married and you're not living on the premises?'

'I'm not sure he's even considered that,' she laughed.

'Then you'd better tell him I fully intend to have you around entertaining *me* in the evenings, not the guests at Penreath.'

'How chauvinistic!' she replied.

'Oh, I can be quite medieval when I want to! There's a lot about me you've yet to discover.'

'Is there?' she innocently enquired.

'A great deal,' he chuckled, drawing her into his arms. 'Just wait until I get this plaster off tomorrow!'

When Charles Morton's party arrived on Friday afternoon, Bryony was pleased to see Jen and Phil among them, and they greeted her like a long-lost friend.

'What's all this?' Phil demanded, seizing her hand and glaring down at the sapphire ring. 'I turn my back for five minutes and look what happens? Didn't you realize I came back to sweep you off your feet?'

'Don't believe him, Bryony!' Jen laughed. 'The rugby season's well underway now and he's been suffering for weeks with his thigh.'

'I did it deliberately,' Phil chuckled, 'so that I could experience your lovely soft hands again. And when I told some of the other guys in the team, they decided to come as well. You're going to be rushed off your feet coping with us all.'

'And how about you, Charles?' Bryony asked, turning to the other man standing quietly beside them.

'Changed my job since we last met. You scared me half to death, you know! Computers are old hat anyway. My uncle's taken me into his art business. Runs a gallery in Windsor. Notice how I'm standing upright now? All that staring up at paintings.' He gave her a wink. 'Not going to find something hazardous about that are you?'

'I doubt it,' she laughed.

'Well, I've come back to thank you,' Jen said, slipping her arm through Bryony's and heading for the lounge. 'Haven't had a single migraine since I was here. *And* I've been trying out all those deep breathing and relaxation exercises you showed me, too. I don't think I get quite so het-up, but perhaps you should ask Charles. He knows me far better than I do myself,' she said, turning to smile at him.

'You should see us in the mornings,' he grinned. 'Laid out there on the bed, doing all our exercises!'

'He's a terrible slave-driver,' Jen declared. 'I'm not allowed to put a foot to the ground until I've practised every one. You certainly made a great impression on him, you know.'

'Put the fear of the devil into me, more likely.'

'Well, it seems to be working,' Bryony smiled. 'And at least you've come back for more.'

'But we always come in December,' Jen observed.

'To get slimmed down ready for Christmas?' Bryony enquired.

'No,' Charles replied quietly. 'It's the anniversary of Tim Maxwell's death. We couldn't be anywhere else, could we?'

Bryony looked at him with startled eyes. 'He died in December?'

Charles nodded.

'But I thought you said he went swimming. His clothes were found on the beach.'

'They were,' Charles replied. 'That's what was so odd about the whole thing. After all, who'd go swimming in this kind of weather?'

'He was drunk, Charles,' Jen butted in, 'but let's not go into all that again. It's so depressing. It's bad enough you dragging us all back to do some sort of homage to his memory.' She leaned towards Bryony and said confidentially, 'I couldn't stand the guy to be honest. At times he was the pits.'

'He was my friend,' Charles put in bluntly.

'Your friend, yes, although I could never work out

why. He got up to some pretty nasty tricks, didn't he?'

'Bit of a dare-devil, that's all,' Charles declared hotly.

'Calm down, children,' Phil soothed. 'There's no need to get so lathered up. Tim Maxwell just isn't worth it.'

'You always were jealous of him,' protested Charles.

'Jealous! Come off it, Charles! Tim Maxwell was the dregs. He thoroughly deserved everything that happened to him.'

'Not to die,' Charles retorted.

'The way he was acting that night, he did.'

'What did happen?' Bryony questioned.

'We'd all been down in Falmouth. Helston was out of bounds – thanks to Tim Maxwell. We'd have been lynched if we'd gone there,' Jen explained. 'He'd got a bit high on a few occasions. Some of the kids there were impressed. Tim had that effect on people.' She glanced sideways at Charles as she spoke. 'Anyway, on the journey home we almost had to tie him down in the car. Everyone was a bit merry on scrumpy, but Tim Maxwell was really over the top. Old Gavin was furious when we came in. Told us all to go to our rooms and stay there until we'd sobered off.'

She gave a little giggle. 'Bit like a Victorian schoolmaster really. Well, Tim rebelled. I thought poor old Gavin was going to have apoplexy. Scarlet in the face. Virtually put the half-nelson on Tim and bundled him up the stairs to his room.' Her expression became serious. 'We didn't see Tim again.'

'Did you all sleep in the tower?' Bryony questioned.

Charles shook his head. 'No, the rest of us were on the other side of the house. I think Gavin put Tim up there because he was so disruptive. Out of harm's way probably.'

'No one bothered much when Tim didn't appear at breakfast. With the amount he'd drunk, he would've had a head like I don't know what,' Phil put in. 'It was around midday when Gavin came along and said he'd just found his dressing-gown and towel down there in the cove.'

'Must've been pretty drunk though. Never usually wore a dressing-gown. Always cursed because his mother insisted on packing one. Took up half his suitcase, he complained,' Charles added.

'How do you know?' demanded Jen.

'Darling, we were at boarding-school together. Same dormitory too. I'd known Tim since we were seven. Both wept buckets for the first week.'

'I wonder why he chose to swim in the sea,' Bryony mused, 'when there was the indoor pool?'

'Don't know why he should choose to swim at all,' Charles retorted. 'Hated swimming. Always had. Gave him earache, he used to say.'

Bryony noticed the decorators had almost finished stripping wallpaper in the room below hers as she passed its open door the next morning. Odd bits scattered the landing where they'd walked in and out, and she could see new rolls and tins of paint heaped on the floor just inside where the men sat smoking as they read the daily newspaper. Gavin won't like that, she thought. Cigarettes were banned at Penreath, although she'd seen the occasional guest having a quick puff out in the grounds.

Her room wouldn't be done until after she'd gone on honeymoon. Only one more week. Then, she and Adam would have their own home. A pretty little whitewashed cottage that Adam had restored, set in a huge rambling and overgrown garden over at Cadgwith, between Penreath and Coverack. Her heart gave a skip of excitement at the thought. This time next week, I shall be married to Adam. Or almost, she decided, glancing at her watch. The wedding was at ten o'clock.

Adam had suggested Brittany for their honeymoon. She could guess why. It was very similar to Cornwall. There was Mont Saint Michel as well, so like their own St Michael's Mount off the coast at Marazion.

She could see his Range Rover parked near the cottages on the cliff, half-hidden by heaps of earth where the water authority men were working. She'd be lucky to snatch a moment to go up there and see him with so many people at Penreath for the weekend. Never mind, she comforted herself. In one week's time we'll be together for always.

She went to bed early that night. Tomorrow was going to be a busy day and her appointment book was already full from first thing. Her footsteps echoed on the bare boards of the stairs as she climbed. They were next to be painted, the men on the final stages of the room below. In a way she felt sad to leave Penreath. Over the months it had become home for her. A haven. And she loved the wide view from its windows.

It was comforting, too, to see lights reflecting out from the cottages on the cliff – like they used to, decades before. Adam and Joe must still be working there, trying to complete the final bathroom so that the pipes could be connected within the next few days. Having his wrist out of plaster meant that Adam could do far more now, and the work up there was progressing rapidly. Soon people would be living in them again. She liked the thought of that. A whole new beginning.

And a whole new beginning, too, for Adam and herself was about to commence as well.

TEN

At first Bryony thought it was her old nightmare returning. The harsh drag at her throat. The fight for breath. That feeling of suffocation. And then her eyes opened, terror drenching into her.

The noise filling her ears wasn't the roar of the sea as it pounded against the shore, nor the buffeting of wind against the cliffs. She'd only heard such a sound once before. The fury of flames.

Her feet felt for the floor, touching the softness of the carpet. On leaden limbs she made her way across the room, her fingers reaching out to slip damply on the handle of the door. It won't be. It can't be, she silently implored. Not here. Not again.

The door yawned slowly inwards, the narrow landing outside filled with a frenzied dancing light, making her cower back in horror. She stood there, staring down at the flames as they rose to curl and lick round the banisters, bursting with explosive force as they reached each tin of paint on the floor below.

Thoughts raced through her terrified brain. The tower was on the far side of the house. Away from everyone else. She glanced at her watch. Nearly half-past eleven. Everyone would be in bed by now. Dr Carthew insisted a good night's sleep as part of his guests' treatment.

There was a phone in her room. She turned. With shaking fingers she pressed each number, listening, waiting. Someone must hear it ring in reception. The roar of the fire echoed around her, filling her ears. She tried again, panic growing. The phone was dead.

This is a dream, she told herself. A nightmare. I've dreamed it many times before. In a moment I shall look from the window and see Tom standing there. And then I'll know it's only a dream.

She moved there, to stare out, seeing the outline of the garden, bushes silhouetted against the night. In the distance the lighthouse blinked. Once. Twice. They must see the flames. Perched high up on the cliff. They *must* see the flames.

Her desperate eyes scanned the pale gleam of moonlight on the sea, the scattered stars in the sky, following the clear-cut line of the cliff, seeing frost sparkle its grass-thick edge. The windows of the cottages were dark now. Adam was gone. Hopelessness engulfed her.

She could see a dark trail of smoke creeping under the bedroom door, watch it thicken and spread. Her eyes stung. Her throat tightened. To swallow was impossible. Fear paralysed her whole body. She could only stand by the window, hands pressed backwards against the chill of the glass, waiting for the door to burst and flames surge in. Already she could feel the heat from the floor on the soles of her bare feet. It was as if her brain had slowed. As if she was watching a video played in slow motion. Knowing it had all happened before.

In a moment I shall hear Tom's voice call out. Turn my head. See him standing there outside. And then he'll be gone. Coming to find me. And this time, take me with him. She closed her eyes, knowing there could only be moments left.

'Bryony!' It was his voice. Calling to her. Slowly, her

eyelids raised and she looked down through the glass. Figures were moving in the garden, darting this way and that. Lights flooding out on to the frosty lawn. One stood apart, gazing up at her. Her mind was a confusion. She heard the voice again.

'Bryony!'

Not Tom, but Adam. Her knuckles beat against the window pane. She saw him move, her voice crying out, telling him not to come; to stay safe there in the garden. And her heart ached with her love for him.

Others, staring upwards, crowded into the space where once he had been. She could see the shape of their faces, pale in the flickering light. But Adam was gone.

No, no, no! The word tore through her, fighting past dry lips to whisper helplessly in the air. Not Adam. Please God, not Adam too.

The sash-window above her was sliding. Her eyes watched it with fascination. Inch by inch. Slowly downwards. She could see the little wheel move as the cord wound round. Then it descended with a rush and Adam's lean body erupted into the smoke-filled room, his arms closing round her, lifting her up to the sweet shiver of cold salt air.

With a surge of fury the door burst inwards, drawn by the sudden draught, long tongues of flame leaping towards them. Adam's foot kicked hard against the glass, shattering the lower pane, scattering the floor.

'The roof, Bryony,' he urged.

Hands were reaching down, fingers outstretched. Phil's rugby team? she wondered hazily. Adam seized her wrists, guiding them upwards until they were grasped and she felt a sudden jerk, her body swaying sideways into a void of darkness. For a moment she spun, hanging there, the chill night air biting into her, and then the rushing blackness of her mind met that of the night.

'Adam.' His name forced its way through her to croak into sound and as his fingers curled round hers, she saw his face, grimed and tense, smile down.

'Rest quietly now,' he whispered.

With a deep sigh of contentment she let her eyelids close again, her hand clasped in his. 'I love you, Adam.'

'I love you, too.'

They had a white wedding. Frost covered the ground, every tree glistening in the sunshine. Fishing-boats swayed at anchor in the harbour and sparkling waves frothed the shore where wading birds dipped and strutted the tideline among the dark rocks.

Inside, the church was decked with Christmas colour. Shaggy-headed chrysanthemums glowed from squat vases. Pale translucent discs of honesty were intermingled with the polished scarlet and green of holly. Tall stately lilies graced every pillar. A froth of gypsophila and tiny white carnations garlanded the end of each pew.

Bryony's dress was white velvet, hooded and cloaked; her bouquet, scarlet roses. And Adam was tall and handsome in his dark morning suit, a sprig of mistletoe edging the carnation in his buttonhole.

The whole village seemed to be waiting, faces smiling, while Adam and Bryony walked the short distance from the church to the reception, drifts of confetti and rose petals scattering round them, rising upwards in tiny swirls of colour, to wing away into the crisp blue sky.

Tom was gone, too, as if he had never been.

Matthew greeted them on their return from honeymoon with the news that on the final day of excavation, the water authority had unearthed a human skeleton from the garden of one of the cliff cottages. It was thought to have been interred there for about three years.

'And,' he continued, 'Gavin Carthew committed suicide the very same day. It's created a great deal of speculation, as you may well imagine.'

'The missing boy. Tim Maxwell,' Bryony breathed. 'It has to be.'

Police files were reopened, tests carried out and finally the body was identified. It was Tim Maxwell; his skull fractured.

Bryony's mind went back to the tower room. The room with a nailed-up window. What had happened that night, after Tim Maxwell was taken there? He was drunk, Charles Morton said. Very drunk. Had he opened that window? Leaned out for fresh air. Fallen?

Or had someone pushed him? Gavin Carthew had taken him to that room. *Gripping him in a half-nelson,* Jen said. Had Tim Maxwell fought back? He'd caused trouble several times before, both at Penreath and in Helston. And Gavin Carthew hated disruption.

But enough to kill?

She recalled the part-sawn floorboards that sent Adam crashing to the ground. The long sliver of glass that sliced into Arthur's arm. Both incidents were callous. Both were deliberate. She couldn't forget seeing that broken pane in the greenhouse at Penreath.

Gavin had once worked in forensic medicine. He understood the way a criminal mind worked. And he knew what methods of crime were hard to detect – and prove.

I'm being unreasonable, she told herself. Too much imagination. Why should he do these things? The accidents hadn't prevented the cottages from being rebuilt.

But did Gavin hope they would? Did he imagine that Matthew and Adam would give up the whole idea and let them fall into ruin, to finally disappear in a heap of rubble, covering the grave for ever? He must have realized that the gardens would be dug up to lay drainage pipes. Bryony remembered his unreasonable anger when he saw the new trenches on his return from London.

And if it wasn't Gavin, who else could it have been? Someone had put Tim Maxwell's things on the beach. Someone had hidden his body. Charles Morton and his friends seemed unlikely to have done it.

But why should Gavin commit suicide? The perfect murder is impossible to prove. Wasn't that what he told the novelist Jill? Had, finally, his confidence shattered?

Or was it remorse? Gavin Carthew was trained as a doctor, on oath to aid, not take, life.

'Who'll run Penreath now?' Adam mused thoughtfully.

'How about me?' Bryony enquired.

He kissed the tip of her nose. 'No, Mrs Veryan, not yet awhile anyway. You're going to be occupied raising our family for the next few years. I was thinking of Penny – Dr Pentland. She's coming up for retirement over at Truro. What better place to be than Penreath? A far more convenient drive for my father.'

'Still matchmaking?' Bryony questioned, snuggling into his arms.

'I recommend married life to everyone now – provided one can find the right wife.'

'And have you?' she asked him curiously.

'The perfect one,' he smiled.

'Sir Toby Balfour will be spending a few days at Penreath soon. He makes a regular tour of all his properties. I think he likes to keep an eye on his investments. How about if I drop a few hints in his ear?'

'Why? Does he want to get married as well?' Adam grinned.

'Can't you ever be serious?' she murmured, lifting up her face to his.

'Only about some things,' he replied. 'Like this.'

Shadows of the Night

One

A thin line of pale gold edged the horizon. The day was still new; the sea like crinkled silk. Only close to the beach were there waves, rising slowly, before thundering in to whiten the shore.

Lauren walked down the four wooden steps. Beneath her fingers the handrail was smooth and warm. Dried seaweed crackled; fine sand gritted her toes and her feet sank into its softness, making every step an effort until its surface became chill and damp.

As the force of the first wave swirled round her ankles she paused, her breath catching in her throat at its coldness. For one hesitant moment her fingers travelled searchingly across her cheek; then she went on again.

The second wave reached her knees, soaking the cotton of her dress, making it cling.

With the third, her body swayed and lifted, spray splashing over her face. Her lips tasted salt. Deliberately she forced herself not to swim.

This was how it had to be. There was no turning back now.

5

The next wave came, and she let the sea close over her, dragging her down into the eternity of its depths.

When her head was forced upwards, breaking the surface of the water, making her choke and splutter as an agony of pain tore through her lungs, she was angry; wanting to scream in protest; kicking out against an encircling, relentless grip.

Her body met the harshness of the shore; her eyes fighting to open, stinging.

An outline loomed, blurrily, over her.

'What the hell were you trying to do?' The words seared into her with their fury.

Again she tried to focus her gaze, only to be checked by the burn of salt. Her teeth began to chatter and she felt the folds of something soft enclose her. Particles of sand scoured her skin and her limbs glowed from the rub of strong, firm hands.

'You could have drowned.' The deep voice was gentle now.

'That's what I wanted,' she raged. 'Why did you have to stop me?'

'You foolish little creature!'

Desperately she caught her quivering lower lip between her teeth, but couldn't prevent one lone tear.

His fingers smoothed back the tangle of her hair. Instinctively she jerked away, twisting her face to one side, pressing it into the shingle.

He was lifting her now, her head cradled into the

comfort of his shoulder, and she felt its muscles strain against her cheek as he bent to pick up his discarded track suit.

'You're renting Trennion cottage, aren't you?'

She nodded, hearing the words tremor in her ear, suddenly too weary to reply, closing her eyes, letting herself sink into the safety of the arms holding her.

The wooden gate creaked as it opened. She felt the rough catch of his chin on her hair when he stooped to go through the door; then he was carrying her up the steepness of the stairs.

Her feet were lowered to the smooth floor of the bathroom.

'What you need is a hot shower,' he ordered, abruptly turning on the tap. 'Are you OK to manage, or do you want me to stay?'

She stood, clutching the thickness of his towel around her, a trickle of dampness creeping down her neck from the mass of tumbled hair that fell around her face and shoulders, making her shiver as she stared back at him.

He was tall; strongly built, yet lean. The firm lines of his sun-bronzed body in brief black swimming-trunks revealed that. Long-limbed, too. Not young. Thirty. More likely thirty-five, she decided, noticing the slight hint of silver that caught the darkness of his hair over well-shaped ears.

But it was his eyes that held her. Wide. Deep. Compelling. An overwhelming, almost navy blue against the tan of his skin.

'I said can you manage?' There was an impatient snap to his voice and his hand stretched towards the towel, making her clasp it more closely round her.

'I can manage,' she said defensively.

'Don't lock the bathroom door. If you faint, or try to drown yourself again, I want to be able to get in there – and fast.' She turned her head swiftly away as he reached out to cup her chin, his voice softening slightly. 'I'll only be downstairs in the kitchen if you need me. Don't be afraid to call out.'

He'd pulled on the faded blue track suit by the time she came downstairs again, and was already drinking coffee from a blue-glazed mug. Another waited, steaming, on the wooden table.

'I've put in plenty of sugar.'

'But I *hate* sugar!' she flared back at him.

'Drink it!' he commanded. 'It'll warm you up and counteract the shock. Then I want an explanation.'

An explanation? To him? Her anger brimmed over. 'Why don't you just go away and leave me alone?' she blazed.

'To do what?' he questioned drily. 'Try again? A beautiful girl like you shouldn't need to kill herself.'

'Beautiful?' The word tore from her lips, and with one violent movement she flung back her head, swinging the damp veil of hair away from her face, tensing herself for his reaction.

The blue gaze didn't flinch. 'Am I supposed to be revolted? Horrified? Shocked? Is that what you want? I'll grant you it's a vicious scar, but I'm a doctor. I've seen far worse.' His eyes were like steel blades, slicing into her. 'And it's not a good enough reason to die.'

He pushed the mug of coffee into her hands.

'Drink this, and after that you'll eat. You don't look as though you've had food for days. Let's see what Mrs Tolly has put in the fridge.'

Stunned by his calm acceptance, Lauren watched him move purposefully across the kitchen and tug open the shiny white door, taking out eggs and butter, then she heard the faint pop as he lit the calor gas stove.

The coffee was hot and her cold fingers curled round the smooth sides of the mug, drawing on its warmth. Her body felt weak now, sapped of all strength, and she sank down on a high wooden stool, leaning her back against the rough whitewashed stone of the wall.

'My name's Daniel, by the way,' he remarked casually. 'Daniel Kerrow.' He was intent on the saucepan, beating in the eggs, while bread browned under the grill. 'You don't mind if I have some too, do you? I'm famished and it's well past my breakfast-time.'

He put two plates on the table and sat down opposite her, cutting into the scrambled eggs, and began to eat.

The savoury smell tantalized her nostrils and slowly she picked up a fork.

'You see,' he said, as her plate emptied, 'I'm not such a bad cook, am I?' A smile widened his mouth, sending tiny lines radiating out from the corners of his eyes to be lost in the thick darkness of his hair. 'But scrambled egg *is* about my limit, I'm afraid. More coffee?'

She nodded silently, her tired gaze following the movement of his hands as they spooned the granules into her mug and refilled it. They were strong hands with long tapering fingers. Dark hairs lightly flecked their tan. She remembered their touch on her skin. Gentle hands.

'You have yet to tell me your name.'

Her gaze moved back to his, aware of the silent reproach.

'Lauren,' she said flatly. 'Lauren Russell.'

One of his hands reached out and curved firmly round hers.

'Hullo then, Lauren Russell.'

For a moment she almost returned his smile, letting her fingers lie in his, until he glanced down at his wrist and frowned.

'Have you any idea of the time? My watch's stopped.' His eyes glinted with wry humour. 'That sudden dip in the sea doesn't seem to have agreed with it.'

Instantly she stiffened. 'Then I apologize.' Her voice was terse.

'What's a watch compared with a life?' he asked lightly, but she refused to meet his gaze.

He stood up, pushing the kitchen stool away with a twist of his long legs. 'I'm afraid I'll have to go now. I've a couple of house-calls to make. Are you going to be all right on your own for a while? I'll be back later.'

'There's no need,' she retorted.

'I think there is,' he said quietly.

The implied meaning infuriated her. 'I'm not your patient!' she flung back at him sharply.

'No,' he agreed, gathering up the still-wet towel from where it lay draped over another stool. 'You're not.'

'Then for heaven's sake do as I ask!'

For a moment he stood there, gazing down at her thoughtfully, then he turned towards the door. 'I'll be back.'

Lauren remained sitting at the table after he'd gone, her fingers still curled round the mug.

Why? she asked herself bitterly. Why did he have to come along? By now everything would have been over. Finished. Ended.

Her hand reached up slowly, tracing the line of puckered skin from the corner of one eye down across the smoothness of her cheek to where it tugged at her mouth.

And she remembered the expression on her fiancé Mark's face when he'd first seen her in the hospital ward the day after the accident. The way he'd turned his head away from her, not even attempting to hide his horror and revulsion, so that in a flood of despair she'd torn his ring from her finger, and thrust it back at him. For in that expression she'd read her whole future.

If Mark, who loved her so much, couldn't bear to look at her, how would others react?

The thought had tortured her.

It was a doctor treating her at the hospital – the same hospital where she had trained and where Mark worked as a pharmacist – who'd suggested Cornwall.

'You need to get away from all your memories, Lauren. Adjust to what's happened. I know just the place. A friend of mine has a cottage. Trennion. It's quiet and peaceful. Just the right sort of surroundings. He lets it out for holidays. I'll get in touch. So early in the summer, it's bound to be free.'

He'd made all the arrangements; taken her to the station. She'd insisted on the overnight train. Darkness hid so many things.

A taxi drove her to the cottage. She hated that. Shrinking into one corner of it. Hiding from the early-morning streets of the town. As the car increased speed, her fingers caught desperately at the edge of the seat, digging deep into the smooth fabric, her body tight with panic.

'Staying long, m'dear?' The driver's voice was interested.

'A while,' she said. Long enough for what she had to do. And she'd already planned that.

'Bit off the beaten track is Trennion. Not much there for a young lady like you.'

She hadn't answered, hoping he'd end the conversation, but his Cornish accent continued its probing. 'Mebbe there's more joining you later?'

'I'm on my own.' Alone. That's how it had to be.

'You'll like it here. Folk always do.'

She leaned forward to stare through the car

window. The town was left behind now and high grass-banks rose on either side, so close she could almost reach out and touch them; banks that were a riot of breathtaking colour. The deep pink of foxgloves, standing tall and erect above the soft blue-mauve of scabious and the sharp glow of knapweed, mingled with pale campion and a few remaining bluebells to bury the lichened grey stones of a wall. She'd never seen such a profusion of wild flowers growing.

'That's Trennion,' the driver told her. 'Down there.'

She followed his pointing finger, seeing the lane twist steeply, trees arching above, and through their leaning trunks saw a brief glimpse of hazy azure sea.

The cottage was almost on the beach itself. So very near that when the wind rose and a gale blew, the spray from the waves would mist its windows and fill the air like thin smoke.

'I said 'twas a lonely spot,' the driver warned, lifting her case and carrying it through the wooden-slatted gate.

Rose-stems trailed upwards over the low roof of the porch to burst into a blaze of scarlet against the whiteness of the walls, heads heavy with scent. Lauren could smell their fragrance blending with the salt as she stepped into the sunshine.

'Key's kept under that tub there,' the man instructed.

Obediently her fingers found the cool metal and drew it out, fitting it into the lock, turning it, feeling the door yawn inwards. A faint spice hung over the darkness of the hall, and the contents of a china bowl of pot-pourri on the polished carved wood of a chest fluttered in the sudden draught.

'There'll be groceries and milk in the fridge. Look like you could do with a nice cup of tea, m' dear.'

He'd lowered her suitcase onto the floor and smiled, but Lauren was acutely aware that his gaze veered swiftly away from her face, and knew the reason.

After the engine-notes of the taxi had died away everything was silent, leaving only the soft surge of the sea.

The sea.

That was her reason for coming here, knowing exactly what she would do. It would be so easy. So easy.

Until Daniel Kerrow came along.

The used breakfast plates lay on the wooden surface of the table. His blue-glazed mug empty in the sink. She could still see those deep blue eyes regarding her thoughtfully over its rim; feel the firm pressure of his fingers around hers; remember his smile.

A wave of anger burned through her. Why did he have to appear there, on the beach at that very moment?

The raw fury of his voice still echoed in her ears.

'What the hell were you trying to do?'

Why did he have to stop me?

Sunshine filtered in through the salt-hazed

window revealing faded colour in the bowl of fragrant dried petals when she went through the hall again. Outside, fat bees hummed lazily round purple spikes of lavender and the sinuous limbs of a tortoiseshell cat were stretched below as it lay on its side, in the shade of the silvery-leafed bushes.

Lauren bent, crouching on her heels to put out a tentative hand. Languidly the cat rolled onto its back, inviting her to smooth the soft fur of its stomach, its head nuzzling against her wrist.

'Hullo, you gorgeous creature,' she whispered, and discovered that her voice was soft again, the anger gone.

It was only yards to the beach and she sat on the top step, staring down at the deep imprints where Daniel Kerrow's feet had carried her across; feeling once more the strength of his arms cushion her head in the curve of his shoulder.

'Good morning, my dear.'

The unexpected voice startled her and she swung round, the long strands of her hair swirling. A plump, rosy little woman stood by the cottage gate, her eyes bright like those of a mouse as her mouth smiled.

And Lauren watched the smile fade, the eyes change to awareness, and she thrust up her palm to cover her cheek.

'I'm Mrs Tolly,' the woman said, her expression now cautious. 'Just popped over to see if you've settled in all right. Young Dr Kerrow passed me on the cliff-path.'

And what did Dr Kerrow tell you? Lauren

wondered, her body tense again.

'I thought, from the letting-agent's phone-call, 'twould be a family staying. Families usually do come. Nice place for surfing, so they say ... I wouldn't know about that. The sea's a fearsome force to me.' She shook her head vigorously from side to side. 'Not to be trusted, my dear. You take care and don't venture out too far.'

Has Daniel Kerrow told her? Lauren asked herself.

'Found the girl attempting to drown herself, Mrs Tolly.'

But somehow she couldn't hear his pleasant voice disclosing such a thing.

And it was a pleasant voice, she had to admit, despite its frequent bursts of fury. The sort of voice that somehow, just listened to, was like a balm. It created a feeling of security. A safeness. A sense of peace.

'Along the cliff is the shortest way to the village,' Mrs Tolly was saying as she pointed to where a track led up from the beach, near the cottage. ''Tis a mile or so by road and that's a winding one. Only a small place, you'll find, my dear, but does us nicely. My cottage is next to the "Dolphin" inn should you want me. "Honeysuckle" 'tis called, though 'tis a long while since any grew there. Nasty old winds we get here in winter. Wither anything to sticks, they do.'

The cat came stalking down the garden path, twisting itself round her legs in a frenzy of delight.

'Old Toby won't worry you, will he, my dear?

Spends most of his time here, though where he come from 'tis anybody's guess.'

Lauren shook her head, careful to keep it lowered, not wanting to distress the kindly woman again. 'No,' she said.

'Milk and bread you'll find over in the village,' Mrs Tolly continued. 'Tregony bakes his own. And don't you forget to call in on me when you're passing. There'll always be a pot of tea ready.'

Reading the woman's eyes, Lauren felt suddenly guilty. 'Would you like some now?' she asked, and saw Mrs Tolly hesitate, tempted.

All Lauren wanted was to sleep after Mrs Tolly had finished her tea and gone again. Her voice had chattered on, giving a history of everyone in the harbour village; their names, what they did, where they lived. None meant a thing to Lauren, wearying her even more after the long overnight train journey.

'Now don't you forget to pop in whenever you're passing, my dear,' Mrs Tolly repeated as she closed the gate. 'Any time. You'll always be welcome.'

The bedroom looked out over the sea, a salt breeze mingling with the fragrance of lavender drifting through the open window. Waves murmured against the shore with a faint drag of shingle as they retreated, then advanced once more. Lauren's eyelids were already drooping when she lay down on the bed, listening to the hypnotic sound.

The wide arc of headlights sliced across the

*rain-spattered windscreen, dazzling her vision with a
myriad splinters of brightness as she tried to fight off their
glare. Brighter and brighter. Closer and closer. Her body
braced itself, waiting for the impact: knowing what was to
come. Mark's head was silhouetted against the side
window of the car. She could see the dark outline of his
sleek hair, the smooth straight brow, the curve of his
mouth and when he turned to look at her, his gaze wide
and shocked in the blaze of light.*

*Then came the rending crunch of metal against metal;
the agonizing pain as the windscreen dissolved into a
shimmer of jagged daggers, and that endless scream rose
in her throat, echoing, echoing ...*

Hands caught her bare arms, their strength
gripping into them, while a voice spoke through
the darkness, repeating her name over and over
again.

In terror her eyelids flew open.

Slowly the shape of his head became familiar; the
dark wind-ruffled hair, the square, angular lines of
his face, the deep concern filling those searing blue
eyes; the soothing hand on her skin.

'Lauren,' she heard Daniel Kerrow say softly. 'It's
all right, Lauren. You were dreaming.'

Instinctively, her hand flew to her cheek to hide
it from his gaze, and his fingers gently drew it
away, their touch running lightly along the ragged
scar-line; but it wasn't pain that sent a fiery pulse of
sensation beating through her, making her close
her eyes and her breath quicken.

'I didn't mean to frighten you, Lauren. I came
back as I promised I would, and heard you

screaming right from the top of the cliff.' His wide mouth curved into a rueful smile. 'It scared me. You see, I wasn't sure quite what you might have done ... this time.'

She understood his meaning, lowering her eyes from the searching depths of his.

'It was a dream,' she said slowly. Only a dream. A nightmare that had haunted her ever since that dreadful day ... 'But it keeps coming back. Over and over again.'

'And it will, for a while,' he said quietly, seating himself on the side of the rumpled bed. 'Until you forget.'

'How *can* I forget?' The words tore across the stillness of the room. 'When *this* will always remind me?'

She lifted her head, pushing the wild cloud of hair away from her cheek, thrusting her face towards him.

'It will fade.'

'Fade!' Her sharp retort echoed through the air. 'Look at my mouth. My cheek. My eye. Grotesque. A travesty of a face. How can I bear that? How can I live with it? Seeing people flinch and turn away, their expressions suddenly blank to hide what they truly feel.'

'And what do they feel, Lauren?' he asked softly.

'Revulsion!' The word was filled with despair.

'Is that what I reveal, now, when I look at you? I am a person, you know, just like everyone else.'

She stared back at him, her eyes blazing with anger. 'You! You're a doctor! You've seen horrific

sights like this many times before. You said so
yourself.'

'But for each time there's a first time, Lauren.
Like when I first saw you.'

His hand caught her chin, firmly cupping it so
that she couldn't turn away.

'When I dragged you from the sea all I saw was a
beautiful young girl deliberately destroying herself. That's what you were doing, weren't you,
Lauren? Destroying yourself.' His grip tightened.
'Didn't it ever occur to you to think what that
destruction would do to others? Those who love
you. Care for you. Haven't you a family? Friends?
Didn't you think of them? Or was it only of
yourself?'

He let one finger stroke across the scar again,
like the soft brush of a butterfly's wing, and
Lauren's breath hesitated in her throat.

'Those who love you don't think about what you
look like, Lauren. It doesn't matter to them. *You're*
the one that matters. You. The person. Not the
visual image. That's only a façade; the wrapping on
a parcel; the icing on a cake. It's what's inside that
matters. You, Lauren. Not what you look like.
People will get used to that. Soon they'll not even
notice. And the physical appearance of it will fade,
I promise you.'

He lifted her chin higher so that he could gaze
into her troubled eyes.

'When you begin to forget, others will forget too.
Only if you try to hide it, to turn away as you're
trying to do now, will others continue to

remember.' He threw an impatient glance round the room. 'I don't think you should be here on your own like this, you know. I'm not sure it's wise after all that's happened. Why don't you come over to the village? Take a room at the "Dolphin" where I can keep a close eye on you. If you want my professional opinion, that would be the best thing for you to do.'

She tugged her face away from his hand and shook her head fiercely, sending her hair into a whiplash about her cheeks.

'I don't want your *professional opinion* thank you, Dr Kerrow,' she said bitterly. 'It was kind of you to call and check up on me, but as I don't intend to become one of your patients, I certainly won't be in need of your attention again.'

Without a word, he rose from the bed and strode across the room to stand in the doorway, filling it with his height.

'Maybe one day you'll be glad that I did bother about you, unless, of course, you fully intend to carry out the act you attempted earlier today.'

She felt the sting of his words bite into her, making her cheeks burn with humiliation. Then, shaking her hair away from her face in a gesture of defiance she glared back at him, matching his anger with her own.

'That, Dr Kerrow,' she stated coldly, 'is entirely up to me.'

The bones of his face stood out palely against the tan of his skin as his jaw tightened.

'Oh no, Miss Russell, there I'm afraid you're

quite wrong,' he said in a low voice. 'I have no intention of letting that happen. And I *shall* be back, whatever you feel about the matter.'

The door closed firmly behind him and Lauren sat, fury sweeping through her, listening to his feet pound down the stairs and, later, the sound of the gate click loudly into place.

Two

Lauren was tempted to run over to the window and pursue their conversation, determined not to let him have the last word, but she guessed it would be pointless. Daniel Kerrow was the kind of man who would always have the final word.

The sun had moved on now, sending shadows from the nearby trees to slant across the white walls of the room. A glance at her watch told her it was past five o'clock. She'd slept for nearly six hours, but her brain now felt clear and fresh, all its weariness gone.

Reluctantly she found her mind was continuing to dwell on Daniel Kerrow.

'I shall be back, whatever you feel about the matter.' His words hung in the air, echoing round her.

He seemed determined to invade her life: like the old man of the sea in the *Arabian Nights*, who perched on Sinbad's shoulders, she thought ruefully, then wound his legs round his neck and refused to budge.

Was the walk across the cliffs from the village a favourite one for Dr Kerrow? Remembering that morning, she guessed he must swim somewhere nearby. He was wearing swimming-trunks when he rescued her, his track suit cast off and lying on the sand.

So was this the place where he always swam?

Was there no way she could avoid him?

She leaned against the sill, pushing the sash-window higher, to gaze down at the cove. It was only small. Secluded. A private place.

Her cove now.

Maybe that would keep him away.

The deep footprints in the sand still remained. Her tongue slid over her lips, remembering the taste of salt where her mouth brushed against his sea-wet skin, and she quickly rubbed them to obliterate the intimacy.

Even now she could feel the pressure of his arms round her; hear the deep rhythmic thud of his heartbeat; sense the prickle of his chin where it caught her hair.

When he spoke, the words had trembled her skin through the deep barrel of his chest, before breathing their way into her ear. It was a voice that soothed; that created a feeling of safety. A voice she could listen to again and again.

'*And I shall be back …*'

Her pulse quickened at the thought. And then she remembered that he was a doctor, taking a professional interest. To keep a close eye on her, as he put it, was part of his job. Nothing more.

Somehow it saddened her.

*

The dream returned to her that night. It always did. There was no escape. She woke shaking.

Slowly the peace of the room lulled her; the soft scent of roses at the open window, the sharp tang of lavender, the sound of the sea. A row of books caught her eye and she spent an hour or two browsing through them, before she finally slept once more.

When she woke again it was to hear the clink of a bottle against the stone of the front step. The sound puzzled her. Mrs Tolly said nothing was delivered to the cottage. Milk and bread could be bought in the village.

Quickly she ran across the room to the window.

A tall dark-haired figure was striding easily across the beach, tugging off the top of his faded blue track suit as he went. Lauren couldn't fail to recognize the tanned, muscular back that emerged from its folds, or that strong, upright figure.

Daniel Kerrow! She might have guessed.

A few yards from the water's edge he pulled off the bottom half, tossing it down on the beach, and splashed into the sea, his arms striking out strongly as he began to swim.

The nerve of it, she thought. It's *my* cove. It belongs to the cottage. What right does Daniel Kerrow have to swim here?

Her indignation grew as she slipped into jeans and tee-shirt, ran down the stairs and out into the porch. A bottle of milk stood there, guarded by the tortoiseshell cat. Daniel was towelling his shoulders vigorously as he walked across the sand.

'Good morning, Lauren,' he called out.

'I'd prefer it, Dr Kerrow, if you swam somewhere else,' she bit out, trying to concentrate her eyes on his face and not the strong contours of his lean body. 'I don't like someone constantly checking up on me.'

One of his dark eyebrows twitched upwards into a question-mark as he started to towel his hair.

'So you'd prefer me to swim elsewhere?' he mused, echoing her words. Laughter was tugging at the corners of his mouth.

'Yes, I would,' she snapped. 'This is my cove. It goes with the cottage.'

'It does,' he agreed mildly, 'but actually it's *my* cove.'

'Yours?'

'My brother and I own the cottage, you see,' he replied simply.

'But … I thought … Mrs Tolly …'

'Mrs Tolly cleans it and generally keeps an eye on it, but it belongs to us. My brother works in America and I live in the village at the surgery, so now we let it out, but officially it is still ours.'

He slung the towel round his neck and stood looking down at her with amusement.

'However, if it's going to distress you so much, then I'll find somewhere else. I'm afraid it's become rather a habit of mine to swim out to the rocks and back each morning.' His mouth twitched more strongly and she could see the laughter lifting the corners of his eyes. 'No one has ever objected before, but I can see your point. The cove does belong to the cottage and should be solely for the use of its occupant – whoever that may be.'

She felt deflated. No wonder he knew his way round the cottage so well. She was the intruder, not him.

'And how are you this morning? Did you sleep all right, or were you troubled by that nightmare again?'

Dr Kerrow's professional manner has returned, she thought as she nodded ruefully.

His eyes changed to concern while they rapidly scanned over her. 'Did it keep you awake?'

'Not very long,' she admitted. 'I read for a while. There's quite a collection of books in my bedroom.'

He turned down the corners of his mouth in a rueful grimace. 'Oh dear! I hope you don't think all those are my taste! They're intended as light entertainment for the holiday-makers. Mrs Tolly is an avid paperback reader.'

'I am a holiday-maker,' she reminded him drily.

'So you are!' he grinned. 'Somehow you've never given me that impression. So what made you choose Trennion for your drowning?'

The edge behind his words annoyed her. He's determined not to let me forget, she fumed, her chin jutting angrily.

Reading the expression in her eyes, he hastily went on. 'I brought you some milk, by the way. You must be running short by now, especially as I see Toby has decided to join you. You do realize how honoured you are, I hope. He can be extremely choosy about whether he stays or not. Ardent surfers who rent the place are disapproved of by him in no uncertain manner and he leaves instantly.'

'What does he do then?' she asked, her interest awakened.

'Oh, he always comes back to me. He knows the cliff-path pretty well, and it's not all that far.'

'Mrs Tolly said he was a stray.'

'He is. Just appeared one bleak and stormy night, drenched and very pathetic. Rather like you,' he grinned.

Why can't he stop reminding me? she thought.

'That's probably why he's decided to stay on. You're kindred spirits – although I must say his temperament's a little more reliable.'

'Thank you for the milk,' she replied tersely, turning away to climb the steps.

'That's OK.' He followed her in through the gate. 'I'll wait and walk back to the village with you. You must be in need of some extra food by now. Mrs Tolly will only have left the bare essentials. My father's taking early surgery this morning. We're in practice together, you see,' he explained.

'There's no need,' she said quickly. Does he think I'm going to leap off the clifftop on the way there or something?

'No trouble.'

She recognized the determined glint in his eyes and knew that, once again, her protest would be ignored.

'Oh, by the way, I brought you a couple of freshly-caught mackerel,' he said. 'The boats were just coming in when I came past the harbour. I thought you might fancy one for your breakfast. They're in the shed round the back, out of Toby's way. I'll gut them for you. It's a bit of a messy process.' His gaze met hers, as if challenging her to refuse. 'And then I'll cook them.'

'I thought scrambled eggs were your only speciality?' she remarked drily.

'And mackerel,' he said firmly. 'Let's get started, shall we? Cutting off their heads isn't for the squeamish.'

'But I suppose it's an everyday occurrence for a doctor like you?'

'Of course,' he grinned. 'How else do you think I managed to qualify?'

Once again she found herself sitting in the little kitchen facing Daniel, both of them eating hungrily. Does he do it on purpose? she wondered, thinking that I won't bother to eat unless he's there to cook for me? But if so, he was right. She hadn't eaten since yesterday's scrambled eggs.

The cat was going frantic on the window-sill outside, yowling and tapping with one paw at the window, until eventually Daniel gave in and opened the door to put out a saucer with the boneless bits for him to gobble.

'The village shop opens at eight,' he said, rinsing his hands under the tap, 'and you'll be having a nice cup of tea with Mrs Tolly by a quarter past, if you're lucky.'

'But I don't need to go to the village,' she protested. She wasn't ready, yet, to meet the stares of strangers.

His blue eyes studied her shrewdly as if reading her thoughts. 'Everything will be all right, Lauren.'

She looked away, pulling a thick strand of her hair across her cheek. 'I told you, I don't want anything from the village.'

'Well, Toby does. You can't expect him to worship you for ever if you don't give him all your left-overs. How else do you think he supports that fat stomach of his?'

He put both his hands on her shoulders, swinging her round to face him. 'You can't run away from people for the rest of your life, Lauren. OK, so people *are* going to stare, but only in sympathy I promise you. And next time, it won't be so bad. And, after that, it's not going to matter any more.' He gave her a little push. 'Go and fetch a jumper or something. It can be a bit windy up on the cliffs.'

Upstairs, she looked round at the bedroom with thoughtful eyes, knowing now that it belonged to Daniel. Old, deeply polished, wooden furniture; smooth shining boards scattered with faded rugs, their finely tasselled edges fraying slightly. Everything suddenly seemed different. Were they his choice? Was, once, this his room? Was it his bed in which she now slept?

She could hear him in the kitchen, clattering dishes into cupboards. His dishes. His cupboards. His kitchen.

Does he have a wife?

The thought jolted through her like an electric shock. It was something that hadn't occurred to her

before. Surely a man as good-looking as Daniel
Kerrow must be married.

'*I live in the village at the surgery,*' he'd said. Was
that because his wife found Trennion far too
isolated? Yet Mrs Tolly looked after the cottage –
why? Wouldn't Daniel's wife do that? Or was she a
doctor too? '*My father's taking early surgery. We're in
practice together.*' So maybe she wasn't.

Lauren pulled a soft mohair jumper from one of
the drawers. The delicate pink reflected faint
colour onto her skin. Dragging a brush through
the thick waves of her hair, she parted it carefully
so that its mass fell over her cheek, then she tied a
headscarf firmly under her chin to hold it in
position.

From his frown Daniel didn't approve of the
action when she appeared in the kitchen again, but
this time he was silent, closing the front door as
they stepped outside, with Toby following on his
heels.

'Are you staying or coming?' he asked, looking
down at the cat. 'Lauren will be back, you know.'

As if understanding completely, the animal
settled down by the gatepost and began to lick its
fur.

The climb to the clifftop was steep, the track
worn smooth over the years by countless footsteps.
Daniel reached out a hand to help her, but she
thrust her own into the pockets of her jeans,
ignoring the gesture, not wanting to let herself
know again the touch of his skin on hers.

Once there, the wind hit them, buffeting in

across the sea, biting into their skin. From here the cottage was almost hidden. Only the red pot of its chimney showed, and she thought she could catch the glint of sunshine on a window in the grey slate roof. Maybe there was an attic room.

Below the cliff-edge the crinkle of azure stretched away into the distance until it met the hazy horizon and merged into soft greyness before turning to pale blue sky. Fat white clouds were banked thickly above like snow-capped mountains. One, she noticed, was the shape of a rounded pig, one hoof raised.

'Don't get too close to the edge,' Daniel warned. 'There've been some nasty falls of rock during the winter. Those vicious gales took their toll, and you can never tell quite where it's going to crumble away next. I should hate to see you disappear in a tumble of rock.'

Does it really matter so much to you? she wanted to ask. After all, you keep reminding me that I was going to drown myself, so why should crashing down onto rocks be any different?

'A fall like that would be far more unpleasant than a swift death in the sea,' he pointed out, shrewdly reading her thoughts once again.

They were at the highest point now, looking down to where the harbour lay, guarded by a long narrow jetty and deep stone walls, its water glinting in the sunshine like a myriad fallen stars.

'There's an outer and inner harbour,' Daniel explained. 'Vital, because winter storms can be pretty lethal round this coast. The outer wall was breached three times last January, and flooded a fair number of the surrounding cottages and cellars. That long, low white building on the opposite side is the "Dolphin". Mrs Tolly lives next door. She gives a hand there with the cooking and her pasties are quite out of this world.'

Lauren could see the village clustered round the harbour: long terraces, whitewashed, slate-roofed, rising away to cover the surrounding hillside. Fishing-boats were still coming in to unload their catch and she could hear the echo of voices float in the air, but not their words.

'How did the accident happen?' Daniel's unexpected question startled her. 'Maybe I shouldn't ask,' he said quickly, watching her expression. 'If it's going to upset you, let's talk about something different.'

'No,' she replied slowly. 'It's all right. It's just ...' She paused, her fingers moving to where the headscarf covered her cheek. 'It's just something I try not to think about.'

'And yet it still haunts you?'

She stared back at him, surprised by the compassion in his voice.

'I haven't forgotten hearing you scream, Lauren.'

The pupils of his eyes were suddenly dark as she gazed into them.

'It is a terrible dream,' she whispered.

'Talking it through can sometimes help,' he said gently, drawing her down beside him on to a wooden seat near the cliff's edge.

Her gaze followed the progress of a little blue boat as it rounded the rocks. Here everything was so different. Her life before was beginning to seem far away. Unreal. Like a dream.

The nightmare flooded into her memory.

'It happened at night,' she began. 'We were on our way back from the theatre. *Aspects of Love*. We'd been waiting months for a seat. A belated birthday treat.'

'We?' Daniel questioned lightly, his eyes following the boat as it turned towards the harbour.

'I was with Mark. My fiancé. He's a pharmacist at the hospital where I worked. We'd eaten first – an Italian restaurant – Mark likes Italian food.'

She could picture Mark sitting opposite her. The scarlet of his napkin against the light grey jacket of his suit. The navy and white striped shirt. The bright red of his tie. It had clashed with the serviette, she remembered.

He'd remembered her birthday. Toasting her with claret. Another, deeper, red.

Red. She'd been surrounded by the colour that night.

Her body gave a shudder and Daniel's head turned sharply.

'After the show we drove home. Mark had parked the car in a side road. We were lucky to find somewhere. It wasn't too far from the theatre to walk. And then it started to rain.'

She'd been wearing a thin wool dress with matching coat, and both were soon soaked. Mark had hurried on ahead to unlock the car, taking the umbrella with him. His suit was a new one. Expensive.

'The motorway wasn't crowded. Not at that time of night. Then we turned off for the last few miles home. The rain was pretty heavy by then. Huge puddles had spread across the road from the gutters and splashed the car with muddy water.'

They were listening to a cassette, the music from *Aspects of Love*. One side had ended. She watched Mark's fingers reach out in the glow of the dashboard to change it over.

When she looked up again, the wide arc of headlights was coming towards them, slicing across the rain-spattered windscreen so that she had to screw up her eyes at the brightness.

It all seemed to happen in slow motion. The dark shadow of the van. The way its lights had dipped and wavered as it met the water stretching across the road. How it had slewed round, almost sideways, in a skid, heading straight at them.

She'd looked at Mark, seeing the dark outline of his profile etched clearly against the side window, waiting for him to swing the car out of line. It was as he were transfixed; his hands rigid on the steering wheel. Then came the horrifying crash of glass as the windscreen disintegrated in front of her.

'It was a builder's van,' she said, 'with an aluminium ladder on the roof, projecting quite a way in front. The force of the impact detached it.'

She closed her eyes, not wanting to remember any more, but the picture was still there. And the pain.

Daniel's voice was a whisper of horror. '*That* was

what came through the windscreen? The ladder?'

She nodded.

'Was Mark injured too?'

Silently she shook her head. Daniel's hand enclosed her knotted fist, his thumb lightly soothing across the back of it.

'The metal pinned me to the seat.' It was a bleak, unemotional statement.

'I'm sorry, Lauren.' His voice was full of remorse. 'I shouldn't have asked. I shouldn't have reminded you.'

His fingers folded more tightly round hers.

'It doesn't matter – now,' she said. 'Nothing can change things.'

'So when's the wedding?' he enquired.

'Wedding?' she repeated blankly.

'Mark is your fiancé, you said.'

She gave a bitter laugh. 'Mark *was* my fiancé. He likes things to be perfect.' Her hand rose to push aside the headscarf. 'But I'm not any more, you see. I read that message quite plainly in his eyes.'

'And the engagement ended because of that?' Daniel sounded incredulous.

'Why not?' she questioned. 'I gave him back his ring. He didn't object.'

'Then he didn't love you, Lauren.' The words were gentle.

'I thought he did,' she whispered brokenly.

The blue boat was directly below them now, coming through the harbour entrance leaving a foaming white wake, while gulls dipped low over its deck.

'So that's the reason why you came here,' Daniel murmured softly. 'Why I found you in the sea ...'

'And why it would have been so much better to leave me there,' she told him bitterly.

'Never say that!'

'Why not? It's true.' Her voice was defiant.

'No life should be wasted.'

'It's my life!' she retorted. 'I can do what I like with it.'

'Don't you care in the slightest about other people?'

'What about them?' she demanded.

'I can't believe you're a nurse. You're totally selfish. All you think about is yourself. Your feelings.' The fury of his eyes unnerved her. 'Don't you know the effect that suicide has on those left behind? Their guilt? Their feeling of inadequacy? Their loss? Have you even bothered to consider that, or doesn't it concern you at all?'

His words flayed like a whip.

'All you have is a scarred face, Lauren. You still have a brain, your sight, your hearing, both arms and legs. You can walk, run, sing, dance, think. You've worked in hospitals, seen what others have to contend with, know how they fight to retain their hold on life.'

With a sudden movement, he caught her shoulders. 'And yet you want to toss yours away as if it were totally valueless.' His fingers bit into her skin, making her gasp in pain. 'Does the gift of life really mean so very little to you, Lauren?'

Three

His eyes, glaring into hers, were cold steel; his face so close she could feel the warmth of his breath feather her skin. His mouth seemed to be growing imperceptibly nearer, or was it the pressure of his hands on her shoulders drawing her closer?

She couldn't move; didn't want to move. Her heartbeat pounded in rhythm with the waves against the rocks far below. Then, abruptly, the dig of his fingers was gone. Daniel rose to his feet, the wind snatching at his dark hair, ruffling it over his forehead. 'It's time we walked on.'

And she could only follow him.

The path ended in stone steps that went down almost to the harbour and met the long out-thrust of the jetty. Here the wind was shielded and she could feel the sun radiate over her.

'You won't need that headscarf any more.'

Daniel's fingers caught the knot under her chin, and she clutched fiercely at his hand to tug it away.

'It only draws attention to your face, Lauren, hiding it like that,' he said.

'I want it hidden.'

He shrugged impatiently. 'Then you're being very foolish.'

The shop was small, set back from the road. Outside it was heaped with bulging sacks of vegetables that threatened to tip all over the pavement beneath a trestle-table loaded with lettuces, cucumbers, tomatoes, celery, and everything needed for a salad.

A rack of postcards fluttered in the breeze, beside another filled with newspapers. Notices and leaflets were crowded onto a large board proclaiming every event in the village, both past and present.

Daniel watched the expression on her face with amusement.

'Even "Harrods" can't compete with our Tom.'

Lauren's bemused gaze studied the crammed window.

The top half was filled with sweet-jars and boxes of chocolates on a shelf; while the lower part contained an arrangement of clotted cream pots advertising a service for posting them to all parts of the country, bordered by decorative notepaper and envelopes in plastic wallets.

Inside, through the open door, she could see lined on one side ceiling-high shelves of magazines and paperbacks that made her wonder if she'd discovered the source of Mrs Tolly's entertainment. The rest were stocked with tins and an enormous deep-freeze occupied the centre, its glass top revealing a wealth of goodies inside.

Daniel bent his head to avoid a string of small

coloured plastic buckets and spades hanging in the doorway and guided her through.

'Morning, Dr Kerrow,' came a rich voice and a gnarled little man emerged from somewhere at the back to greet them, his button-bright eyes almost lost in the deep furrows of his skin.

'Good morning, Tom,' Daniel replied. 'This is Lauren Russell, who's rented Trennion.'

The man's toothless mouth smiled at her as he shuffled a pile of newspapers into tidiness. 'Maudie – Maudie Tolly that is – has mentioned you, m'dear. Worries her that you're a bit lonely over there, though I see young Dr Kerrow's keeping an eye on you. Now what can I get you? There's baskets over by the door and 'tis all self-service.'

Lauren looked round at the haphazard collection, mentally comparing it with the supermarket back home. Somehow here, in the confusion, there was a more welcoming atmosphere.

She caught the humour in Daniel's eyes and guessed that, once again, he was reading her thoughts. Was her mind always so transparent?

He took charge after that, helping her fill the basket until she looked at the growing heap on the counter with dismay.

'Don't worry. Take whatever you're going to need for lunch and Tom can put the rest in a box. I'll collect it in my car and bring it over after afternoon surgery. Now how about coming to meet my father? He should still be there.'

With a carrier bag of salad stuff and some eggs and ham, Lauren followed Daniel up the hill to where a red-brick wall enclosed a garden and large house.

'I thought rectories were only for the clergy,' she said as they entered the arched gateway and she read the name.

'This was a rectory once upon a time, but the vicar now has to cope with three different parishes, and lives in the next village, so my grandfather bought the place when it came up for sale years ago. It's big enough to hold the surgery as well.'

'Do many of your patients survive that hill?' she asked wryly, looking back to where it wound down to the harbour-side.

He grinned. 'It is a good test for them. If they can walk up here, I reckon they can't be too ill. Come on in, I'll make some coffee.'

The kitchen looked out over a long lawn with wide herbaceous borders on either side, then disappeared into an orchard at the far end. A tall, grey-haired man, just finishing his breakfast when they entered, looked up from the newspaper he was reading, and she could see an older Daniel in his smile.

'This is Lauren, Dad — the girl staying over at Trennion I was telling you about.'

Lauren's back stiffened. Exactly *what* had Daniel been telling his father?

'Ah yes.' Clear blue eyes, almost as dark as his son's, studied her closely, the gaze narrowing slightly.

Instinctively her hand flew to her cheek,

shielding it. The silk headscarf had slipped back
from her face, loosening her hair.

Daniel turned away to switch on the kettle and
she wanted to reach out and draw him back to
protect her from his father's piercing regard.

'What do you think of that scar? It appears to be
making good progress, wouldn't you say?'

She couldn't believe that Daniel was saying such
a thing, his fingers lifting her chin and turning her
face towards the light.

His father leaned forward, putting on a pair of
gold-rimmed half-glasses as he did so.

'Mmm. Not bad at all,' he replied.

As if, Lauren fumed indignantly, I were a
specimen on a slide under a microscope.

'You see,' Daniel said, handing her a mug. 'I told
you it was going to be all right. Now, do you take
sugar or not? Last time I made you coffee, I believe
there was some protest.'

Speechlessly she regarded the pair of them.
Everything was so matter-of-fact. As if nothing was
out of the ordinary. And, she supposed, thinking
rationally, to them nothing was unusual. It was a
scar. Something they came across as part of their
everyday work. But to her …

To her it was the whole meaning of her life.

Daniel's father carefully folded the paper and
glanced down at his watch. 'Best not be late or
Karen will read me the riot act. Nice to have met
you, my dear. If you're over at Trennion, then I
dare say we'll be seeing a lot more of you while
you're here.'

He gave her another smile and then was gone.

'How could you!' she burst out after the kitchen door had closed.

Daniel's eyebrows shot up in surprise. 'What have I done now?'

'Discussing me like that with your father,' she blazed.

'Like what?'

'I'm not a patient!'

'No,' he agreed calmly.

'Then how dare you thrust my face forward for his inspection?' she demanded.

'I wanted confirmation that the scar tissue was healing properly. What's wrong with that? Aren't you pleased? Isn't that what's been worrying you?'

'Yes,' she admitted grudgingly.

'Then why all the fuss?'

'I don't like being used for demonstration purposes.'

'Oh really, Lauren!' he laughed. 'You make it sound as if I was dissecting you on a slab and holding up the bits for open viewing.'

'To me,' she said stiffly, 'that's exactly what it's like.'

His face sobered. 'Then I'm sorry. I didn't mean to upset you once again.' He gave a rueful sigh. 'I seem to do that rather frequently, don't I? Let's take this out into the garden. It's my father's pride and joy. He'd be pleased for you to see it.'

Under the shelter of the red-brick wall, it was hot. Lauren tugged off her jumper and dropped it onto the stone of the patio, and laid the headscarf on top of it, shaking her hair forward round her face.

'You don't need to do that,' Daniel said softly. 'Not with me.'

I'm forgetting his professional interest, she told herself bitterly. Forgetting I'm just a specimen on a slab to him. Forgetting he's *Doctor* Kerrow. But unconsciously her hands lifted away the thick tumble of curls as she leaned back on the swinging seat to rest her head against its flowered canopy, and she was aware of his eyes following the movement, colour flooding into her cheeks at the way they darkened.

'Can you wind-surf?' he asked abruptly.

Surprised, she shook her head.

'Then you must learn while you're here. You have the ideal build for it. No one can come to Cornwall and not experience that. It's exhilarating. You'll love it.'

'I broke both my ankles in the accident,' she remarked drily.

'I guessed as much when we were climbing the cliff. With exercise that stiffness will ease. Wind-surfing won't hurt you.'

He doesn't miss a thing, she thought, swiftly tucking her feet up onto the swing beside her out of his view.

'Where are you nursing? London?'

Those annoying eyebrows were questioning her again.

'I've given up.' The words were terse and abrupt.

'Given up? But why?'

'Didn't you say I was too selfish and callous to be a nurse?' she enquired acidly.

'Not exactly, although from the behaviour I've witnessed so far, that's probably true. So what was *your* reason?'

She turned her head towards him, tossing back her long hair. 'Can you imagine what effect *this* would have on a patient?' she challenged.

'I've already told you, it will fade in time.'

She gave a bitter laugh. 'I doubt the nursing profession will want a geriatric.'

He stretched out his long legs and leaned his head against the wall while he thoughtfully studied her over the top of his coffee-mug.

'You really are a prickly little creature, Lauren, like a hedgehog on the defensive all the time. Are you sure that wasn't the reason why your fiancé was so content to let you go?'

Furiously, she swung her feet to the ground and stood up, leaving the seat to sway rapidly to and fro. 'It's time I went back.'

'To do what?' he enquired lazily.

'Anything, rather than be put through ill-mannered cross-questioning by you.'

She picked up the headscarf and tied it under her chin, deliberately avoiding the disapproval of his eyes, then slung the mohair jumper round her shoulders.

'Don't forget your shopping's in the kitchen,' Daniel reminded her. 'And I'll bring the rest over this evening.'

'Then leave it in the shed,' she snapped.

'If that's what you want.'

The mildness of his tone reproached her.

'I'm sorry, I'm being ungracious,' she said.

'Don't worry,' he replied, putting an arm round her shoulders as he walked her to the door. 'My skin's quite thick.'

His fingers were lost beneath the thickness of her hair, just touching her neck, and she had a sudden desire to move her head a fraction to feel their caress, quickly resisting the idea with horror.

'Can you find your way back to Trennion all right?' He paused in the doorway to look down at her.

She regarded him gravely. 'I think so,' she said, letting herself smile, 'provided I keep in a straight line.'

His eyes crinkled at the corners. 'And avoid the cliff-edge,' he murmured teasingly.

Mrs Tolly was standing outside her cottage when Lauren reached the village again, chatting to a girl pushing a pram. As Lauren grew near, they both looked up and she caught nervously at the scarf, pulling it closer.

'Morning, Miss Russell. I thought I saw you go past with Dr Kerrow a while earlier. Lovely man, that one is.' With a smile, she continued: 'Kettle's nearly boiling. Have you got time to stop for a cup of tea?' Her button eyes turned to the girl beside her. 'This is my youngest daughter, Morganna. Anna, we always call her. Rest 'tis rather a mouthful.'

Morganna looked up shyly and Lauren could see her eyes flicker towards the headscarf. Obviously Mrs Tolly had warned her daughter and she was trying hard to avert her gaze.

'And this is my grandson, Oliver. Four boys and three girls now there are. Not all my Anna's though,' the plump little woman chuckled. 'Although 'twouldn't surprise me is that's what she finishes up with.'

Lauren noticed the daughter's cheeks turn an even brighter colour, and realized she was heavily pregnant, even though the baby in the pram was scarcely at the sitting-up stage.

'All my daughters keep young Dr Kerrow busy,' Mrs Tolly smiled. 'If 'tisn't one, then 'tis another. I think they're all a bit sweet on him.'

'Mother!' Anna reproved and Lauren decided the embarrassed girl's face couldn't turn a rosier shade.

'Are you coming in for a cup, too, then, my love?' her mother demanded, but Morganna shook her head.

'Promised I'd be over at our Wenna's to keep an eye on the little ones, while she crosses to Truro on the ferry. I said I'd give them their tea when Davy comes out of school.'

'Now I could have done that for her,' Mrs Tolly admonished.

'What about the "Dolphin" lunches?' Morganna reminded her.

'Well that would've been awkward,' her mother

mused, shaking her head. 'Never mind though, I'll be up to give you a hand when I'm finished there.'

'I can manage,' the girl pouted with a sideways look at Lauren, who guessed from it that the daughters had trouble casting off their mother's apron strings.

'Near three o'clock, I'll be there,' Mrs Tolly said firmly. 'Don't want you tiring yourself out with Wenna's unruly brood, not in your condition.'

She bent her plump body to kiss the sleeping baby and tuck its curled fist back under the cover, then led the way in through the front door which opened straight from the cobbles outside.

'Always something when you've a family,' she sighed, patting up a cushion before Lauren sat down.

'How many daughters have you, Mrs Tolly?'

'Just the three, though does seem like half a dozen at times.' Mrs Tolly's face saddened. 'One son, I did have, too. My youngest, he was, but I lost him. The sea's a fearsome force, my dear. Never to be trusted.'

'He was drowned?'

The woman nodded. 'Last winter, it was. Fishing out by Nare Head. Weren't no warnings about a gale. Blew up quite sudden. Four of them lost, there were.'

'I'm sorry.'

Mrs Tolly regarded her with tear-wet eyes and blew her nose on a pink paper tissue from her apron pocket. 'You see, 'tis they that's left behind that feel it most. Grieving never stops. No matter how long.'

And Lauren remembered Daniel's bitter words to her earlier that morning.

'But this won't get that tea made, will it, my dear?' Mrs Tolly observed, hurrying away into the kitchen. 'Forgetting my manners, I am, with my troubles. And you've enough of your own to deal with.'

For a while, Lauren had forgotten the scar.

The sky had clouded by the time she walked back over the cliffs again, making the wind feel cold. Lauren wished she'd brought an anorak. The grey surface of the sea was whipped into white-topped waves and she could hear it thunder against the rocks hidden below the grassy edge. Her headscarf had already blown back and her hair streamed out to sting ferociously across her cheeks.

Even the little cove looked unfriendly when she reached it. Rolling surf pounded the beach and sand swirled in little twists along the edge of the shore.

The tortoiseshell cat was crouched in the porch looking pathetic when she opened the gate, and it waited impatiently for her to unlock the door, then headed inside as she cried, 'Oh, you poor little darling.'

Upstairs a window rattled, and she hurried to close it, pulling in the curtain that had twisted itself round a rose-stem. Everywhere there was a damp chill.

I still have to master that gas stove, she remembered, feeling hungry, and wished she'd brought a tin of soup with her from the packed box. Doubtfully, she studied the contents of the carrier bag. Salad wasn't going to warm her very much.

She felt a pang of remorse for the way she'd snapped at Daniel when he offered to bring the rest later.

Or was it just another excuse for him to keep an eye on her? she wondered. He was so persistent.

Just because he'd found her out there in the cove …

The remains of the loaf were still in the bread-bin, cut earlier that morning when he'd made toast to go with the mackerel. A faint hint of their smell still hung in the air, teasing her nose, reminding her of how he'd sat there, on the stool opposite, eating the crisply cooked fish.

Slicing the last hunk of bread, she put it under the grill trying to recall how Daniel had lit it, finally succeeding, then as one side browned, she turned it and spread cheese on top to melt under the flame.

Around her ankles Toby began to go frantic, weaving in and out, until she was certain he would trip her up.

'For goodness' sake, be patient!' she protested laughingly, filling a saucer with milk and soaking in the breadcrumbs, watching as the cat began to gobble.

A smell of burning made her grab at the grill-pan to blow out a tiny flame scorching the edges of the toast and then she, too, began to eat hungrily.

*

It was after four when she heard the sound of a car engine coming down the lane.

Daniel! she thought. She'd intended to be out when he arrived with the groceries, but since her lunch she'd settled into reading one of the books – a history of the village – and was too fascinated to put it down again.

In it, she discovered that there had been a Dr Kerrow living there for over a century. Were they all as persistent as this one? she reflected. I could just not answer the door. But Daniel's sure to glance in through the window and see me, or even hear me breathing. He's that sort of person. Besides, the front door is open for the cat to come in and out.

'Where do you want these?'

The kitchen was suddenly filled by his presence as he carried in the box and she was annoyed to find herself smiling as she said, 'On the table, please, then I can unload it into the cupboard and fridge.'

He took out the contents for her, watching her stow them away.

'Would you like a cup of tea?' she asked hesitantly, reluctant for him to leave when the last tin was on the shelf.

'No, thanks. I'm off to visit a patient. Like to come with me? It's only a mile or so from here.'

She shook her head quickly.

'Because of the car?' he asked, and once again she saw compassion darkening the blue of his eyes.

His hand reached out to take hers. 'Come and

see it first before you decide,' he suggested, leading her into the hall.

She stopped in the doorway not wanting to go further, but he didn't wait, tugging her on towards the gate.

Outside in the road was an open tourer, glistening with polished chrome. The sight surprised her.

'It's a Lagonda. Isn't she beautiful? Centuries old. Well, 1933 to be exact, and my pride and joy,' he smiled, watching her reaction. 'We'll keep the roof down if it's not too draughty for you, then you won't feel shut in, but you'll need a jacket. I'll get that one in the hall.'

He was gone, in through the front door, and had returned carrying her anorak before she could object. Putting it round her shoulders, he helped her up on to the running-board and into the high seat, then climbed in the other side next to her.

As the engine roared into life her fingers gripped the door-frame, clinging in terror, not knowing whether it was her own trembling or the vibration of the car making her shake as it began to travel slowly up the hill.

'OK?' Daniel's head turned slightly. 'If not, we can easily reverse down again.'

'No,' she whispered, determined not to let him see her fear. 'No, I'll be all right.'

'It's not far,' he said, swinging the huge vehicle round the next corner, long strands of grass brushing against the shining red paintwork as they passed, and his voice brought its now familiar sense of calm.

Gradually her body began to relax, sinking back into the deep leather of the seat, her legs untensing from their rigid pressure against the floor. Her knuckles lost their whiteness on the door-edge and her hand moved slowly to rest in her lap.

They stopped outside a collection of farm-buildings where cows gathered near the fence. Lauren wrinkled her nose at the pungent smell.

'This way.' Daniel stretched up, and she was swept down, her body held close, his cheek warm against hers, before her feet met the muddy ground.

The door of the farmhouse opened and with a shriek of excitement a child's voice called, 'It's Dr Dan, Mum.'

A small boy came stumbling down the path towards them, a couple of collies barking frantically at his heels. With puzzled eyes, Lauren watched his awkward progress until, when he reached them, she understood.

The child was blind.

His face, under its shaggy thatch of fair hair, was a picture of delight, mouth smiling widely to display a couple of missing front teeth.

'Hi, Matthew!' Daniel had caught him up in his arms and was swinging him round while the child laughed excitedly. 'How's your Mum?'

His mother appeared in the doorway, wiping her hands on her flowered apron, and gave a smile of welcome. Lauren saw that she, too, was heavily pregnant like Morganna. It must be something in the air, she thought wryly.

'Come on in, Dr Kerrow. And you too, Miss. Excuse the mess,' the woman apologized. 'Matthew's been doing one of those jigsaws you brought him.'

Lauren glanced down at a table by the window seeing the big wooden pieces, their surfaces raised in relief. Already the picture of a tractor was half-finished.

'Let's check that blood pressure then, Mary. And are you going to give me a hand, Matthew, like you did at the surgery?'

Daniel ruffled the tumble of thick fair hair as he lifted the little boy onto his knee.

'I can remember what to do, Dr Dan,' the child gabbled eagerly. 'It's that sviggy thing, isn't it? You wrap one bit round Mum's arm and I blow it up with that squeezy thing.'

'Sphyg-mom-an-ometer,' Daniel said very slowly. 'You've a good memory, Matthew. Ready now? Put your fingers here, next to mine, and we'll pump it together, then stop the second I say so. OK?'

Lauren watched him take the child's small hand as he spoke and guide it into position.

'That's it. Now we'll let the air out v-e-r-y slowly while I read the numbers off this little dial.'

'Is this it?' The little boy's fingers moved to smooth carefully over its surface.

'No problems are there, Doctor?' his mother asked anxiously.

'None whatsoever, Mary,' Daniel assured her. 'But it's not long now until the baby's due, and your blood pressure can shoot up towards the end, so I need to monitor it fairly closely. It's certainly lower now than when you had to traipse all the way down to the surgery, so I'll call in whenever I'm over in this direction, if that's OK with you, and see how you're going.'

'Are you sure it's not too much bother, Doctor?'

'No bother at all,' he smiled and Lauren saw the relief that flooded over her face.

Matthew knelt up on the sofa, his small fingers exploring Daniel's face while he was speaking. 'Your eyes are all crinkly at the corners when you laugh,' he said, touching them lightly. 'Dad's go like that only he hasn't got all fuzzy eyebrows like you have. They're just the same as the woolly caterpillars that live in our hedge.'

'He's a brave little boy,' Lauren said quietly as they drove the short distance back to Trennion.

'He knows nothing different,' Daniel replied, easing up a gear so that the car increased speed. 'He's been blind since he was born, you see. We believe Mary had German measles early in the pregnancy. Sometimes the rash is so slight, no one really notices. She used to teach at the village school so could easily have contracted it there, or maybe from someone on holiday.' He turned down the corners of his mouth in a rueful grimace. 'I'm afraid not all parents bother to have their children immunized.'

He slowed down for the final bend, then drew the Lagonda against the hedge outside the cottage.

'That's why I'm being extra cautious this time

and keeping a close eye on her. Not that I want to create any alarm. Mary's under enough stress already what with the farm and Matthew to cope with.'

'What about her husband?' Lauren asked.

'He's a nice enough chap, but he has to work all hours. Farming's not something youngsters are keen to do nowadays, so he finds it increasingly difficult to get help. Some people have a lot to contend with, you know, but they don't give up easily.'

And Lauren read the unspoken message his eyes conveyed as he turned his head to gaze at the footprints, still showing deep in the sand by the four wooden steps.

Four

Daniel climbed down from the car and came round to open her door.

'Look, it's not much fun eating here on your own, is it? I'll collect you around seven and take you out somewhere.'

'No!' The word rang out like a pistol shot.

His eyes widened, turning them into dark blue lakes, and she felt herself begin to drown in their depths. 'Why not? The "Dolphin" does very good food. Mrs Tolly sees to that. And it's usually pretty quiet in there on a Monday.'

'I'd prefer not to,' Lauren said firmly.

'Prefer not to eat, or prefer not to eat with me?' he challenged. 'My table manners are quite civilized. You should know that by now. We've had breakfast together a couple of times.' His voice softened as he smiled at her. 'Or is it the thought of eating in public?'

She turned her head away, bending to stroke the cat as it peeped out sleepily from under the lavender bush.

'Actually the "Dolphin" is quite a gloomy place

inside,' he continued. 'All low ceilings and tiny windows. You eat by candlelight, so it's a bit like being down a tin-mine. And if that's completely put you off, then come and have dinner with my parents instead. They'd be only too pleased. My mother's a nurse over at Truro, so you've probably quite a lot in common.'

Not any more, Lauren thought ruefully.

The cat moved to nuzzle its head into her hand, eyes closed, contentedly purring, and a fragrance of lavender drifted in the air as the stems of the bush stirred.

Daniel crouched down on his heels to smooth the cat's twitching ears, his shoulder touching hers. His face was so close she could see the shadow that was beginning to darken the strong line of his chin and his mouth part into a smile. A strand of his hair blew across his forehead and feathered her cheek.

'So what's it to be?' he said softly, his thick eyebrows raised in question.

She rose quickly to her feet, away from his disturbing nearness, and heard her voice betray her with its tremor.

'I'd like to try the "Dolphin".'

'Seven o'clock it shall be then.'

The old car revved into life with a low throb and backed slowly away. She saw him wave one hand, then the Lagonda rounded the bend and disappeared.

Why did I say yes? she asked herself frantically. All that wretched man does is constantly haunt me. Is he really so fearful of what will happen if I'm left on my own for more than half an hour? I don't even *want* to spend an evening in his company.

But she knew it wasn't true. Being with Daniel gave her a feeling of safety. To him, her disfigured face was nothing. It had aroused his professional interest and now become a matter of fact. It was like a case of mumps, a sprained ankle, an attack of 'flu. An everyday occurrence. He didn't even notice.

Others would though.

The thought of entering a crowded bar, seeing heads turn, eyes curious, then their expression change, become deliberately blank and look away, distressed her. She'd seen it happen so many times, and each time was worse than before.

I don't have to go, she told herself. When he comes back I can say I have a headache; that I feel too tired; anything. I don't have to go.

At ten minutes to seven she was waiting, dressed in a summery frock, her ears listening for the sound of Daniel's car coming down the lane; and when she heard it murmur in the distance, she was in the hall, opening the door before it had even reached the final bend.

His eyes studied her approvingly as she climbed in beside him.

'Are you sure you'll be warm enough?' he asked, one hand lightly running the length of her bare arm. 'There's a sheepskin jacket on the back seat if you're chilly coming home, or would you rather have it now?'

'I'm fine,' she murmured, her skin already turning to fire under his touch.

The car didn't worry her any more. With its open roof, there was nothing to confine her and this time she sat relaxed, watching the countryside go by, familiar now with every twist in the lane.

A sweet musky smell caught at her nostrils as they passed a field of yellow rape, its glaring colour harsh, almost dazzling, to her eyes. It stretched away down into a valley and then rose again to brighten the hillside with fierce radiance.

The journey by car to the village was far longer than that over the cliffs, the road winding its way inland for a mile or so before turning back towards the sea once it had crossed the hills.

Daniel didn't speak, his eyes concentrating on every turn and bend, his hands firm on the steering wheel, and she guessed that he was driving more slowly than he would have done without her there.

She found her gaze constantly drawn to the strong contours of his tanned face, noticing the way his hair grew smoothly down his firm neck to curl slightly over the edge of his collar. There was a faint hint of grey flecking its darkness where it was cut close above his ears, and she wondered once again exactly how old he was. It intrigued her.

The corners of his eyes were etched by fine lines, white in the suntan, emphasizing the laughter that so frequently puckered them, as did the sharp upward tilt of his mouth.

It was a nice mouth, the bottom lip slightly fuller

than the top. Wide and generous. Mobile. She rarely saw it still as it was now, almost serious for once.

And she wondered what it would be like to be kissed by it, the thought making her swiftly look away, her skin burning once more.

They approached the village from the far end, winding down past the old rectory and the little shop, the pavement in front now empty where earlier the piled sacks of vegetables and trestle-table had been.

The water of the inner harbour glinted rosily in the setting sun, its surface rising and falling to slap gently against the shadowed stone. Boats were held at mooring by bobbing orange balls and only the faint rattle of rope against mast disturbed the stillness.

Gulls, far larger than she'd imagined, stalked the cobbles on leathery legs, huge yellow beaks probing, the gleaming slant of their eyes alert as their grey-topped heads bent.

A few early holiday-makers strolled along the jetty to watch fishermen who patiently sat, lines dipping.

The tall clock, rising like a sentinel behind a row of sombre, granite terraced houses, chimed a quarter as the car stopped near the water's edge.

'I've booked a table for 7.30. Is that all right?'

She nodded, her apprehension returning as she thought of entering the crowded room, her hand moving to her cheek.

'There's nothing to worry about, Lauren,' Daniel said quietly.

'It's the first time …'

'There's always a first time for everything,' he smiled, taking her hesitating hand and tucking her arm through his. 'How about a drink first to give you courage?'

She nodded slowly, letting herself be drawn forward past long wooden benches filled with people outside the whitewashed walls and in through the low doorway.

A hubbub of noise met her and she stopped, wanting to turn and back away but Daniel held her arm firmly, his blue eyes looking searchingly down into hers.

'OK?'

She bent her head, shaking her hair forward, and then lifted it again, her eyes meeting his.

'OK,' she replied with a wavering smile and felt his fingers squeeze hers encouragingly.

The room was dark-beamed. Its windows, small and leaded into diamond panes and curtained in willow-green, made the light shadowy and dim. A thin pall of smoke blurred the air. Thick-set men gathered at the curved wooden bar in one corner, their voices and laughter loud and noisy.

Lauren hesitated again.

'There's an empty bench by the window.' Daniel nudged her towards it and she sat down, turning herself sideways to look out over the harbour.

'White wine?'

'Please.'

He strode across the room, his head almost brushing the beams, and was greeted by the others at the bar, their heads twisting to glance across at Lauren.

She sat fixedly staring through the salt-misted glass, her body tense, until she heard the wood of the bench creak when he sat down beside her.

The wine was cold, chilling her fingers as she held the glass.

'To the future,' Daniel said, raising his, and she saw his mouth tighten when she gave no reply.

A yacht was heading in through the outer harbour, its sails flapping as they slid down to the deck. A slender girl in a jade-green outfit hauled at the ropes while a sun-bronzed young man in a navy anorak steered. As it reached the still waters the boat paused, swinging round, then continued its leisurely progress past the window and out of Lauren's view.

'Do you sail?' she asked, aware of a growing silence between them.

'My father has always had a boat. He taught my brother and I when we were quite small.'

She noticed there was a slight edge to his voice.

'Is your brother a doctor too?'

Daniel nodded.

'But not in the same practice as you and your father?' she enquired.

'He's a neurologist. In America.'

Again, she was conscious of a terseness in his tone.

'Older or younger than you?'

'Two years older. He'll be thirty-five in October. He ... and his wife ... have lived over there for four years, since they got married.'

Lauren heard the slight hesitation in his words and was curious. Could Daniel be envious of his brother? Would he, too, like to work abroad, and not as a general practitioner in a remote little Cornish village? Did he wish that he had specialized?

She noticed that for once Daniel's eyes didn't meet her own directly but were lowered, concealing their expression.

'Your meal's ready, Dr Kerrow,' a voice called from the bar.

As they passed there was a sudden silence, heads turning with interest to study her, and she wondered how often Daniel came in to the "Dolphin" accompanied by a girl.

The dining-room was candle-lit. Wavering flames cast shadows on the pale-cream walls. Two of the small tables were already filled. A middle-aged couple ate at one, two elderly ladies at another. Lauren wondered whether they were local, or staying at the "Dolphin" for a holiday.

When she read the handwritten menu she realized how hungry she was. That toasted cheese seemed a long time ago.

'The prawns will be freshly caught this morning. And the crab,' Daniel said, leaning forward across the table into the flickering circle of light that shut out the rest of the room, including only the two of them in its close intimacy.

'Then I'll start with that, please – the prawn and crab salad.'

'And to follow?' he asked. 'I can recommend the

steak. It's always good. But don't let me influence you. The duck is delicious, and fish is a speciality here.'

'It's all so tempting,' she sighed, scanning the menu again.

'Next time you can try something different.'

She raised her eyes to his. Next time?

'Then I'll have the duck in orange sauce.'

'The vegetables of the day are courgettes, broccoli, carrots and new potatoes.' Lauren looked up in surprise at the familiar voice to find Mrs Tolly beaming back at her while she stood patiently awaiting their order.

'I told you it would be a good meal,' Daniel smiled, 'with Mrs Tolly cooking it.'

"Tis flattery, my dear. Take no notice. Terrible flatterer is young Dr Kerrow,' Mrs Tolly chuckled, her rosy cheeks glowing even brighter. 'Just making sure he gets an extra spoonful of prawns, that's all.'

'How's Morganna?' Daniel asked her.

'Worn to a shred by my Wenna's riotous brood,' Mrs Tolly frowned. 'Makes me cross, that does, when my Anna's so near her time.'

'Another month surely, Mrs Tolly?'

'I reckon 'twill be early, Dr Kerrow. She's carrying very low.'

'Well, so long as it's not this evening, before we've had a chance to eat,' he grinned, with a wink at Lauren.

'Then I'd best be getting on,' Mrs Tolly answered, bustling away.

'Quite a chatter-box is Mrs Tolly,' he said. 'And into all the local gossip.'

'So I noticed this morning when I had a cup of tea with her.'

Daniel laughed. 'Then you didn't escape!'

'She was waiting outside her cottage when I went back. I think it was Morganna who was with her – with a baby in a pram. Oliver, Mrs Tolly said.'

'Yes, that's Morganna. Very fertile collection of daughters Mrs Tolly has. Young Oliver won't be a year old until a couple of months after the new one's born. And Morwenna has four, with the eldest only just five. It's eating prawns that does it, you know,' he said with a mischievous glint in his eye as he watched her spoon into them. 'Fantastic aphrodisiac! That's why there's such a demand for them round this coast.'

'Truly?' she questioned, regarding her heaped dish rather doubtfully.

'Would I lie?'

'Probably,' she smiled.

'That's better,' he said, leaning back in his chair.

'What is?'

'You're smiling. It's rather a rare occurrence.'

'It must be the wine,' she replied.

'Then do have some more.' He lifted the bottle.

'Oh, heavens, no!' she protested.

'It'll help you to sleep,' he said seriously, 'and dispel any nightmares.'

'I could become an alcoholic, you realize,' she teased.

'Then I shall find a cure for that too.'

Her laughter faded. He was a doctor. She'd forgotten that.

'Why didn't you specialize, like your brother?' she asked abruptly.

'I did.' She thought she could detect a note of regret in his tone. 'Paediatrics.'

No wonder he can cope with young Matthew so easily, she thought.

'Then why ...?'

'My father had a heart attack nearly five years ago,' he interrupted, anticipating her question. 'He couldn't manage the practice here on his own. I came back and joined him.'

'And gave up a career like that.'

'And gave up a career like that,' he echoed. 'Thankfully, my father's made a good recovery but needs to take things easy even so. I know he'd be heart-broken if the practice had to go to someone else. I shall take it over completely when he retires in another year's time.'

Lauren recalled the local history she'd been reading. There'd been a Dr Kerrow in the village for over a century. She frowned slightly, 'But surely if your brother is the elder ...'

'Simon is far too good a neurologist to give it all up and become a general practitioner, especially in a small area like this one. It would be a tremendous waste of his training and experience.'

'You did,' she reasoned.

'I have no ties like Simon.'

'A wife, you mean?' she said.

'A wife. Simon's wife is ambitious for him. And

for herself.'

'You don't like her?'

He gave a strange laugh. 'Like her? No,' he said slowly. 'I don't like her.'

He seemed to linger over the word *like* in a way that puzzled Lauren.

Mrs Tolly appeared from the kitchen to take away their empty dishes, and then returned with their second course. Lauren spooned baby carrots and thick green slices of courgette onto her plate, and then the tiny potatoes and broccoli.

'Is it all right?' he asked as she began to eat.

'Beautiful! I've never tasted duck that's so delicious. This sauce is wonderful. I'm surprised the "Dolphin" isn't more crowded.'

'When the summer season gets underway you won't be able to book a table for at least a week in advance,' he smiled. 'Mrs Tolly's third daughter, Demelza, helps out then.'

'She's certainly chosen some unusual names for her children,' Lauren mused.

'I told you she's an ardent reader.'

'So what was her son who drowned?'

'Arthur,' Daniel replied solemnly.

Lauren wrinkled her nose in thought. 'Tintagel? The knights of the round table?' she suggested.

'After her husband,' he said.

She laughed. 'So what does he do?'

'He's the barman, and Tom, her father, owns the village shop.'

'Quite a close community,' Lauren replied.

'There are only about three original families in

the place,' Daniel grinned. 'Everyone is related to everyone else. Mrs Tolly has five sisters and four brothers. And Arthur was one of eight, three of whom didn't survive. So you can see that her daughters have quite a way to go to catch up.'

'They seem to be doing pretty well, or is it the prawns?' she smiled.

'I must admit their babies are always rather a pink shade,' he observed, making her laugh even more. 'Now, what about a sweet? The trolley's over there. Can you see?'

'I could have rum baba or even sherry trifle and really get tipsy,' she suggested.

'You could,' he said drily, 'but I think you're probably well over the top already with three glasses of wine.'

'Three?' she questioned.

'And a half,' he replied, the corners of his mouth tilting upwards. 'I'm driving, don't forget, so you've emptied most of this bottle.'

She pushed back her hair with one hand, holding it there, to study the sweet trolley Mrs Tolly wheeled towards the table.

'Then it'll have to be the fruit salad. It looks gorgeous, doesn't it?'

She smiled across at the two elderly ladies sitting nearest them, and then froze into silence. Both were staring at her with stricken eyes before rapidly looking down at their plates again.

Her hand flew from her hair to her cheek and at the same moment Daniel caught her fingers, folding them into his own, holding them tight as she struggled to release them.

'All evening you've forgotten, haven't you? It's been wonderful, watching you so totally relaxed. Don't change now,' he pleaded.

'You didn't see their faces,' she choked.

'I did, but what do they matter? When they look again, it won't be the same. You'll see.' He turned in his chair to smile across at the two ladies. 'Are you staying at the "Dolphin"?' he enquired.

They hesitated, dabbing at their lips with their serviettes before replying in unison, 'Yes. Yes, we are.'

'Then perhaps you'd like to join us for coffee in the lounge after you've finished your meal?'

Lauren stared at him in horror. What on earth did he think he was doing?

Shy smiles flittered across their bird-like features. They must be sisters, she decided.

'Why, yes. How kind of you. We'd like that very much.'

She struggled through the fruit salad, dreading the minutes to come. At the end, Daniel rose to his feet and requested coffee for four, then guided her and the two ladies in to the tiny lounge.

A fire crackled noisily in the wide open grate, spitting tongues of flame high up the chimney from its piled logs. Daniel pulled two chintz-covered armchairs nearer to a small round table, then sat down on the deep sofa next to Lauren, shadowing her from the lamp with the breadth of his body.

'Are you here for long?' he asked.

'Just one week,' the more positive of the ladies told him. 'My sister and I always come in May before the season begins.'

'It's cheaper then, you see,' the other joined in, and was reproved by a sisterly glower.

'And you? Are you local? From your tan we thought you might be,' the first enquired.

'I live here, but Miss Russell is recovering from an accident.'

Their expressions conveyed their dismay, and they smiled uncertainly across at her.

'We did wonder ...' the elder one began, and her sister said quickly, 'We couldn't help noticing your beautiful hair. And then, of course ...' Her voice faltered.

'Same thing happened to me, you see,' the other interrupted. 'Years ago now. During the war. Caught in the blast from a bomb. Hardly find it now, would you?'

She bent closer, turning her face to the lamp. Lost among the wrinkles, Lauren could just make out an extra criss-cross of lines.

'Nothing unusual then, of course. Flying glass everywhere, but to me it was the end of the world. I'd just started teaching. You know what children can be like.'

'My sister really dreaded facing them when she came out of hospital,' the second lady revealed. 'But our dear father insisted that she went back, didn't he, Helen? And no one would ever dare to oppose him.'

'Treated me like a war-hero those children did,'

Helen went on. 'Truly amazing. Curious, of course. Had a good old stare. Then, all over and done with. Thought I'd be in for a few sly names behind my back, but I don't think they even noticed after the initial excitement.'

Lauren shot a sideways glance at Daniel. Had he engineered this? Found a scar-faced lady and positioned her strategically? But from the way he was leaning forward full of interest, to study the withered skin, she had a feeling that it was all a coincidence, even though a strange one.

The two ladies sat, eagerly chatting to them for an hour or so, then with many apologies trotted off to bed.

'Don't worry about it, my dear,' Helen smiled, pausing as they went towards the stairs. 'Besides, it hasn't prevented you from catching a handsome young man like this one, has it?'

With her face flaming with embarrassment Lauren watched them go, hardly daring to turn and meet Daniel's laughing eyes.

'So now you know,' he grinned.

'Typical spinsters!' she muttered.

'More likely widows,' he observed. 'Both were wearing wedding-rings.'

'Were they?' she said in surprise.

'And now I'd better take you home. It's almost ten and I'm on call tonight.'

'I could walk back. There's almost a full moon.'

'Heavens, no! You never know who you might meet up there on the cliffs.'

'In a quiet place like this?' she scorned, glancing

round the empty lounge.

'Quiet! Listen to those guys in the bar. And don't forget the prawns!'

'You ate them,' she reminded him.

'Yes,' he said with a tantalizing smile, 'so I did.' And his mouth softly brushed her lips, hesitating for a moment, before the kiss deepened.

Instinctively she found her arms move upwards, her fingers disappearing into the thickness of his hair where it peaked to his collar; her mouth respond.

Mark's kisses had never roused such an overpowering desire in her; a desire to be totally possessed, by one man and no other. This man.

Slowly, reluctantly, they broke apart, Daniel lightly tracing a path along her cheek-bone with his thumb-nail as he gazed for one long moment down at her, then the mischief was back in his eyes again.

'I never realized quite how effective they could be!'

The cottage was very still after Daniel had gone. From the sea came a soft sigh of sound that soothed in through the open bedroom window as she lay there, breathing in the delicate scent of the roses.

It had been a long day.

Her mind began to wind its way backwards. Their conversation with the two elderly ladies. Daniel's fingers firmly holding hers when she tried to cover her cheek. His touch had sent a tingle of sensation through her, but not like the fire of his kiss.

Her mouth parted at the memory, and she forced her mind away.

Daniel was a children's specialist. Trained in paediatrics. She understood now his complete rapport with the little boy that afternoon. Was it only that afternoon? The day seemed so much longer. It was as if she'd always known Daniel, not just for a brief while.

What a sacrifice, to give up such a career.

Why Daniel and not his brother, Simon? A neurologist in America. But Simon had a wife. She was ambitious, Daniel had said, and then, 'No, I don't *like* her,' with that strange inflexion in his voice.

But why? she wondered. She couldn't imagine Daniel disliking anyone. There must be a reason.

Somehow it troubled her.

Five

The telephone woke her next morning. Drowsily she picked up the receiver, glancing at the little alarm-clock on the chest of drawers below the open window as she did so.

Ten! It couldn't be.

'Lauren?' She recognized his warm deep voice.

'Mmmm.'

'Aren't you awake?' She could hear his laughter and her own mouth smiled.

'No,' she said.

'But it's ten o'clock! I saw the cottage was silent when I came for my swim earlier, so thought I'd better let you sleep on a while, but this is ridiculous!'

The note of his voice changed. 'No bad dreams?'

'No.'

She hadn't dreamed at all. Just deep refreshing sleep.

'So how about helping me with Matthew this afternoon? I thought we might take him for a boat-trip. I've four hours free between surgeries.'

'Well …' she said doubtfully.

'I will need a hand,' he urged.

'All right …'

'Morning surgery ends around 11.30. Can you organize a picnic lunch? It looks as though it's going to be fine. I'll collect Matthew on the way over. OK?'

'OK.'

She leaned contentedly back against the pillows. Through the open window she could hear the murmur of the waves; a whisper of soft sound as they tugged at the shingle. Quickly she put on her bikini and went for a swim.

The cat was sitting at the top of the wooden steps when she returned and paused from the grooming of its fur to look at her with huge topaz yellow eyes, then continued to lick one paw. As she began to towel-dry her hair a spatter of water made it lift its head again in disapproval, before it stalked away towards the cottage gate.

Lauren studied the contents of the fridge, then grilled bacon and toast wishing Daniel was there to share it with her. The kitchen seemed empty without him on the stool opposite. She'd begun to accept his presence at breakfast.

A picnic lunch, he'd said. What do small boys like to eat? she wondered. Maybe Tom at the village shop would be able to advise her, or if the worst came to the worst, Mrs Tolly.

She knew the path over the cliff now, avoiding the deep gaps where it had fallen away in a tumble of granite to join the rocks below. In the dark it would be treacherous.

The little shop was crowded at this time of the morning and she hesitated in the doorway to pull the headscarf more closely round her cheek, before going in. For a moment there was silence as heads turned to look curiously at her, then faces smiled a welcome and conversations continued.

With a wire basket in one hand, she scanned the shelves, slowly filling it with a collection of assorted packets of crisps, little cheeses, bananas, apples, biscuits and some small cartons of fruit juice. She wondered what Daniel would like to eat. Probably the same schoolboy fare, she decided, but Tregony the baker would have rolls, and there was still plenty of salad left to fill them.

She joined the queue at the counter to pay, recognizing Mrs Tolly's Morganna with Oliver clutched on one hip. The baby was placidly eating the chocolate drops his mother fed him, his small rosebud mouth liberally smeared, while his great-grandpa Tom rang up the bill. Morganna gave Lauren a shy smile as she passed on her way to the door and murmured a quiet hullo.

She's probably younger than I am, Lauren mused, watching the girl go out. Eighteen or nineteen, she judged, although it was difficult to hazard a guess with the huge swell of her body. People married early in a place like this, she supposed.

Tom greeted her cheerily as he began to tot up her purchases, his knobbly fingers tapping on the keys of his up-to-date cash register.

'That'll be four pound twenty, m'dear,' he

smiled. 'Tea-party, is it?'

'Dr Kerrow's taking Matthew Tulliver and me for a picnic,' she replied, seeing heads nod to each other as the customers listened.

'Poor little mite,' Tom said. 'Life can be cruel, can't it?' and she heard murmurs of agreement around her. 'Likes those little savoury twiggy things, does young Matthew. Here, you have some from me. Pass me over a packet, will you, Mrs Tregony? Right next to your shoulder on that shelf.'

A small box progressed across the shop from customer to customer and Tom tucked it into her carrier bag. 'Enjoy your day.'

Lauren was aware of interested eyes studying her as she walked out, and heard the hubbub of conversation begin again when she reached the pavement, wondering if their comments were about her. Old Tom had been friendly enough, she decided. And kind too.

Tregony the baker also had a queue and by the time she'd reached the counter his wife had returned and joined him to serve.

'Likes they little soft finger-rolls does young Matthew, Miss Russell,' she told Lauren. 'And Dr Kerrow is partial to that ginger parkin. Shall I put you in some of both?'

Lauren smiled. The whole village must know about the picnic by now.

'We do a nice fruit-cake too. Filling, that is. Here, let me sort out that carrier for you or you'll squash those bananas.'

'I know you won't have time to stop this morning, my dear. Not if you're off on a picnic,' came a voice from behind her, and Lauren found Mrs Tolly standing there, beaming as always. 'But don't you forget there's always a pot of tea waiting whenever you're passing. Did you enjoy your meal last night at the "Dolphin"?'

Tucking a loaf of bread under her arm, she followed Lauren out onto the pavement.

'Proper pair of old biddies are those two you had your coffee with, my dear. Sisters. Both in their seventies. Used to be schoolteachers up in London. Live in Dorset now.' She fell into step beside Lauren down to the jetty. 'We don't often see Dr Kerrow eating out, although he used to come in to the "Dolphin" at one time with his young lady.'

Lauren's interest sharpened.

'Well, I mustn't keep you, my dear,' Mrs Tolly observed as they reached her front door. 'Time's getting on and you'll need to get back and prepare that picnic. If I'd known I'd have made you some pasties.'

Lauren wished she could go in to continue the conversation. She was curious to learn more about Dr Kerrow's young lady – and why they didn't visit the "Dolphin" any more.

By the time she arrived at Trennion she was breathless. The carrier bag had grown heavy during the walk and its handles rubbed her fingers, making them sore.

Swiftly she sliced and buttered the rolls and washed the salad, then put everything into plastic boxes she found in the cupboard. There also she discovered a large thermos-flask and filled it with coffee. When she'd finished it was almost twelve and she flew upstairs to get ready.

A boat trip, Daniel had said. So even though it was hot here in the sun, out at sea it would probably be chilly. She pulled on a denim skirt and short-sleeved blouse, and gathered up her mohair jumper. Then, in a last-minute decision, she threw her anorak on top of the basket of food.

Toby wound himself round her ankles in a frenzy of excitement, apparently trying to convey that it was time to eat, so she opened a tin of pilchards and gave him half the contents.

'Now, out you go,' she said firmly, 'and eat that in the porch.'

As she put down the saucer, she heard the sound of the Lagonda coming down the lane and her heart gave a little skip of excitement.

Matthew was perched in the back, chattering excitedly to Daniel and she climbed in beside the little boy, tucking the basket down by her feet.

His hand stretched out to touch it, then with a great grin of pleasure he whispered, 'Is that the picnic?'

Lauren nodded. 'Yes,' she said.

'What's in it?'

'Wait and see,' Daniel teased, but his gaze was on her. 'Good morning, Lauren. I trust you're fully awake by now.'

'Fully awake?' she demanded. 'I've been over to the village, gleaned all the local gossip, staggered home with my purchases and fed the cat.'

'Toby?' Matthew questioned, listening intently.

'Yes, Toby,' she replied. 'He's extremely greedy and ate two pilchards almost before I'd put the saucer down for him.'

'He's very fat,' Matthew agreed. 'And cuddly. You've got lovely hair, Lauren.'

She stared back at him in surprise.

'It smells all spicy, like hot cross buns. Lovely!' the child continued. 'And it keeps tickling my nose when the wind blows. Where are we going?'

'Over to the harbour,' Daniel said. 'I've borrowed a friend's boat.'

'One with sails?' Matthew questioned.

'No, one with an outboard motor. Very fast.'

'Faster than your car?'

'Much faster.'

'I can smell the yellow field,' Matthew said, turning his head. 'Dad says it's like buttercups, but they don't smell the same. He grows it to make special oil, you know. I like corn best. It feels nice. Dad grows lots of different sorts. Oats are thin scattery ones. And wheat has thick rough ends that scratch your fingers. I can't remember what barley's like though. He didn't grow any last year. We're on the big road now, aren't we?'

Lauren listened to his constant stream of chatter, marvelling at the knowledge he had. He seemed to know far more than a sighted child, and she recalled that his mother was once a teacher. As the car began to descend the hill to the harbour, he leaned forward to speak to Daniel again.

'Are we going past your house now?'

'Exactly now. Why, do you want to stop?'

'It's not apple time,' Matthew chuckled.

'Not for months yet, Matthew, the blossom's only just over.'

'Can I help pick them again when it is?'

'Of course you can,' Daniel replied laughingly, 'provided you don't take a bite out of every one like last time.'

'I was only little then,' Matthew pouted indignantly. 'Now we're almost at the harbour, aren't we? The road's gone all bumpy. That's cobbles, Lauren.'

Daniel lifted him down into a gleaming white boat moored against the inner harbour wall, and sat him on the seat while he helped Lauren, his fingers lingering on hers as she stepped over the side.

'There's a life-jacket for each of you. Can you fix Matthew's, Lauren?'

'Is that in case we fall in?' the little boy questioned. 'I can nearly swim. Can you, Lauren?'

She caught the look Daniel threw at her, and felt her cheeks flush.

'Yes, Matthew,' she said firmly. 'I can swim very well.'

'Then why does Lauren have to wear a life-jacket too, Dr Dan?'

'Everyone has to wear one,' Daniel replied. 'Even me. Now, are you both ready?'

He untied the mooring rope and started the motor, then the boat began to inch slowly away from the wall. Lauren slipped her arm round the child's narrow body as their speed increased when they reached the open sea.

'Tell me what you can see, Lauren. I've never been here before.'

Holding him tightly, she described the gaunt rocks they were passing near the harbour mouth; the black and white oyster-catchers darting along the water's edge; the dark shags and cormorants holding out their wings to dry as they perched on a tiny islet; the seagulls bobbing on the water; the tall clock-tower disappearing into the distance.

'It's nearly one o'clock,' Matthew announced.

'How do you know?' Lauren asked.

'It chimed quarter to something when we were climbing into this boat and Dr Dan collected me at nearly twelve o'clock, so it must be,' he declared triumphantly.

The wind lifted the thick fair hair from his forehead revealing tiny freckles dappling his skin and she saw the pleasure on his face as spray from the wake of the boat splashed over it.

'Did you bring your fishing-rod, Dr Dan?'

'Of course, and I've promised your mother that there'll be mackerel for your dad's tea, so you're going to have to work hard later. Now, hang on tight, we're going to go fast.'

With a roar of sound the boat lifted and skimmed over the water, bouncing as it hit the waves, the sinews in Daniel's arms taut in their control of the wheel.

Matthew gave a shriek of excitement and Lauren

hugged him more closely, nervous that he'd slip off the seat.

The speed continued for a minute or more, then slowed as Daniel cut the engine, until the boat finally came to a halt and swayed gently on a flat, calm sea.

'Lunch!' he announced, turning to smile at them, his tanned skin wet with spray. 'And now we'll see what feast Lauren has for us.'

After they'd eaten and dabbled their fingers in the cool water to get rid of the stickiness from the ginger parkin, Daniel produced three fishing-rods, one extra small.

'Where did you get all this?' Lauren questioned, amazed at what could come next.

'My friend, John, who owns the boat, has an enthusiastic little fisherman of his own. Hence the mini-life jacket and rod. He was quite happy to let me borrow the lot, especially when he knew Matthew was to be using them. His son's a year older, and at school.'

'I go to school too,' Matthew protested, not missing a word of their conversation.

'Yes, but not every day,' Daniel observed.

'I go on Monday, Wednesday and Friday mornings to give my Mum a rest,' Matthew declared. 'A mini-bus comes and takes me, doesn't it, Dr Dan?'

He turned his face towards Lauren again. 'Mum's going to have a baby. That's what makes her get tired. She's growing it in her tummy. It keeps kicking her, you see. I was sitting on her lap and it nearly pushed me off.' He gave a little chortle of delight as he remembered. 'It must be a boy baby, mustn't it, Dr Dan?'

'We shall have to wait and see. Now are you going to bait this rod or shall I?'

'You do.'

'Right, and what about Lauren's?'

'Oh, you do mine too,' she said hastily, seeing laughter darken his eyes. 'I've never been fishing before.'

'Then Matthew can tell you what to do,' replied Daniel.

'Hold the end of the rod in both your hands, Lauren,' the little boy instructed. 'The liney bit goes into the water. Then you wait until you feel something tugging on the end of it, and pull up the fish.'

'Suppose it's a shark. Then what shall I do?' Lauren asked him.

Matthew chuckled. 'It won't be, Lauren.'

His face went thoughtful for a second, then he turned his head towards Daniel. 'Could it be a shark, Dr Dan?'

'If it is, Lauren can buy us all an ice-cream to celebrate, when we get back to the harbour again,' Daniel grinned, tweaking the child's button-nose.

'I hope she does. Can I have one of those with a crumbly bit of chocolate in it? They're my favourite.'

Lauren felt sleepy sitting there with the sun warm on her skin as the boat swayed gently. Too much food, she decided, idly flicking crumbs from her skirt. Matthew leaned sideways against her, his head resting against her bare arm while he waved the fishing-rod backwards and forward in the water. Only Daniel seemed to be concentrating properly.

He'd pulled off his navy sweatshirt and the tanned skin of his back was sleek and smooth, the muscles rippling as he swung the line up into the air and far out into the sea. Then, with one hand, he drew a denim cap from the pocket of his jeans and put it on Matthew's head.

'Can't have you getting sunstroke, can we, young man?' he said, tipping it forward.

'Is it your hat?' Matthew questioned.

'My best one,' Daniel replied.

'It's a bit big.'

'There's a buckle at the back to adjust it,' Lauren said, reaching out to do so, and found her fingers meet and touch Daniel's, startled by the surge of pleasure that flooded over her at their contact. Even though his hand moved away instantly, her own still trembled as she drew the material through the metal and fastened it.

'Is that better?' she asked Matthew, concentrating her eyes away from Daniel, aware that his own were gazing intently back at her.

Carefully the child nodded his head up and down, then from side to side, experimentally, before he answered, 'Yes.'

The first fish Daniel caught caused a great deal of excitement, although Lauren had to turn away while he disentangled it from the hook. His second was greeted with not quite the same enthusiasm and by the third, Matthew enquired plaintively why the mackerel didn't like his line as well.

'It's because you keep flapping your fishing-rod around,' Daniel explained. 'The poor fish don't get a chance to nibble the bait.'

'Poor fish!' Lauren commented wryly. 'Yours are the poor fish, getting hooked like that.'

'They don't mind really,' Matthew interrupted quickly in Daniel's defence. 'Dr Dan doesn't hurt them. He's very gentle.'

Yes, Lauren thought, glancing up at him through her lashes. He is very gentle. And as she watched Daniel pulled in the end of Matthew's line and attached one of his own fish, before sliding it back into the water again, then gave it a jerk.

'Come on, Matthew,' he chided. 'You haven't nodded off, have you? You've got a bite! Wind it in slowly.'

He placed the little boy's fingers in the correct position, helping him reel in the line, then laid the fish on his outstretched hands.

Lightly the child smoothed over the glistening scales, stopping at each fin, feeling it, before moving on to where the tail forked.

'Can I really eat it for my tea?' he said, his cheeks dimpling.

'All to yourself,' Daniel told him.

'I've never caught a fish before. Now it's your turn to catch one, Lauren,' Matthew said, 'so's you can have one for your tea too.'

'After all that picnic-dinner?' she demanded.

'That was ages and ages ago! I'm nearly hungry again.'

Daniel glanced at his wrist, then turned down his mouth ruefully. 'I keep forgetting my watch is still being dried out. What do you make the time, Lauren?'

'I'm not wearing one either.'

'Look at that tower-clock then,' Matthew told them.

Lauren turned her head to gaze back at the shore. Thick mist hid the cliffs like a pale-grey wall.

'Daniel!'

The horizon was obliterated too. Everywhere she looked, mist surrounded them.

'I've been too intent on those fish to keep an eye on the weather,' Daniel groaned. 'Never mind, we'll soon be back.'

He pulled at the cord to start the engine and it spluttered feebly, then died again.

'Damn! It's probably caught up in some seaweed. I'll have to go over the side and have a look. Avert your gaze, Madam. I'd hate to shock you.'

Lauren watched him begin to strip off his jeans and hastily looked away as a miniscule pair of navy briefs were revealed, then she heard a slight splash as he dived in, making the boat rock.

His head appeared, flicking wet strands of hair from his eyes as he took great gulps of air, before he dived again.

Three times he surfaced, and by the fourth Lauren was starting to worry. The mist was thickening rapidly, closing in densely on either side. Without the engine for a couple of hours, the boat must have drifted and she had no idea in which direction the village lay.

Finally, Daniel was clambering back over the side again and she clung to Matthew at the violent motion as the boat dipped alarmingly.

'It was a bit of old net,' he said, trying the engine again and this time, after a few wheezes, it trembled into life.

'You're going to freeze. Put my anorak round you.' Lauren pulled it from the basket.

'I'll dry off in a minute or two.'

'Not in this chill, you won't,' she declared. 'Do as you're told.'

His lips twitched with laughter. 'What a wonderful bedside manner you're going to have, Nurse,' he grinned, cautiously easing his muscular arms through the sleeves until his hands and wrists protruded from the tight cuffs. 'Now all we have to do is try to work out which way to go.'

'That way,' Matthew said, pointing.

They both stared at him, then at the dense wall of fog.

'I could hear the clock chiming when you were in the water, Dr Dan. It's over there.'

Daniel silently raised his eyebrows at Lauren and eased the boat round. With a shiver, she pulled the little boy onto her lap and tucked her jumper round them, huddling him close for warmth, wishing she could do the same for Daniel.

He must be frozen, she thought. The jacket barely went round him and droplets of sea-water

meandered their way down his body and long legs
to vanish beneath his toes.

The fog held a clamminess that clung to her hair
in thin beads, turning it into rat's-tails. Matthew
snuggled himself closer, his cheek against hers.
Then his head lifted, one hand reaching up to
travel searchingly across her skin.

She felt his fingers pause, then slowly move on
again along the scar and up to her eye.

'When did you hurt yourself, Lauren?' he asked.

'Oh, a long time ago now,' she answered.

'Did it make you cry?'

'Yes,' she said softly.

His voice lowered and he whispered in her ear.
'Sometimes I do. The tears just come and won't go
away again. Do you mind you didn't catch a shark?'

'I didn't catch anything at all,' she mourned.

'You can have my fish if you like. Fishes are a bit
prickly when you eat them.'

'I thought your fish was for your dad's tea.'

'He won't mind if you have it, Lauren. He
doesn't mind about anything ... 'cept sometimes.'

'No, I'll have one of Daniel's. He caught so many,
he won't even notice. Maybe he'll cook it for me, if I
ask him nicely.' She looked teasingly up at Daniel
when she spoke, seeing a smile curve his mouth.

'We're nearly back now,' Matthew said, leaning
away from her, his head turning. 'I can hear the
cars.'

Within minutes the end of the jetty loomed out
of the mist, then Daniel was steering the boat
through the outer harbour entrance.

'I think Matthew deserves an ice-cream, don't you, Lauren, for guiding us safely home again?' he said as he tossed the rope up and it was caught by one of the fishermen and tied. 'And a cup of hot coffee for us wouldn't go amiss either.'

'Isn't a hot shower your professional recommendation after sudden immersion in the sea?' she enquired drily.

'Your place or mine?' he whispered, bending over her with a wicked smile.

Six

'Oh, you're safe back. I've been so worried.' Mrs Tolly came hurrying over the cobbles. 'You come on indoors and get warm. That poor mite must be frozen.'

'This poor mite is a trifle chilly too, Mrs Tolly,' Daniel complained.

"Tis not surprising, Dr Kerrow,' she said, her shocked eyes skimming down over the anorak to his long bare legs, 'but I'm quite sure a nice cup of tea will soon put that right. In you all come before you all catch your deaths.'

She picked up Matthew and carried him through the open door, sitting him gently on the sofa, then turned to Lauren. 'There's been a lady looking for you all afternoon. Been over to Trennion, she said, then on down here. I offered to make her some tea, but she wouldn't come in. Said she'd have a drink over in the "Dolphin". Think she's still there. Would you like me to go and see while the kettle's boiling?'

'Looking for me?' Lauren was puzzled. She knew no one round this area.

'I'll see if I can find her,' Daniel offered.

'You go on up to my bathroom and get yourself dressed first, Dr Kerrow,' Mrs Tolly said disapprovingly. 'Walking around like that, half-naked. I don't know what folk must think. Now, young Matthew, would you like orange or blackcurrant to drink?'

'Lauren did say I could have an ice-cream,' the child ventured cautiously.

'I'll buy one on my way back from the "Dolphin".'

'With a chocolate bit in it, please, Lauren.'

'That tea'll ready by then, my dear. I'm just going to fill the pot.'

Lauren went into the inn next door where a group of fishermen were chatting round the bar.

'Just going out to make a search for you and young Dr Kerrow, we were,' one said, giving her a grin. 'Nasty sea-fret that one. Blew in quickly too. Didn't expect you to find your way back so easily.'

She returned the man's friendly smile. 'It was thanks to Matthew Tulliver. He heard the clock strike and told Daniel which way to go.'

'Sharp ears that little lad has. Always amazes me. Knows every seabird round this coast too, yet he's never seen one of them. Glad you made it safely. Saved us calling out the life-boat.'

'Your wife said there was a lady looking for me, Mr Tolly,' she said to the barman.

'Talking to they two old school-marms, she is, m'dear. Through in the lounge,' he replied, polishing a glass and placing it carefully under the bar.

When she reached the doorway, Lauren felt her heart sink.

'Darling!' came her mother's welcoming voice. And then. 'Oh, my sweet, do find something quickly to cover that cheek.'

With a shock of surprise, Lauren realized she'd completely forgotten her face. Her hair was clinging damply to her head from the mist, leaving her cheek exposed. And yet, she hadn't been aware of any reaction when she'd been in the bar with the fishermen, even from the man she was talking to so closely.

'Have my silk square, darling.'

Her fingers reached out numbly, taking the cool softness, then she was automatically twisting the material round her head.

'My sister and I have been so anxious,' the younger of the two schoolteachers told her. 'We watched you go out in that lovely boat with your young man and the little boy, and when we saw that awful mist come in soon after we'd finished our lunch and were sitting here in the lounge, we didn't know what to do.'

'What on earth were you doing in a boat, Lauren?' her mother asked. 'I quite thought you'd be tucked away safely in that sweet little cottage. It really gave me a horrible shock to know you'd actually ventured into the village. Do you think that was wise? And with nothing round your head too.'

Lauren's fingers caught at the edge of the silk, drawing it more closely round her.

'Well, we'd better be going back to the cottage,

darling,' her mother said, rising gracefully to her feet and smoothing down the straight skirt of her cream linen suit.

'But what are you doing here? Where are you staying?'

'With you, darling! At the cottage. Where else? I've come to look after you. I knew you'd never be able to cope on your own down here alone.'

'There's no need.' Lauren stood squarely, facing her mother, who glanced round apologetically at the two elderly ladies.

'You're causing embarrassment, darling,' she murmured in a low voice. 'Let's go out to my car and discuss things there.'

'I don't want to go out to your car, Mother. There's nothing to discuss. I'm perfectly all right on my own here. I don't need you.'

'Now don't get hysterical, Lauren. It's quite obvious I've arrived in the nick of time. Come along, darling, and don't make a fuss in front of these ladies. I'm so sorry,' she said, bending towards them. 'My daughter is still in a very emotional state after her dreadful accident, and I doubt this trip in a boat has helped her either.'

Lauren felt the grip of her mother's fingers round her arm, as she marched her steadily towards the door of the inn and then they were outside in the chill of the mist.

'Please don't speak to me like that, Lauren. In front of strangers too.'

'They aren't strangers to me, Mother.'

'Now for goodness' sake, calm down and let me

talk to you sensibly. Get in the car.'

'I'm sorry, Mother. People are waiting for me.'

'People? What people?' her mother enquired.

'My friends,' Lauren replied abruptly, and turned away towards Tom's little shop.

Her mother was still waiting in her car when Lauren came out again with Matthew's ice-cream, but she hurried past and in through Mrs Tolly's partly-open front door.

'Dr Dan was just coming to find you,' Matthew greeted her, eagerly taking the dripping cone.

'You were rather a long time,' Daniel explained, his eyes quickly taking in the flowered silk covering her hair. 'Are you all right?'

'Fine,' she replied tautly.

'There's a nice cup of tea waiting and a slice of ginger parkin, if you'd fancy some,' Mrs Tolly interrupted. 'I put it on one side before these two had gobbled up the lot. Did you find who was looking for you?'

'Yes,' Lauren replied in a tight voice.

'Someone you know?' Mrs Tolly enquired.

'My mother.'

She saw Daniel's glance flash towards her, his brows slanting upwards.

'Then you'll want to drive back with her to Trennion,' he said.

'No,' Lauren answered swiftly.

'But surely she'll stay at the cottage? It's too far for only a day's visit.'

'I don't want her to stay there, Daniel,' Lauren jerked out. 'Hadn't we better be taking Matthew back home again? You'll be late for your surgery if we don't.'

'I've hung your anorak over the boiler,' Mrs Tolly told her. 'Should be dry now, 'though I hope Dr Kerrow hasn't stretched it too much.'

'I didn't fasten it up, Mrs Tolly,' he remarked, 'so it should still be all right.'

'We all know you didn't fasten it up,' the little woman said indignantly. 'Walking down that road wearing nothing but your underwear. What tales your mother and father are going to hear, I dread to imagine. The gossip that goes round this village is something shocking.'

'Then I shall leave it to you to make sure my image remains untarnished, Mrs Tolly,' he told her with a grin. 'And now before you burst with all that ice-cream and parkin, young man, we'll take you home.'

'Were you really only wearing your *you-know-whats*, Dr Dan?' Matthew whispered with a little giggle, as he was carried out to the car.

'Now don't you go telling tales on me as well,' Daniel chided, dumping him down on the back seat.

Lauren saw her mother walk purposefully across the narrow street towards them.

'So you're my daughter's "young man" those old ladies were referring to,' she said acidly, taking in the faded jeans and sweatshirt. 'A local fisherman.'

Lauren felt her face burn with humiliation at the scathing tone.

'You're married, I take it? I presume this is your son.'

'No, Mrs Russell, I'm not married and this is not my son. Matthew is one of my patients and Lauren and I have been on an outing with him.'

'One of your patients?'

Lauren saw her mother's eyes travel over Daniel again.

'I'm Dr Kerrow,' he said, holding out a polite hand to her. 'And now, if you'll excuse us Matthew's had rather a long day and we must take him home.'

The Lagonda roared into life and began to bump its way over the cobbles towards the hill.

'Goodbye, Mother. I'll be in touch,' Lauren called out to her, and sitting Matthew on her lap, pulled Daniel's sheepskin jacket round them.

'I'll put the roof up when we reach the top of the hill, but I felt you wanted to make a quick exit.'

'I did,' Lauren told him gratefully.

'It's been a lovely day,' Matthew sighed contentedly, leaning his head against her chin.

Lauren reflected later that she must have been very rude to her mother. But seeing her there, so unexpectedly, had startled her. And now, once more, she was only too aware of her scarred face.

She looked down at the crumpled silk headscarf lying on the table.

I'll have to phone her and apologize, she decided. Tomorrow.

But the phone rang soon after she was back in the cottage again, and she heard the injured tones of her mother's voice.

'Lauren? Are you feeling better, darling? I realized after you'd gone and I heard those people in the bar talking, that you must have been suffering from shock after your terrible ordeal in that boat. It was so silly of you to go out in it, darling. Who was that young man? And that poor little blind boy? He said he was a doctor. Have you been ill? What's happened, Lauren? You will let me come over this evening, won't you?'

'Mother,' Lauren said gently. 'I'm fine. Really I am. I've settled in here. I like it on my own. I don't want to upset you, but it's far better that way. I'm learning to forget about my face. I don't want you to remind me again.'

'Oh, Lauren! How can you say such a thing? I'm only thinking of you, darling. I know how cruel people can be. I want to protect you from that. You *are* my daughter, darling.'

'There's no need, Mother. I'm coping.'

'Just let me come and talk to you, darling.'

'Mother! Please!'

'Maybe tomorrow then? I shall be staying at the "Dolphin". It seems quite a pleasant little place. I'll ring you in the morning, darling. Maybe you'll feel differently about things then.'

When Lauren woke the following morning thin mist and drizzle still hazed the cove, merging sea and sky into one. Daniel won't be down there swimming today, she decided regretfully. The walk over the cliffs would be too hazardous.

On the end of her bed, the cat was curled in

sleep, one paw outstretched. Carefully, she slipped her feet from the covers without disturbing him, and lowered them to the floor. The polished wood was cold.

Downstairs she looked at the fire laid in the grate and wondered whether to light it, then decided it would spoil the careful arrangement of logs and fir-cones if she did. Maybe it was only for decoration and not meant to be lit at all. She'd hate to fill the place with smoke from a blocked chimney.

It's a comfortable room, she thought, looking round. Had Daniel chosen the furnishings? The two armchairs and wide sofa covered in a deep blue chintz patterned with pale cream roses matched the curtains and cushioned seat under the window.

There were long white-painted shelves on either side of the fireplace, reaching from wall to wall. She knelt down to study his choice of books. Most were medical textbooks, but there was also an expensively bound set of Dickens and Shakespeare, well-worn; a series of boys' adventure stories, their spines showing signs of great use; a vast number of books about Cornwall, and even more of seabirds.

The bottom shelf surprised her with every book written by P.D. James and Ruth Rendell, while a pile of Agatha Christie paperbacks were stacked at the end. She hadn't realized that doctors had a taste for crime. Perhaps that was a way of unwinding after a stressful day.

Somehow breakfast didn't appeal to her, although Toby had other ideas, light-footing down the stairs to join her.

'How do you manage when there's no one living here to feed you?' she asked, emptying the last pilchard onto his saucer. 'Do you go back to the rectory?'

She was relieved when her mother didn't phone. She hated upsetting her, but the continual fussing annoyed her. Her mother was trying to be kind, she knew, but it only made things worse. Here, she was beginning to relax and, somehow, the scar didn't seem quite so terrible.

Her fingers smoothed over the uneven surface of her skin. When I forget, others will. That was what Daniel had said. And she was forgetting. She didn't want to be reminded all over again.

Toby had finished his meal and she let him out of the front door, closing it quickly again as dampness began to seep in, then went to make a cup of coffee. What could she do on a day like this? The walk over the cliffs to the village didn't appeal. Not with those yawning gaps in the path. She viewed the contents of the fridge. There was plenty to keep her going for a day or so at least. Not that she felt hungry. On her own, breakfast wasn't the same.

Lauren wandered back into the lounge to peer out of the window. The mist didn't seem quite so thick now. She could see the wooden handrail of the steps now and Toby sitting there, waiting.

Well, Daniel was going to disappoint the cat this morning, she decided. Swimming was definitely out. He was probably taking surgery by now. It was after nine.

There were pictures on every wall of the room, she noticed. Small, neatly framed water-colours. Sea scenes. She recognized the cove on a bright summer's day, and again at early morning, the gold of dawn brightening the water; the fury of a storm with wind-lashed waves sending columns of spray up over the rocks; sunset, rosy with colour. All were of the cove.

She went to study them more closely. In one corner of them was the scrawled word Kerrow. Daniel? Did he paint? Was that what he did, here, in the winter months when he couldn't swim?

She wondered if, or where, he had a studio. The cottage only had two bedrooms and they were used by the holiday-makers who stayed there. There was nowhere else. Unless … She remembered sunshine glinting on a window in the roof.

Quickly she ran up the stairs and stood on the tiny landing staring up at a trapdoor in the ceiling. She hadn't noticed it before, but then she'd never thought to look before.

So how to get up there?

In the second bedroom there was a long pole standing behind the wardrobe. She carried it back and heaved at the trapdoor, watching it slowly rise and the end of a ladder project. A quiver trembled down her spine at the sight of its metal rungs, and in her mind she heard the shatter of glass as the windscreen dissolved into a million pieces.

Abruptly she pushed away the memory.

There was a hook on one end of the pole and she tugged at the lowest rung, bringing the ladder down with a rush of noise. Above she could see daylight.

Slowly she climbed, her head emerging to find that the space under the roof had been made into a painter's paradise. A long window ran the length of one side, overlooking the cove, and below it was a bench where everything was tidily placed. A couple of stools like those in the kitchen were tucked under it.

And every wall was hung with paintings, not all of the cove. On one was a series of portraits, of a girl with short dark hair. Lauren moved across the room to study them. She had a striking face: huge dark eyes, thickly lashed; a small straight nose; high cheek-bones; and a full, almost pouting mouth. Was this the girlfriend Mrs Tolly had spoken about? It had to be. Why else would Daniel have painted so many pictures of her? And where was she now? Had she stayed here once? With him? Was that why he kept coming back to the cove – to remember her? Who was she?

The whine of an engine tremored the eerie silence of the mist. Daniel! Hurriedly she climbed down the ladder and pushed it back, closing the hatch, then went downstairs. The shadow of a car darkened the hall window and she opened the door, her heart beginning to pulse faster.

'Darling!'

Her mother stood in the porch.

'I told you not to come!' Lauren burst out.

'You were upset then.'

'I don't need you here, Mother.'

'You're being childish, Lauren,' her mother frowned. 'For goodness' sake stop acting so melodramatically and let me come in. I'll freeze in this wretched mist. It wasn't so bad inland or I'd never have attempted to drive round here.'

If only you hadn't, Lauren vowed silently.

'What a gloomy little place,' her mother commented, glancing round. 'No wonder it's affecting you so much. You've always been a sensitive child.'

'I'm twenty-two, Mother.'

'A child. And you take after me. Atmosphere can have a terrible effect. Shall we have some coffee?'

Lauren went into the kitchen. Her mother followed.

'There was a cat outside so I shooed it off. You don't want stray creatures like that getting in. Never get rid of them if you do and you don't know where it's been. Probably flea-ridden too.'

'That was Toby, Mother!' Lauren protested. 'He lives here.'

'Well it took off as if the devil was chasing it when I clapped my hands.' Her mother eyed her uneasily. 'Do put something round your face, darling.'

'I don't need to. You've seen my scar before.'

'Yes, but you know how much it distresses me. Have you a comb? I'll do your hair the way you used to have it. Tied back like that doesn't suit you.'

'It's how I want it, Mother. Shall we take our coffee into the other room or do you want to sit out here in the kitchen?'

Her mother glanced round with a shiver. 'Oh no, it's so depressing with that dreadful rock looming over me.'

'How long did the drive down take you?' Lauren asked, hoping to draw the conversation away from herself. 'Or did you stop off on the journey?'

'I did it in three stages, starting on Sunday, the day after you'd gone. I stopped overnight with those friends of mine, Andrew and Myra, in Dorset, and with your Aunt Jane in Bideford on Monday, then arrived here yesterday just after lunch. I was so worried when I couldn't find you, darling, so I drove on to that village and those women in the pub told me you'd gone out in a boat. I really couldn't believe it!'

'Why not?'

'A boat! After that accident!'

'The accident was in a car, Mother,' Lauren said impatiently.

'Even so, it was foolish of you. Suppose the thing had capsized? And then, when I saw that fog, I almost went frantic.'

'You seemed quite calm when I found you,' Lauren commented drily.

'Well I had had a couple of brandies by then. I needed them. My nerves were shattered. And those women were droning on and on. I had to be polite.' The hurt look returned to her eyes. 'Not that you were.'

'I'm sorry, Mother, but I really didn't expect to see you. Not here.'

'Well I realized the moment you left that you'd

never be able to cope on your own. It's all very well trying to be independent, but an accident like that takes its toll. And of course I knew how distraught you were about Mark.'

'I'd rather not talk about him, Mother.'

'But you must, darling. You should try to understand his feelings. He's such a poppet. It was an awful shock for him, seeing you so soon after the accident. There was bound to be some reaction.'

'Not like that!'

'He loves you, darling. And it was your looks that attracted him in the first place. To see you … so disfigured … what else could you expect?'

'I didn't expect revulsion, Mother,' Lauren said quietly. 'Or rejection either.'

'Of course he didn't reject you! You should have seen him again. He did try. He told me so. But you wouldn't let him anywhere near you.'

'After the way he'd behaved?' Lauren demanded angrily. 'You didn't see his expression when I went to kiss him that day, Mother. He turned away and actually shuddered. The man who was supposed to love me. I needed him then. I needed his support, his comfort. And he turned away.'

'You should give him a second chance, Lauren. It wasn't his fault. I can quite understand how he felt. I was revolted too.'

'Mother!'

'It's something you must learn to live with, darling. The sight of you does repulse people. But we can overcome that. Together we can overcome that. Now, let me do something with that hair of yours. That should help a little. You've such lovely hair.'

Lovely hair. Lauren remembered Matthew's words. All spicy – like hot-cross buns. It hadn't mattered to him that her face was grotesque. Even when he touched it, his only thought was of the pain she had felt. Only a child, but such a caring one.

Like Daniel. It didn't matter to him either.

And with them she'd been happy.

Seven

She couldn't avoid her mother's company for the rest of the day. It would have been unkind to try. By midday a strong breeze had blown away the drizzle and mist and was sending strong waves up the beach.

'If I don't swim now, it's going to be too rough,' Lauren commented. 'I'll put on my bikini.'

'Swim!' Her mother's voice was horrified. 'Oh no, darling, for goodness' sake don't do that.'

'Why ever not?'

'You could pick up an infection in that wound, darling. The sea's a sewer nowadays.'

'But I swim here every day. So does Daniel, and he's a doctor. That's the Atlantic out there, Mother. Not a silted-up estuary.'

'You'll be very unwise if you continue to do so, darling, although heaven knows what harm you've already done.'

'It's salt water, Mother. Isn't that supposed to be good for healing?'

Her mother gave an impatient shrug. 'Don't blame me if you suddenly break out in oozing sores.'

'I won't,' Lauren replied grimly.

The sea was rougher than she had imagined, freezing-cold and buffeting too. If she hadn't been determined to defy her mother, she would have stayed in only for seconds. Even so she could feel the current sweeping her sideways, towards the rocks, and had to strike out strongly to get back.

It worried her that Toby wasn't in his usual place on the top step when she ran up the beach and climbed them. He wasn't under the lavender bush either, and when he didn't appear for his dinner, she checked the shed in case he'd been shut inside.

Maybe he's gone over to the comfort of the rectory, she decided. Daniel had said the cat was very choosy about the company he kept.

'The phone rang while you were swimming,' her mother told her when she returned.

'Who was it?' Lauren asked quickly.

'Donald Kerry, I think he said.'

Lauren's heart gave a leap. 'Daniel Kerrow. I'll phone him back then.'

'No, don't bother. Someone was having a baby. That's what he was phoning to tell you. He didn't know when he'd be back.'

Morganna? Lauren wondered. Mrs Tolly had said she thought the birth would be early, and in the shop the previous day her daughter had certainly looked as if it could well happen.

'We'll eat at the pub where I'm staying, shall we?' she heard her mother suggest. 'I'll go and run the car-engine. The damp seems to affect it since I've been here.'

'I'll walk,' Lauren said hastily.

'But, darling …'

'It's not far over the cliffs.'

She couldn't face the confines of her mother's car. It was the same make as Mark's had been.

The wind was very strong up on the clifftop, sending clouds streaming in long straggling mares' tails across the sky. She'd put on the anorak Daniel had borrowed, recalling how he'd looked with his long suntanned body and legs. Its hood blew back after a couple of yards and she felt her hair snake round her face, destroying the careful arrangement her mother had created.

Waves rose high up the walls of the outer harbour, swirling across to crash against the stone and she could taste the salt on her dry lips.

Her mother's car was already parked outside the "Dolphin" in line with several more, indicating a full restaurant, and Lauren began to dread making her entrance.

She went into the little cloakroom just inside the door to comb her hair into position then, reluctantly, went through to the bar.

'Morning, Miss Russell.' Mr Tolly's cheerful round face smiled as broadly as his wife's. 'Your mother said to tell you she was in the lounge.'

'Thank you, Mr Tolly,' she replied. Should she enquire about Morganna? she wondered, but another group of people swept in through the door, so she hurried on.

'Darling!'

Everyone looked up, and Lauren quickly lowered her head, shaking forward her hair.

'I've brought our drinks in here, darling. Not so many people. I knew how you'd feel.'

Lauren was sure her mother's voice carried to every corner, alerting ears, and bent her head even further.

'Quite a gale coming, the barman says. I'll book a room here for you tonight. Maybe you could share mine. It has twin beds.'

'I don't need to,' Lauren muttered desperately. 'The cottage is perfectly safe. It's been there for centuries.'

'Not in the winds we've been getting lately, darling,' her mother said firmly. 'Hurricane force, they've been. And the west country has suffered every time. I'll have a word with the manager after lunch. We'd better go in now, before the rush begins.'

Lauren was only too thankful to see Mrs Tolly's comforting shape appear through the swing doors of the kitchen.

'Is it Morganna's baby?' she enquired.

Mrs Tolly's mouth broadened into a beam of pleasure. 'Fancy you remembering that, my dear. Started labour this morning, she did. Around six o'clock. 'Tis nearly a month early, though I thought she would be. All that coping with our Wenna's young ones didn't help and Oliver's quite a heavy one to carry.'

'Daniel phoned to say he was with her,' Lauren explained.

'Such a kind man, that one is, my dear. Took her over to the hospital himself. Going to stay with her for a while. Poor Anna's that nervous. Husband's in the army, you see. Over in Ireland. Would've been home on leave if she hadn't gone into labour so soon.'

'We'd like to order,' Lauren's mother cut across their conversation.

'Sorry, Madam. Chatter on a bit, I do. My Arthur's always telling me. Now, what'll you have to start with? 'Twas prawns you fancied last time, wasn't it, my dear?'

She and Daniel had sat at the table in the corner, Lauren reflected. Candle-lit and secluded. Now the sun was blazing in across the room directly onto her.

'Just melon, thank you, Mrs Tolly.' She didn't feel hungry. 'And ham salad to follow.'

'Oh, the prawns and then the mackerel for me,' her mother enthused, unfolding her serviette.

It wasn't the same, here, in the daylight. Or maybe it was just that the company was different, Lauren mused. Somehow the magic was gone.

This time yesterday they'd been on the water, laughingly feeding gulls that swooped round the boat, before the mist came. Yesterday. She wondered what Daniel was doing now? Was he home? But if Morganna's baby had arrived surely Mrs Tolly would be the first to know? What would this one be called? Did the daughters favour literary names as well? Oliver. Perhaps he was named after Cromwell. Or could it be Reed? A smile curved her mouth and she saw her mother's eyes question it.

'Your hair looks so much better like that, darling. No one would ever know.'

For a moment Lauren was tempted to sweep it back deliberately to see what effect it would have, but her mother was right. The sight would revolt people.

From across the room the elderly schoolteachers smiled at her. The younger one waved.

Were they enjoying their holiday? What did they do all day? They seemed always to be there, in the lounge or dining-room of the "Dolphin", whenever she saw them. Both wore wedding rings, Daniel said. Men noticed things like that. Probably an instinct developed early, she decided. A safeguard maybe. Were they widowed? Thrown together for comfort in their ageing years? Or even divorced?

She looked across at her mother. Divorce had changed her. Before that she hadn't been so over-protective. At least not to Lauren. Maybe it had been centred on her father then. She'd never really noticed.

It had come as a shock when he walked out – to both of them. After eighteen years of marriage too. She'd been still at school: her 'A' level year. Not that anyone there thought it unusual. To have divorced or remarried parents was normal. It was those who had only the original pair who seemed strange. At one time she'd even been jealous when friends boasted about gifts their mother or father had given them, and how that had been bettered by their new parent. She'd felt quite deprived.

Her father had married again. Sarah was a pleasant girl; more like a sister in a way. Her mother objected strongly when first Lauren went to visit them, so she'd stopped going for a while. Now when she went, she didn't mention it to her. It was the simplest way. It seemed disloyal to her mother until she realized that not seeing him would upset her father as well. She was his daughter. And *she* still loved him.

Since her accident she sympathized with him even more, knowing how dominant and overbearing her mother could be. That had been the reason he left them. Now she could understand.

'Darling.' Her mother was leaning across the table towards her. 'Your hair.'

Unconsciously, Lauren had pushed it back, hating the way it obscured her vision. Hastily she shook it forward again, glancing round at the other diners to see if she'd caused offence.

'The cheese-cake's good, though I say it myself.' Mrs Tolly returned, wheeling the sweet-trolley.

'Just coffee,' Lauren said, wanting to get away from the crowded room.

'Are you sure, darling? Wouldn't like some of that gorgeous gâteau? I'm going to have a piece.'

'No thank you, Mother,' she said wearily.

'You're all right?'

'Yes, fine.'

'It was such a silly thing for you to do yesterday, you know. You're bound to have a reaction.'

'A reaction?' Lauren stared at her mother, puzzled.

'That boat. The speed. The noise. It must have brought back all the horror of your accident.'

'I was perfectly all right, I keep telling you.' Lauren's voice rose on a high note.

'All right, darling. People will hear you.'

'Look, Mother, will you please let me forget about the past. I don't want to be reminded. I've got to learn to accept what's happened and start my life again.'

'Yes, darling. Of course you have,' her mother soothed.

'Then why can't you believe me and let me get on with it?' Lauren cried, throwing her serviette onto the table, and rushing from the room.

The sky had turned overcast when she arrived outside. Dark banks of cloud were growing over the cliffs. She couldn't tell whether it was the spray of the waves that made the air damp, or fine rain starting to fall.

I'll go up to the rectory, she decided. Daniel might be back by now. She needed to talk to him. Be with him. Just the thought of seeing him again calmed her.

Her footsteps turned towards the hill, passing the village shop, closed now for Tom's lunch. Tregony's window had the blind down too and she remembered that it was Wednesday. Maybe everywhere closed for the afternoon.

The metal gate clanged as she opened it. Surgery was from nine o'clock until 10.30; three o'clock until four that day, she read on the gatepost; Dr Stephen Kerrow and Dr Daniel Kerrow in attendance. She hadn't known his father's name before. It wasn't the surgery she wanted.

Figures caught her eye through one of the windows. The family were still eating lunch. She'd forgotten her own had been early. That silvery-haired woman must be Daniel's mother. His father sat at the far end. Daniel was in the middle, his back to the window. And opposite him …

Lauren felt her body tense.

Sitting opposite him was a dark-headed girl. A girl with enormous eyes, a small straight nose, high cheek-bones and a full mouth. A mouth that was smiling across the table towards him as he bent to kiss her. It was the girl in the paintings.

Swiftly Lauren turned and went back through the gate, running down the hill to the harbour. Rain was sweeping in from the sea now, driving into her, stinging her cheeks, soaking her hair. Her feet slipped and slithered on the cobbles.

Why has he never told me?

And then she remembered. His was only a professional interest. Daniel Kerrow was a doctor.

At the "Dolphin" she ran in through the doorway. Her mother was still in the lounge.

'I'm going back home with you, Mother.' Breathlessness choked her words.

'Darling! How sensible,' her mother replied.

'Will you collect me from the cottage? I'll pack straight away.'

In the cove waves roared up the beach towards the steps. Every footprint was gone now. Obliterated. Hidden by the swirling water. She could feel the ground tremble as sea pounded against rock.

Fallen lavender flowers trampled under her hurrying feet. Rose petals scattered the path. She pushed through the door and stood in the hallway, seeing her reflection in a small round mirror on the wall. Her hair clung to her skull; her face was ghostlike and pale; her mouth and eye dragged sideways, linked by a thin trail. She closed her eyelids tightly, but the grotesque image still remained. Her mother was right. She was repulsive. No wonder Mark had turned away. But Daniel had been different. With him it didn't matter.

In her mind's eye she could see the dark-haired girl sitting there, her pretty face smiling across at him, her skin soft and clear; read the expression in her eyes as her lips met Daniel's.

Upstairs, Lauren bundled clothes into her suitcase, snatching her washing things into their drawstring bag. A phone call told the letting agent she was leaving. And then she was ready, waiting for her mother: impatient; desperate to be gone.

As the car drove slowly up the winding hill Lauren sat, her fingers clinging to the handle of the door, her eyes frantic, watching the glaring yellow of the field pass by, smelling its sickly scent.

'I phoned Aunt Jane, darling, before I left. We'll stay at Bideford with her overnight. She's terribly busy running that old people's home of hers. Can't think why she does it. So depressing. They're probably all senile and incontinent too. I thought we might stay there for a day or so. You could give her a hand maybe. It would help to take your mind off things, wouldn't it?'

From Truro they took the road past St Erme, then travelled across Bodmin Moor, through Launceston to Holsworthy and Great Torrington, and finally reached Bideford around eight in the evening. For

Lauren, despite her mother's cautious driving, every mile had been an agony and she felt drained when they arrived.

Aunt Jane's house was large and imposing, set on a hill between there and Westward Ho! As a child, Lauren had stayed every summer, revelling in the company of her four older cousins, but that was before it became a nursing-home when Aunt Jane and Uncle Don were left on their own.

She steeled herself for the meeting, seeing their eyes flinch away as a gust of wind caught her hair and blew it from her cheek. Her hand rose instinctively to shield it.

'Now, don't make any comment, Jane darling,' her mother declared brightly. 'Poor Lauren's terribly sensitive about her face. Just take no notice. That's what I do. You'll soon get used to it.'

She felt the comforting hug her aunt gave her, and the sympathetic look from Uncle Don as he kissed her. They knew her mother too.

'I think I'll make it an early night and go straight to bed, if you don't mind,' Lauren murmured. 'It's been a tiring day.'

'Shall I bring you up some supper on a tray?' her aunt asked gently.

Lauren shook her head. 'No, thanks, Aunt Jane. I'll be asleep in minutes.'

The nightmare returned that night. Seeing those headlights dazzle through the raindrops. Hearing the shatter of glass. Feeling the metal tear into her skin ...

Her mother's voice soothed, and for once

Lauren was glad she was there.

Afterwards she lay awake in the darkness, tears still burning her cheeks. At Trennion her nights had become peaceful. She remembered the soft scent of the roses around her window; the lavender growing by the front door; the soft surge of sea down in the cove as waves tugged at the shingle. And Daniel.

Watching his dark head as he swam out in the bay. Sensing again the touch of his hand on hers. The way the corners of his deep blue eyes crinkled when he smiled. Those eyes. Always so caring, so full of compassion. Her fingers lightly brushed over her lips, remembering the burn of his kiss.

What had Morganna's baby turned out to be? she wondered. How many grandchildren did that make for Mrs Tolly? Six, or was it seven? She'd never met Demelza or Morwenna. Demelza lived near Helston. Married to one of the Air Sea Rescue crew at Culdrose, Mrs Tolly had told her.

In only a few short days, she'd learned to love the little harbour village and the people who lived there. And not only the village ... She pushed all thoughts of Daniel out of her mind. He had the dark-haired girl.

How would Mary Tulliver cope when she had her new baby? Life on a farm was never easy. Quite a contrast from teaching in the village school. No wonder Matthew was such a bright little chap. Without him in the boat that day how would they ever have reached the safety of the harbour? Blindness was said to make the other senses acute, but even so the striking of that clock was a sound neither she nor Daniel had noticed.

She could visualize Daniel shivering in the chill mist as he steered the boat, his tanned limbs wet from the sea. And she remembered the taste of salt when her mouth brushed his sea-wet skin as he carried her on that other day, quickly banishing the memory.

What would have happened if we hadn't found the harbour? she wondered. The rocks round that coast were vicious and cruel. Supposing that little boat had struck one. What then? She and Daniel could both swim. But Matthew? Would he have panicked in his own darkness, there in the water? Daniel would easily have coped with him, she felt quite sure. As he had coped with her that first day. She'd gone to the cove with only one intention then. And now ...

She buried her face into the pillow. It would have been so much easier if Daniel had never found me that morning, she thought. And if I'd never fallen in love with him. Shock jarred through her. Fallen in love. Was that why it had hurt to find those paintings of a girl whose expressive eyes revealed so much? And then to see the girl herself ... with Daniel?

It was the right thing to do, leaving Trennion. Staying would only have caused heartbreak. Forgetting Daniel would be easy. She'd known him for only four days.

Eight

Lauren didn't sleep any more that night and when the first strands of dawn brightened the sky, she silently dressed.

The walk over Northam Burrows and down to the sea was one she knew well. It was a favourite with her cousins years back. A few ponies and sheep were grazing the short, dew-wet grass and their heads rose to stare as she passed. Here and there she skirted black patches of boggy mud and reed until she came to the high pebble-ridge.

It was all such a contrast to the granite rocks and high cliffs enclosing Trennion's tiny cove. Was Daniel swimming there at this moment? His head dark and sleek as his arms struck out strongly, curving their way through the water to reach the far side? His daily swim, he said. It had become a habit.

And Toby. She'd forgotten the tortoiseshell cat in her haste to get away. Who would feed him? Had he returned to his hidden spot under the lavender bushes after her mother frightened him away? Was he curled in the sunshine, waiting for

Daniel, at the top of the wooden steps? Was the dark-haired girl sitting there with him? Or was she, too, swimming in the sea with Daniel?

Lauren thought it was strange she'd never seen her before. A girl so distinctive would be hard to miss in such a small village. And yet she was there. At the rectory. Sitting opposite Daniel at lunch. Looking at him in a way that could only reveal their closeness.

Does she work at the surgery? The receptionist perhaps? Was that it? On duty each day. Then Daniel must see her constantly. But he'd never mentioned her.

Used to go to the "Dolphin", Mrs Tolly said. *Dr Kerrow and his young lady. Used to go.* And yet, from the way they kissed …

In the distance she could see golfers out on the burrows. An early morning round before the day began. She started the long walk home.

'Darling!' her mother greeted her. 'You had us all so worried! When I woke and your bed was empty … Well, I just didn't know what to expect.'

'I'm fine, Mother.'

'Are you quite sure, darling? You look rather pale. And after that terrible nightmare …'

'I said I'm fine.' Lauren could hear the edge to her voice and tried to soften it. 'Really, Mother, I'm quite all right.'

'Your mother suggested you might be able to give me a hand, Lauren,' her Aunt Jane broke in quickly. 'It would be an enormous help if you could. I have three part-timers, but with the holiday season starting, one or other will be away for the next few weeks, and it isn't easy to get in extra staff. With your nursing training …'

'I'll leave you two to talk shop then,' her mother declared, rising gracefully to her feet from the breakfast table and moving towards the garden. 'Just bring me out a cup of coffee when it's ready, darling, will you? I'll be under that shady tree on the lawn.'

'I really should be doing something useful for a change,' Lauren admitted slowly, 'but to be quite honest I'm a little reluctant to face the outside world again.'

'You're not going to waste all that training, are you?' her aunt asked bluntly. 'Good nurses aren't easy to find.'

Lauren gave a rueful laugh, remembering Daniel's comment on the clifftop that day. 'I'm not sure I will make a good nurse, Aunt Jane.'

'Of course you will. And now it's just a matter of getting back your confidence. Your mother doesn't help, you know.'

Lauren stared at her in surprise.

'Well, she *is* my sister and I know what she's like. Being the eldest of us three girls, she ruled the roost at home. And as for your poor father … Don and I always felt so sorry for him. He couldn't do a thing without Tess breathing down his neck. Then, when he left home, it was you she turned her attention to. Why don't you stop on for a while? It would help me no end.'

She didn't actually say *and get out of her clutches*, Lauren decided, but she had a strong feeling that was what her aunt meant.

'At least it would get you back into nursing again. Although most of the old darlings staying here are pretty active, they still need a great deal of care and attention. TLC, we call it. Tender loving care. It does far more good than any doctor's prescription, you know.' Aunt Jane gave a smile. 'And I think some of that might do you the power of good too.'

'Let's give it a try, shall we?' Lauren replied.

'You can use the little bedroom overlooking the garden.'

'Sarah's old room?'

Her aunt nodded.

'How is Sarah? And the others?'

'Oh, everyone's fine. Sarah will be down when the university term finishes in about four weeks, but she's going straight off to France for the summer, otherwise I'd get her to give me a hand. She always did when she was at school, but with her finals coming up next year, she hopes practising the language will help.'

Aunt Jane placed glass bowls of cereal on pretty flowered trays and began to fill small pots with coffee. 'You know Lynne's wedding is at the end of September, don't you? And Karen is expecting her second baby in mid-July. John's the problem though. He's leaving his job yet again.' John was the youngest in the family, and Lauren always felt that he suffered from being the only boy. 'Why he couldn't have gone on to university like the rest of them, Don and I will never understand. He's bright enough. His exam results were outstanding.'

'So what's he going to do this time, Aunt Jane?' Lauren asked, slicing toast into triangles.

'A life-guard over at Woolacombe,' her aunt replied regretfully. 'One way to get away from home, I suppose. He'll be living over there for the summer.' She gave Lauren a despairing look. 'His current job is labouring in the local garage. It really horrifies us. He could do so much. It seems such a pity. Don always hoped he'd join the bank with him.'

'John is only nineteen, Aunty,' Lauren reasoned. 'There's plenty of time yet for him to decide what to do.'

'Your uncle and I feel that all this wasting time isn't going to be much use to him. And now he has a girlfriend who's intent on settling down. What future will there be for him without a proper job?'

'Well I'm looking forward to seeing him again. He'd already gone before I got back from my walk.'

'If you do see him, you'll be lucky! He's out more often than he's in,' her aunt replied sadly. 'Now, if you like to take those trays upstairs ...'

There were only ten elderly guests, as Aunt Jane called them. An extension had been added to the rear of the house so that each had a single room, and Lauren found that most of them were furnished with some of their occupants' own personal belongings.

All were disabled by age in some way, but greeted her cheerfully when she appeared and by the end of the morning, she found she was already beginning to settle into a routine.

When John arrived home during his lunch-hour, arms and hands black with grease, his mother instantly confined him to the garden to eat. Lauren brought her plate out to join him in the shade of the trees, but was disconcerted to see him stare quite openly at her cheek.

'Trust Aunt Tess to exaggerate!' he remarked candidly, slicing into a thick chunk of cucumber, and continuing with his mouth full. 'She said it made you look … what's the word … grotesque.'

'Not repulsive?' Lauren enquired.

'Probably that as well,' he grinned. 'It'll fade though, won't it?'

'In time, so they say.'

'Bet it was a bit of a shock – when you first saw it,' he said, starting rapidly on a dish of apple pie. 'Anyway, you'll soon forget about it. People do,' he went on. 'Remember Peter Burley? Used to be at school with me. Always hung around here in the holidays.'

'Curly red hair?' she asked.

John nodded, spooning in a final scrap of clotted cream. 'Came off his motorbike a year or so back. Made a terrible mess of himself. You should see him now though. Grown a beard. The girls go crazy over him.'

'It might be a bit difficult for me to do likewise,' Lauren commented drily.

'I didn't mean the beard, Lauren! It wasn't that part of his face he smashed up anyway. Just his nose and forehead, and around his eyes. He was terribly self-conscious about it. Used to wear an old trilby hat, pulled down, like those classic films of Bogart. Made it all the more obvious really – like the way you've done your hair.'

'My mother thinks it looks better like this,' Lauren said.

'Well it doesn't!' he declared. 'Must dash now. Thanks for eating out here with me. I'm a bit of an outcast really. Have to be kept apart from the oldies, or I might give them a heart attack or something.'

'As bad as that?' she laughed.

'I'm glad you're staying for a while, Lauren. You always did side with me, didn't you, when the girls ganged up? I'll take you for a burger one evening! Remember that place? It's still there. 'Bye now.'

John always had been her favourite cousin. Probably because she had no brothers of her own. His older sisters used to complain bitterly when he wanted to join in their sophisticated games. Being a young outsider too, she and John often joined forces.

Lauren had trouble persuading her mother that she wanted to stay on with Aunt Jane in Bideford.

'But, darling, you know how much I adore looking after you. I've been so looking forward to it, having you all to myself again. I'd forgotten just how lonely I am,' her mother wailed. 'And all these depressing old people – are you sure it's a good idea when you're still recovering?'

Finally though, the combined force of Jane and Don convinced her that it would be for Lauren's good and that helping others would take her mind off her own problem.

'Do make sure your Aunt Jane doesn't overload you, darling,' her mother warned as she climbed into her car. 'I know what she's like. As a child she was always the one to slide out of her share of work. She'll have you doing everything around here, while she sits and reads a book in the garden. Don't forget you're still in a very low state, will you, darling? I really don't feel at all happy about leaving you here. If there wasn't so much happening at home, I'd stay on too.'

'Aunt Jane has enough to cope with without another guest, Mother,' Lauren told her firmly. 'Besides, your bridge friends will be needing you, won't they? You play most afternoons, don't you? And what about all those cocktail parties? You must be missing a tremendous amount of local gossip. I'll be fine here. You know how well Aunt Jane looks after people.'

'Rubbish!' her mother replied. 'She has no idea at all. Never has. I really can't imagine how she's managed to bring up a family.' She gave a sniff of disapproval. 'Well of course she hasn't. Look at that awful boy! The sooner he's off life-guarding, the better. At least he'll be clean, instead of covered in oil all the time. He's been nothing but trouble to Jane and Don from the minute he was born. Such a shame he wasn't another girl.' She gave a tearful smile. 'Daughters bring so much pleasure, darling, even if they can frequently be callous and ungrateful.'

"Bye, Mother. You don't want to get caught up in the traffic, do you? Have a safe journey.'

'If you need me, just call, darling. I'll be here in a trice. And don't forget to keep your hair that way, will you? People will hardly know about your face if you do. And when you go out, don't forget to wear a headscarf.'

Lauren remained in Bideford for almost a month until Aunt Jane's permanent staff were all back on duty again. By then May had passed into June.

And during those weeks her mind returned to Daniel far too often for her own contentment. Four days, she thought, that's all I was with him, and yet their memory was etched deep in her heart. She was disappointed that he hadn't tried to contact her, but then why should he? She was merely someone who'd spent a brief stay in his cottage. Dozens of people must come and go during the season. Why should one be any different?

Besides, there was that girl. In comparison with her, no other could stand a chance. But when Lauren was by the sea sometimes of an early morning, and she saw a dark head swimming, she was reminded of Daniel, and her heart ached with sadness.

Her cousin Sarah returned from university two days before Lauren left Bideford. Of her female cousins, Sarah had always been the closest. At twenty-one, she was only a year apart in age.

Her gaze flickered casually over the scar as Lauren brushed her hair that night.

'Do you mind?' she asked.

'Mind?' For a moment Lauren was puzzled. 'About my face?'

'About Mark,' Sarah replied.

Once upon a time they'd shared all their secrets. Boyfriends had been one of them. Giggling together down on the beach, or hidden in the branches of an old apple-tree at the end of the garden, out of hearing of the two older girls, whispering together.

'You loved him, didn't you?' Sarah said. 'You must have done. You were engaged to be married. Wasn't it awful when he just dropped you like that? I'd have been devastated.'

'I was.'

'Oh, Lauren, I'm sorry. I do know what it can be like. There was this gorgeous hunk I met when a group of us went over to Paris in the Easter vac. I was with him for almost the whole week and then, quite out of the blue, his *wife* turned up at the flat. I couldn't believe it. He was an absolute pig, but I still keep thinking about him. I suppose it's the same with you – Mark must be constantly in your thoughts too.'

Was he? Lauren tried to remember when she'd last thought of him. It was Daniel who filled her mind.

'So what are you going to do?' Sarah probed.

'You can't go on pining for him for ever, can you?'

'I'm not.'

'Yes, you are. Every so often there's this dreamy sort of look in your eyes. If you still fancy him, why don't you write and tell him so? Maybe he feels the same way too.'

Lauren gave a hollow laugh.

'You didn't see his expression when he visited me in hospital, Sarah.'

'Yes, but it's different now. Then you probably did look dreadful.'

'And don't I still?' Surprise filled Lauren's voice.

Sarah pulled Lauren's hair back behind her ear, studying her cheek critically. 'It'll never be perfect, I suppose, but it isn't all that bad. Anyway, I've known you so long I don't really notice what you look like. You never do, do you, with people you're close to? And Mark certainly must have been close to you. Why don't you get in touch again? I hate seeing you look so sad and wistful.'

'I didn't realize I did,' Lauren laughed.

'Well you do! There's a sort of far-away look in your eyes and a little half-smile round the edges of your mouth, as if you're remembering something fantastic. I've noticed it several times today since I've been back.'

On Lauren's arrival home her mother's welcome was enthusiastic, then critical.

'Darling, what *have* you done with your hair, piling it on top of your head like that? I know you think that that sun-bronzed look suits you, but damaged skin like yours never tans properly. It only makes it more obvious. Here, let me borrow your comb. I want you to look your best – guess who's waiting for you in the lounge?'

For one moment her mind turned to Daniel. Then she knew that could never be. Unwillingly, her body moved forward, guided by her mother's arm. She heard the rustle of a newspaper as it was hastily cast aside, then heavy steps cross the room when the door opened.

As she guessed, it was Mark. Once upon a time it would have been all that she wanted. Seeing him. Being with him again. Now ...

He was just as handsome as ever. Suppose he had been the one to be scarred in that accident? Would she have turned away that day as he did? Shocked by what she saw? The idea had never occurred to her before. Maybe it was an instinctive reaction. Maybe she, too, would have done exactly the same.

His hands were drawing her close. She closed her eyes. Mark's lips were on hers now. Purposeful. Demanding. And she remembered Daniel's kiss. The touch of his mouth tantalizing hers.

Mark stood back, his hands firm on her shoulders, his brown eyes staring back at her. She waited to see them change.

'Lauren, darling! I've missed you so much.'

She sensed the hostility in her own gaze, the tightening of her mouth.

'You knew where I was, Mark. I dare say my mother told you.'

His gaze lowered. 'But, darling, how could I come to you again, after the way you reacted last time? How was I to know how you felt about me? Your poor, lovely face. Did you think I was to blame for that accident? Did you hold me guilty every time you looked at yourself in the mirror?'

Had he forgotten his own reaction that day at the hospital? The expression in his eyes that he wasn't able to conceal? The way his head had twisted away? Or that he'd never returned?

'I still love you, Lauren.'

Her mother had discreetly vanished from the room, leaving them together, but now Lauren heard her give a light tap on the door.

'Darlings! Can you bear to tear yourselves away from each other to come and eat?'

Lauren gave a sigh. This was the kind of thing that used to happen. After dinner, she pleaded a headache and tiredness.

'Of course, darling,' her mother said. 'It has been a long day for you and then, of course, the excitement of seeing your beloved Mark ...'

He took her to the theatre the following evening. To the cinema a day or so later. A meal in a quiet pub down by the river. Places where it was dark and secluded.

Where no one can see me, she thought. And she reflected that Mark was a perfectionist. To be seen with her flawed like this must irk him. She realized, too, that they could so easily drift back into the companionship that had led to their engagement. And then, marriage would follow. The pattern was

repeating itself as it had once before. She'd known
Mark a long time. He was a part of her life. And
could be in the future. It was what she had wanted
– once upon a time.

'Who was that letter from that I posted on to you at
Jane's, darling?' her mother enquired almost a
week later. 'I didn't recognize the writing.'

'Letter?' Lauren asked.

'It was here when I returned from Bideford
weeks back. I re-addressed it and sent it on. Surely
you received it?'

Lauren shook her head.

'There was quite a heap of post on the mat when
I got back,' her mother said. 'Mostly bills, of course.
A statement from my bank. Two postcards.
Everyone seems to go abroad at this time. Oh yes,
and a letter from Andrew and Myra saying how
lovely it had been to see me. They'd just received
an invitation to their new granddaughter's
christening in America, and were going to stay
there for a month. It was a spur-of-the-moment
decision, but being so expensive, they thought
they'd make the most of it.'

'And there was a letter for me?' Lauren
prompted.

'Yes, darling. I re-addressed it straight away and
popped it in the letter-box when I went out
shopping a while later. I needed some more coffee
and you know Jaffe's grind their own beans.' She
paused, a frown wrinkling her brow. 'I don't
suppose ...'

'What, Mother?'

'Well, my mind was so full of Andrew and Myra's news, I wonder whether I put *their* address on it instead of Jane's. Their letter was open on the hall table when I redirected yours. Never mind, darling. They'll post it back when they return home again.'

'And they've gone to America for a month, you said?' Lauren remarked acidly.

'But that was weeks ago now, darling. They should be back any day.'

When Mark produced her engagement ring from his pocket, she looked at it with a strange heaviness in her heart.

'Please, Lauren. Wear it again.'

It was Mark's free day from the pharmacy. They'd taken a picnic down by the river, miles out in the country, and eaten it, deeply hidden by long trails of willow that reached down into the water and drifted sideways like slender pale-green fish.

She remembered the last time she'd seen that ring – the day she tore it from her finger and threw it onto the covers of her bed. The day Mark had been to visit her in the hospital. It had lain there, glittering. She'd never wanted to see it again then. She was not sure she wanted to see it now.

Mark held it out to her.

'Put it on. Please, darling,' he said softly.

He dropped it lightly into the palm of her hand and she looked down at it with thoughtful eyes. A shaft of sunshine filtered through the thin green leaves and caught the diamonds, sending them into a myriad rainbows. Sparkling like those raindrops on the windscreen so many months ago.

'Can you forgive me?' he whispered.

'For what?'

'For what I did.' He took the ring and slid it slowly onto her finger. 'I froze that night. My fingers were gripping the wheel, but I couldn't do a bloody thing. There was no reason why I shouldn't have avoided that accident.' He lowered his head, pulling her close. 'Then, when I saw you the next day ... I couldn't believe what I'd done to you. It horrified me. Even now, every time I look at your face ...'

'It repulses you?' she questioned.

'Oh, Lauren, please don't sound so bitter,' he replied brokenly. 'I feel so guilty. Every time I look at you, it reminds me.' His mouth was searching for hers. 'Now all I want to do is make up for all those months. We'll get married as soon as we can, Lauren. It doesn't have to be a church wedding, does it? All that fuss ...'

She gave a thin smile. 'My mother will feel deprived. And what about the veil? A veil hides so much.'

'Oh, Lauren!'

He kissed her passionately, but her mouth and body didn't respond. Behind her closed eyes all she could see was the image of Daniel's face, his dark hair blowing in the wind, his eyes full of caring.

Nine

When they returned late that evening, there was a letter waiting. It must have arrived by the midday post. Her mother had left it propped against a vase of blue irises on the hall table. Lauren didn't recognize the thick scrawled writing, but as she picked it up the postmark caught her eye. Cornwall.

'Aren't you going to invite me to stay for coffee?'

She raised vague eyes to Mark while her fingers trembled on the envelope, knowing instinctively who it was from.

'It's late, Mark. I'll see you tomorrow.'

'But, darling ...'

'Tomorrow, Mark. I'm tired now.' She gave him a weak smile. 'All the excitement,' she said.

'Aren't you going to kiss me?'

She could hear the hurt in his voice. Quickly she raised her face and brushed her lips across his cheek, feeling his hands grip her shoulders, and his mouth close over hers in the fierce act of possession.

As the door shut behind him, she was already slitting the envelope, eagerly tearing out the single closely-written sheet. It was from Daniel, and the sting of his words bit into her:

Dear Lauren,

I'm sorry you chose not to answer my previous letter, but can't say I'm all that surprised. Why should you? All I wanted was to know what made you leave so suddenly and that you were all right. However, I realize now that you would have taken it as me 'checking up on you', and I know how much that would have angered you. After all, who am I? Merely someone who owns a cottage where you once stayed — and annoyed you by swimming in the cove. Nothing more.

Enough. That is not the point of this letter. Matthew had a bad fall recently — climbing a tree, would you believe? Fractured both femurs. They're using gallows traction so you can guess the effect it has on such a lively little chap. I see him every day and all he does is talk about you, Lauren. The lady with the lovely hair. And about that day we spent in the boat. He goes over every detail. When is she coming back? he keeps asking.

I know that's impossible. You have no reason to do so any more. At least, I hope you've finally banished that idea from your mind. But would you do something else? Matthew has a small cassette-player and listens to it all the time. Could you do a tape for him? Nothing in particular. Just talk. As if you were sitting there beside him. I know he'd love that.

I've 'borrowed' a sheet of the hospital's notepaper, so you have the address.

His name filled the bottom of the page.

Lauren read it over and over again. *My previous letter*. Was that the one her mother had redirected, and she'd never received? It had to be. And it was there, waiting when her mother returned from Bideford. He'd written straight after she left Trennion. So what had he said, then, to her?

At the station she bought every children's story-cassette she could find. If Matthew already had them, then it didn't matter. He could give them away.

The train didn't go fast enough. The hands of her watch seemed barely to move. She tried to read, but every magazine word meant nothing. The hours crept by. Heat filled the carriage, sunshine blazing in through the windows. Everywhere it was airless. Her head ached. People dozed. One man snored, his head lolling almost to his shoulder; his mouth wide.

She stared restlessly out at the countryside; the rush of a town; the empty expanse of green where young corn grew. That field of yellow rape beside the lane would be cut now. Would Matthew's father have planted something else in its place?

Sheep huddled under a cluster of trees, trying to find shade. A white horse galloped away into the distance, startled by the train's noise. Canada-geese skeined across the sky to land in a rising trail of spray on the surface of a lake.

She drank a cup of coffee. Its taste could have been anything. For a while she dozed. The angle of the sun had changed when she opened her eyes again, but the heat was still unbearable. A hard clear blue glared above. People were gathering coats and suitcases; searching pockets and hand-bags for tickets. She found her own and tugged the small roll-bag from the rack.

A taxi took her to the hospital. The receptionist consulted a list.

'Matthew Tulliver. Third floor. Room 33. Check with the sister on duty.'

'Lauren Russell?' The grey-haired nurse smiled and Lauren thought her face was familiar. 'Daniel, my son, has spoken of you. You stayed at Trennion, didn't you? Young Matthew keeps on about you too. He's asleep at the moment. Would you like to go in and sit there? It shouldn't be too long before he wakes.'

He lay flat on his back, both plastered legs held at right angles by slings attached to cords over pulleys on a frame. One thumb was tucked in his mouth as he slept. She could see the scattering of freckles stand out against his skin; his little face crumpled by pain, like an old man's.

She remembered that day in the boat; his hair blowing silkily across her cheek, dampened by the spray; the wiry strength of his body as she hugged him close; his laughter. Her finger reached out gently to stroke across the back of his hand. A tiny smile began to hover round his lips, his head turning slowly.

'Lauren,' he whispered. 'I can smell your lovely hair. All spicy.'

'Like hot-cross buns?' she asked softly.

He nodded, his fingers reaching out to touch a curl, then smooth lightly across her cheek. 'Is your poor face nearly better now?'

She felt the tears burn her eyes and blinked rapidly, hoping to chase them away before they fell.

'It's fine, Matthew,' she answered. 'Much better.'

'Does it still hurt?'

'Not any more.'

He smiled. 'If our baby's a girl, can we call it Lauren too? You won't mind, will you? It'll be born soon.'

'No,' she said. 'I won't mind.'

'And if it's a boy, we're going to call it Daniel, like Dr Dan. He doesn't mind either. I asked him.' He sighed. 'I don't know what I want it to be most. Sometimes I wish it could be two babies.'

'I've brought you some tapes, Matthew. Stories you can listen to. Is this your cassette-player?'

'Dr Dan brought me that. I can do it all myself,' he said proudly. 'You push this button and it talks and this one to make the cassette jump up when it's stopped. Sometimes the cleaning-lady moves it to a different place and I get a bit lonely. Her voice is like Mrs Tolly's. All cuddly.'

'What's Morganna called her new baby?' Lauren asked.

'Jason,' Matthew replied. 'Dr Dan told me. It was born in this same hospital too. Before I came.'

He gave a little chuckle.

'What was that wickedness about?' Lauren asked him.

'Mrs Tolly was very cross, wasn't she?'

'When?'

'You 'member! When we went out in the boat and the engine got all tangled up and Dr Dan jumped in the water to mend it and got all wet and you said he had to put on your anorak. Mrs Tolly was all cross when she saw him in his ... *you-know-whats*, wasn't she?' He giggled again. 'Did Dr Dan look very funny wearing your anorak, Lauren?'

She thought back to that day. It seemed so long ago now.

'It wasn't a very big anorak,' she said, with a little smile.

'That ice-cream was very nice. I like that flaky chocolate. It goes all crumbly on your tongue. Mum says it makes a mess though. She always buys ice-cream you have to eat in a dish at home. I do like it really, but not quite so much. Mrs Tolly's ginger parkin was nice too, wasn't it? All sort of burny.'

'Not spicy like hot-cross buns?' she teased.

He laughed again and wrinkled his nose.

'Different,' he said.

'Are you tired, Matthew?'

'A bit,' he admitted. 'It does make you sleepy living here. I have to eat lots of funny medicine. If I go to sleep now, will you come back and see me tomorrow?'

'Yes,' she said.

'Promise?'

'I promise.'

She saw his lashes flutter down again, his head turn sideways, the thumb creeping into his mouth.

'See you tomorrow, Matthew,' she whispered, and gave him a light kiss.

Outside, the sun burned down relentlessly. The air barely moved. Even the pavement scorched her feet through the thin soles of her sandals. She needed a cup of tea.

There was an estate-agent's next to the café and when she came out, feeling better after toasted teacakes and a pot of Earl Grey tea, the name caught her eye. It was the letting agent for Daniel's cottage. Impulsively she went in.

'Dr Kerrow's property. Trennion,' she said breathlessly. 'Is it vacant?'

The young man looked at her doubtfully. 'I should very much doubt it at this time of year. From June onwards everything's fully booked right through until late September.'

He pressed the keys of his computer and gazed intently at the screen.

'Just as I thought. No, hang on a minute ... A family booked for a fortnight. This week and next. Then their eldest child broke his ankle windsurfing on Tuesday. They received a phone-call on Thursday to say their house had been broken into and vandalized. The wife and youngest child were suffering with bad sunburn too. So they decided they'd had enough and went home yesterday. Brought the keys in on the way. New people take over Saturday week.'

'So it is vacant at the moment?'

He nodded.

'Then could I stop there? I'm Lauren Russell. I was down early in May.'

'Oh, yes, Miss Russell. I see from the records that you left early too.'

'I had to go home unexpectedly,' she said.

'Trennion doesn't seem to be having a very good run of luck at the moment,' the young man observed. 'I can't see why you shouldn't rent the place though. I'll be able to send that other lot a refund if you do. Might cheer them up a little.'

She stopped to buy food, then found another taxi to drive the final miles. Ahead she could see heat shimmer on the road, making it quiver. Tar oozed. A thin layer of dust coated the hedgerows where dog-roses and honeysuckle now twisted and bloomed.

'Sticky old day, m'dear,' the driver observed when they drove down the lane, long stems of dry grass leaning down from the banks to whisper against the sides of the car. 'Shouldn't be surprised if there's a storm later on. Might clear the air though. We could do with that.'

Trees overhead formed a dense arch, giving the road a welcome shade. Lauren pushed her heavy hair away from her face and leaned her head against the open window. By the sea it would be different, she decided.

Every twist and turn was familiar. Her eyes eagerly took in every detail. Was it the right thing to do? To come back? The final bend was rounded.

She could hear the surge of the sea. The soft salt air surrounded her like a balm once more.

As she walked up the path something rustled, then a long paw patted the air and the tortoiseshell cat strolled from under the tall spikes of lavender, bringing a trail of sharp fragrance.

'Toby!' she cried in delight, bending to stroke him, feeling his dusty head warm against her hand. A faint tremor of sound vibrated through him, rising to a contented purr as he rolled onto his back, paws languidly stretching to display his most ticklish zones.

Nothing has changed, she thought contentedly, stopping to gaze at the cove where a dark line of dried seaweed bordered the sand, curving its way along the edge of the water.

The roses were gone from the windows, only their leafy stems remained, reaching the grey slates of the roof. And she remembered the attic room filled with paintings.

'Will you be all right?' the taxi-driver's voice questioned.

She nodded.

'Yes,' she said. 'I'll be all right now.'

A gust of warm breeze stirred the hair from around her cheeks and she noticed the slight frown that folded over his eyes as he looked at her. Once it would have mattered so much.

The bowl of pot-pourri had lost its fragrance. Its petals were brown and crumbled in the heat. Only a faint memory of roses still remained, held in their midst.

She recalled the first time she'd entered the cottage. Her terrible despair. And her gaze went back to the cove where the sea lapped lazily against the shore. Here her life could have ended.

The cat had followed her indoors, weaving itself anxiously around her feet, and she made her way into the cool dimness of the kitchen to open the shopping-bag. She hadn't forgotten his pilchards.

Upstairs the bed was tidy, clean sheets neatly laid at the head, blankets in a pile at the foot, pillows resting in the middle. Mrs Tolly had been busy. The furniture gleamed.

Lauren opened all the windows, trying to let in some air, but the rooms remained heavy with heat. A swim, that's what she needed, but in her haste to reach Cornwall she hadn't brought her bikini.

There wasn't time to walk over to the village and buy one. Besides it was far too hot. Her bra and pants were no different. Probably far less revealing, she decided. Seizing a towel, she ran down to the beach.

The heat of the sand seared into her bare feet, the sun scorching her back, so that the first splash of water was welcome. Even so its depths were warm, the waves sluggish as if they were too weary to move towards the shore. A strand of seaweed twirled round her ankle, and she kicked it away, rolling onto her back to stare up into the harsh blue of the sky, closing her eyes against its glare. In the distance she thought she could hear a faint tremor, the rumble of thunder, and swam towards the shore.

Once out of the water the heat bit into her again, turning the tiny beads of moisture to white salt. She licked her lips, tasting it, as she began to rub her hair dry with the towel.

It was past six o'clock now, and yet the temperature showed no sign of lowering. She made a sandwich with ham and tomato, then sat on the steps to eat it, joined by the cat who carefully curled himself in her shadow. A scrap of meat fell onto the wood beside him but with a languid turn of his head, he ignored it.

Another grumble of thunder echoed far away.

What would it be like, here, in a storm? she wondered, a tremor of apprehension prickling her skin. It was difficult to imagine that placid sea roused into a fury. And yet at times it must be. The last day she'd been here, the waves had been rough, lashed by rain and wind. It was bleak then.

That day.

The paintings of the girl haunted her mind. And seeing her, seated at the table, looking up at Daniel. She could still visualize the straightness of his back as he sat; the sleek gleam of his dark hair. And she hadn't forgotten the expression in the girl's beautiful eyes. Their possession of the handsome man facing her. Maybe I shouldn't have come here, Lauren thought despairingly. It was a foolish thing to do.

The diamond ring sparkled as she twisted it round and round on her finger, each stone catching and reflecting the light. I should have taken it off when I swam, she thought. Mark would be furious if I lost it. Mark. He says he loves me. Still loves me, despite ... I did love him too. Once upon a time. But now ... His touch no longer thrills me. His kiss rouses no desire. So why am I marrying him?

Everything was moving too fast for her: their old days together catching up, becoming a repetition of before. Mark took it for granted she felt the same way about him. He never even questioned it. So why didn't he know? Why didn't he sense? In time, will I grow to love him again?

He'd be wondering where she'd gone so suddenly. And her mother too. Maybe she'd better phone. Dried sand powdered down from her legs onto the wood as she stood up. The cat shook himself fastidiously, twitching each shoulder in turn, before preceding her to the garden gate.

There was a sullen glare about the sun now, patterning bloodlike across the surface of the sea to reflect from the whitewashed walls. And the thunder sounded to be nearer.

'But why, darling?' her mother's voice shrilled. 'Why go back to that place? It's such a bleak and lonely spot. Why not stay at the "Dolphin" if you must be down there at all? Who is this child you have to visit?'

'It's only for a few days, Mother,' Lauren soothed into the phone.

'And what about Mark? He's totally bewildered, poor lamb. Just when you're engaged again too. I was thrilled when he told me. But why didn't you mention it in that scrappy little note you left? *Gone back to Cornwall*. Not a word about your other news. I'm devoting my evening to planning all the arrangements, darling.' Her mother sighed. 'Well, someone has to, don't they? Mark wants the wedding as soon as possible. Make up for all that lost time. He's so eager. It's quite understandable, darling. He loves you so much.'

'Can't everything wait until I come home again?' Lauren protested.

'We don't want any more delay,' her mother reproved. 'I do rather agree with Mark that perhaps a church ceremony would be a weeny bit daunting for you. Meeting all those relations who haven't seen you since ...'

'The accident, Mother? Since I became grotesque?'

'Darling! There's no need to talk like that. After all, Mark *is* prepared to marry you still. You really are very lucky about that.'

The line began to crackle.

'Look, Mother, I'll ring you tomorrow. There's a storm blowing up.'

The nightmare surrounded her. She could hear the rhythmic beat of the windscreen wipers; the roar as the van grew close; see the dazzle of headlights through her closed eyelids. With terror pulsing through her she forced them to open and meet the brilliance, seeing raindrops glitter on the glass, her head twisting to avoid the agony she knew was to come.

Her fingers felt the soft covers of the bed. The sounds of the storm were everywhere. Lightning made a pale square of the window. A rose-stem frantically rapped against its pane. Sea crashed against rock. Waves pounded the shore. Every inch of the cottage seemed to vibrate with its fury.

Somewhere she heard a thin pathetic wail. Toby! The cat was somewhere out there. Lauren ran down the stairs. She could see his outline through the hall window, crouched on the sill, ears flattened by the beat of the rain. Her hands reached to the door-catch. With a slither of noise, a slate rattled down the roof, and crashed on to the path. She saw the shape of the cat leap upwards, then it was gone.

Her voice sounded thin as she called his name, snatched and lost in the wind. Ahead, she thought she could see a movement and went out on to the path, feeling the wet wood of the door slip from her grasp, to slam behind her.

Another shimmer of lightning lit the sky. Something was running up the cliff-path. She turned to follow, the hem of her nightdress twisting itself damply round her ankles. Mud slid between her bare toes.

'Toby!'

Her voice was lost in another crash of thunder. The howl of the wind shrieked in her ears. Her body leaned into it. Every step was an effort.

'Toby!'

He was there, she knew. Terrified, as she was.

The path disappeared. Now she could feel only the slip of wet grass under her feet.

A leathery strand of wind-borne seaweed slapped across her cheek. Her lips felt its wet chill before it was gone again, making her shudder. Once more the sky became day, quivering round her, and she saw the cliff-edge yawn inwards only inches from her. Terror rooted her to the spot. She stood quite still. Or as still as the wind would let her. Not knowing which way to go. In front lay a chasm. While behind … Rain made her nightdress cling to her cold skin. She could scarcely breathe as the gale raged round her. If I move … What then?

The next flash of lightning came with a crescendo of thunder. Her eyes strained, trying to make out a shape near the cliff-edge. Someone was moving towards her. A beam of torchlight wavered. Then strong arms closed round her and she was lost on Daniel's rain-drenched shoulder.

Ten

'Oh, Lauren, Lauren.' The movement of his lips trembled against her hair, his mouth softly brushing her skin until it found hers, and she gave a little sigh, feeling herself lifted and carried back along the path.

'The door slammed behind me,' she started to warn him, but he had already drawn a key from his pocket and was fitting it into the lock. And then they were in the hall, his arms still holding her as purposefully he began to climb the stairs. In the warmth of the bathroom he put her down gently, sitting her on the stool, turning on the shower so that a rush of hot water sent steam rising to mist the air.

This has happened before, she remembered wistfully. Oh, such a long time ago. Daniel had brought her upstairs that day. After he'd rescued her from the sea. But then he had been angry.

By the time she went downstairs again, he'd lit the log-fire in the lounge, and the sweet smell of pine drifted through the room to mingle with hot coffee.

His arms reached out to pull her down beside

him into the depths of the sofa, and she rested her head against the damp collar of his shirt, letting his mouth possess hers once more.

'I love you, Lauren,' he murmured huskily. 'I love you so much,' and her voice whispered words of her own.

Then his head bent swiftly, his lips burning their way down the column of her neck to scorch across the taut skin of her breast as his hand rounded it, until his mouth met the upraised tip of her nipple, and enclosed it fiercely. Her back arched forward and her fingers twisted themselves into the wet tangle of his hair, bringing him even closer, a faint groan shuddering the length of his spine. The heat of his body flamed through her and she knew that any moment, any second, they would move together in an age-old rhythm of desire.

A log crashed with a muffled thud into the grate, startling her. Tiny pin-pricks of light were spiralling towards her like a myriad splinters of broken glass, and her mouth formed itself into a scream.

With a faint oath, Daniel pulled away, staring down at her, his eyes ink-blue and smouldering.

And she knew then, the moment was gone.

'I'm sorry, Lauren, I frightened you.'

Violently she shook her head. 'No. It wasn't you.'

'Something did. What was it?'

'Just memories,' she whispered.

His fingers stroked her hand, finding the ring, his eyes turning to hers.

'Like this?' he asked, his voice hardening.

'Who is the girl in the paintings?' she countered and saw him frown.

'You found the studio?'

She nodded.

'When?'

'The day I left. And then I saw her. At the rectory. With you.'

'But I wasn't there,' he retorted.

Why must he lie?

'I phoned. Spoke to your mother. Didn't she give you the message? Morganna was having her baby.'

'I saw you, Daniel.'

'But when? Where?' His voice was a desperate pleading. His eyes were one mute appeal.

'I told you. I came up to the rectory. That lunch-time. The day I left. She was sitting opposite you at the table. I saw her, Daniel. I saw you too.'

His fingers gripped into her shoulders, making her meet his gaze.

'I was with Morganna at the hospital in Truro, Lauren. Ask her. Ask anyone. I stayed till she had the baby.'

'But I saw you, Daniel,' she insisted.

'You saw my brother, Simon.'

She stared back at him, perplexed. 'Your brother? But he's in America.'

'He flew back to attend a medical conference in London. Nerissa came with him.'

'Nerissa?'

'His wife. The girl in the paintings. Simon did those. We shared the cottage when we were students. It belonged to our grandparents. We inherited it after they died. Simon paints. It's his studio. All the paintings are his. Those on the wall there. Mostly of the cove. And Nerissa.'

'Did she live in the village?'

Daniel shook his head. 'I met her when I was at medical school. She was training too.'

'*You* did?'

'Nerissa was engaged to me — until I chose to come down here to live after my father was ill. I said once that she was ambitious. A village doctor's practice wasn't what she wanted for me. And Simon was already destined for a far better life.'

'You make her sound so cold.'

'Not cold, but maybe calculating. Simon loves her anyway. As once I did. I'm glad of that.'

'And they were staying here that day?' Lauren asked.

'They arrived the night before. Soon after I got back. They had a couple of days to spare before they returned to America, so decided to come down. There'd been a phone-call lunch-time, when we were out at sea.'

Lauren remembered the expression in the girl's eyes. Total possession. But it hadn't been for Daniel after all.

'From the back you and your brother are very alike,' she said.

'Are we?' Daniel smiled. 'I wouldn't know.' His arms closed round her again, drawing her to him. 'Was that why you left so hurriedly?'

She nodded against his chin.

'Why?'

'I thought you loved her.'

'Once I did,' he said softly. 'But not any more. Not for a long time now. Not once I realized what she was like.'

'How did you know I was staying here at Trennion?'

'Matthew told me. I went to the hospital this afternoon. He was over the moon. Bubbling with excitement. You made such a difference to him. He missed you. And so did I.'

'So why didn't you come and find me sooner?' she teased, lifting her face to his again.

'A patient thought he'd had a coronary. I had to go straight out when I reached home. He was in an acute state of panic.'

She felt his mouth smile against her cheek.

'Too many pickled onions, I'm afraid. He'll survive.'

His fingers were toying with the ring again and she felt his jaw clench. 'But what about this, Lauren? Haven't you some explaining of your own to do? This wasn't there on the day you left, was it? Or is it just that I've never held your hand like this before?'

'You wouldn't have missed it,' she smiled, remembering the two schoolteachers and how Daniel had known they were married.

'So?'

'I was engaged before the accident. To Mark.'

'The man who found you so repulsive? Has he changed his view?' There was a sharp note in Daniel's tone.

'I think he has.'

'You're going to marry him?'

'No,' she said. 'Not any more. How can I, now?' A thought suddenly occurred to her, making her stiffen. 'Should you be here, like this? You're a doctor. Aren't they supposed to be ...'

'Above all moral sin?' he ended for her, and she heard the humour in his voice again. 'Only with their patients and, thankfully, as you pointed out so many times, you're not one of them. Besides, just after I arrived here, the lightning struck a tree. The lane's completely blocked by a fallen branch. You wouldn't want me to risk my life on that cliff-path, would you? Shall we take this off?'

She raised her startled eyes to his and met their laughter.

'Your ring, Lauren. What else did you think?'

They lay, curled together, in the firelight, until finally they both slept, and when the morning light filtered through the salt-hazed window, Lauren opened her eyes. Grey ash littered the fireplace, while here and there a charred shred of wood glowed fitfully. Sunbeams danced through the haze of smoke.

Daniel's head rested on her shoulder, his hair rumpled, the stubble of his chin dark against his skin. She ran her finger lightly over it before bending to kiss him, sensing the instant alertness that ran like fire through his body, so that his arms tightened round her, and his mouth turned to meet hers.

'What will Mrs Tolly say if she comes in now?' she whispered softly when he finally released her.

'Mrs Tolly has three daughters. She must understand the laws of nature by now,' he grinned. 'And those girls certainly do. Morwenna's fallen for a fifth.'

'She'll be here any second to check up on me,' Lauren warned.

'Then it's time for my morning swim. Going to join me? The storm's died away completely and the sea should be calm.'

'I didn't bring a bikini with me. Yesterday I swam in my bra and pants, but I need those to dry.'

'So?' His eyebrows were raised tantalizingly. 'I can assure you, my dear Miss Russell, that as a doctor there's nothing I haven't seen before.' His voice lowered as he leaned forward to kiss her, then continued: 'Or will do again.'

She felt the colour rush to her face as his fingers moved gently across her shoulders, drawing away her robe.

The sea was a limpid-blue as if the night had never been. Only the litter of seaweed and broken spars of wood covering the sand revealed its tumult.

Toby was waiting for them in his usual place on the top step when they came out of the water, and Daniel swathed one of the towels round Lauren before carrying her up the beach.

'What shall I cook you for breakfast?'

'Scrambled eggs,' she said. 'It has to be.'

It was as though they'd never been parted. As if those weeks had never been, Lauren thought, watching as he lit the gas and slid bread to toast under the grill. And things would have ended so very differently, if he hadn't been there that morning in May.

Her hand crept slowly to her cheek, to touch the faint outline of the scar, and Daniel noticed the movement, capturing her fingers in his own, to kiss them.

'It doesn't matter, Lauren,' he whispered. 'Not to anyone, even you.'

'What will happen to Matthew?' she asked abruptly.

'We shall know very soon.'

'And then?'

He buttered the slices of bread quickly, and spooned over the egg. 'No one ever knows for sure. So many things can happen. But Matthew's a determined little chap. He's overcome most things in his life so far. He will again – with the help of those that love him. And we all do that.'

They walked together over the cliffs to the village. There was no other way there. Matthew's father would remove the tree blocking the lane later that morning. Until then it couldn't be passed.

Mrs Tolly gave them a beam of welcome from her open front door.

'Saw you coming over the path. Now what about a nice cup of tea, my dear, while Dr Kerrow's taking his surgery? There's lots to catch up.'

After lunch Daniel drove her to Truro. He'd bought Matthew a blue denim cap. All afternoon the child put it on and took it off again, trying it frontways and back to front, laughing with happiness, chattering away excitedly.

'I listened to one of those stories in the nighttime,' he confided. 'Sometimes I don't go to sleep. It was about Paddington Bear. And I've lended four of the others to the nurses to let some of the very ill children hear. When I come back home, will it still be summer? Can we go for a picnic again?'

'Out to sea or on the beach?' Daniel asked him.

And Lauren saw the mischievous smile that crossed the little boy's face.

'Out to sea please, Dr Dan, only you mustn't make Mrs Tolly cross walking about in your *you-know-whats*, must you?' His expression grew anxious. 'I hope our new baby doesn't get born before I come home or it won't know me, will it?'

'If it does, then I'll bring your mum over from the maternity ward so that it can meet you,' Daniel declared, lightly stroking the little boy's thick hair.

'Promise?' Matthew asked.

'I promise.'

'Lauren or Daniel, I don't know which one I want it to be. You will be here to see the new baby as well, won't you, Lauren? You won't go away like you did before? We missed you lots and lots, didn't we, Dr Dan?' Matthew murmured sleepily, snuggling his head down into the covers.

'No, Matthew,' she replied, but her gaze was on Daniel. 'I won't go away again.'

'Promise?' Daniel whispered huskily, the word feathering her skin before his lips met hers.

'I promise.'